Thr...
vehicles skidded to a stop

Nine longblasters were poked up over the cabs and aimed at Jak, J.B. and the members of the collective.

"People of the Silvertide collective, you are ordered to surrender immediately, or we will be forced to open fire!" The voice that boomed over the loudspeaker sounded familiar. "You have ten seconds to comply."

All through the camp, fighting men and women looked up at the voice. When they saw the overwhelming force arrayed against them, they turned to J.B., who shook his head.

"Stop! It's over," he shouted.

"Not serious," Jak muttered.

"For the moment, yeah, I am," the Armorer whispered. "But stay ready."

"Lay down your weapons, put up your hands and walk toward the sound of my voice."

The driver's door of the main truck opened and a tall man stepped out into the light. When they saw him, both J.B.'s and Jak's jaws dropped.

The newest leader of the kidnappers was Ryan Cawdor.

Other titles in the Deathlands saga:

JAMES AXLER
DEATHLANDS®
HIVE INVASION

A GOLD EAGLE BOOK FROM
W💧RLDWIDE®

TORONTO • NEW YORK • LONDON
AMSTERDAM • PARIS • SYDNEY • HAMBURG
STOCKHOLM • ATHENS • TOKYO • MILAN
MADRID • WARSAW • BUDAPEST • AUCKLAND

Recycling programs
for this product may
not exist in your area.

First edition January 2015

ISBN-13: 978-0-373-62630-4

Special thanks and acknowledgment to
Travis Morgan for his contribution to this work.

Hive Invasion

Printed in U.S.A.

The brain may be regarded as a kind of parasite of the organism, a pensioner, as it were, who dwells with the body.

—Arthur Schopenhauer,
1788–1860

THE DEATHLANDS SAGA

This world is their legacy, a world born in the violent nuclear spasm of 2001 that was the bitter outcome of a struggle for global dominance.

There is no real escape from this shockscape where life always hangs in the balance, vulnerable to newly demonic nature, barbarism, lawlessness.

But they are the warrior survivalists, and they endure—in the way of the lion, the hawk and the tiger, true to nature's heart despite its ruination.

Ryan Cawdor: The privileged son of an East Coast baron. Acquainted with betrayal from a tender age, he is a master of the hard realities.

Krysty Wroth: Harmony ville's own Titian-haired beauty, a woman with the strength of tempered steel. Her premonitions and Gaia powers have been fostered by her Mother Sonja.

J. B. Dix, the Armorer: Weapons master and Ryan's close ally, he, too, honed his skills traversing the Deathlands with the legendary Trader.

Doctor Theophilus Tanner: Torn from his family and a gentler life in 1896, Doc has been thrown into a future he couldn't have imagined.

Dr. Mildred Wyeth: Her father was killed by the Ku Klux Klan, but her fate is not much lighter. Restored from pre-dark cryogenic suspension, she brings twentieth-century healing skills to a nightmare.

Jak Lauren: A true child of the wastelands, reared on adversity, loss and danger, the albino teenager is a fierce fighter and loyal friend.

Dean Cawdor: Ryan's young son by Sharona accepts the only world he knows, and yet he is the seedling bearing the promise of tomorrow.

In a world where all was lost, they are humanity's last hope…

Chapter One

"Gaia, Ryan, just do it!"

Taking a deep breath, Ryan Cawdor flexed his fingers, then picked up the scalpel. He wished there was some other way to do this, but just like the last time, it was the simplest, more direct way of solving the problem, despite the potential fallout. "Now, hold still—"

"I am! Just get on with it!"

Ryan had faced countless dangers during his life: power-hungry barons holding the lives of countless people in their hands and willing to kill whoever they thought might take that power away; mechanical nightmares, created by long-dead mad whitecoats, that still roamed the land to hunt and kill; monsters of every stripe, from the tiny to the gargantuan, all roaming the hellscape called Deathlands.

He'd lost count of the number of folks he'd chilled during his travels and never even thought about how many muties and other freakish creatures had lost their lives at his hands. But every few months he took his own life in his hands; even worse, each time he did so willingly.

Before him, a gorgeous, flame-haired woman knelt on the dry ground. Only her fingers tapping her thigh revealed any tension. Tall and well built, Krysty Wroth turned heads wherever she went. She was also smart, levelheaded, good with a blaster and a deadly hand-to-hand fighter.

Ryan stepped closer to her, weighing how best to begin. Choosing a thick lock of her long red hair, he pulled it away from the rest with one hand and wasn't surprised when it trembled and curled around his fingers.

Krysty was also a mutie. She could sense things, such as the life force of nearby people and creatures, and their emotional state. And she also had strange, prehensile hair that reacted to her moods. Getting Krysty drunk was the best—and only—way to cut her hair. Unlike everyone else's, from Ryan's thick curly black hair to Jak Lauren's blindingly bright white mane to J. B. Dix's close-cropped pate to Doc Tanner's silver-white tendrils to Mildred Wyeth's beaded plaits, Krysty's hair was alive on her head.

Cutting it hurt—a lot. She compared it to taking a blade and dragging it across your skin hard enough to draw blood, then multiplying that pain by a thousand.

They stood on a plateau overlooking what would have been a bucolic river valley a century ago. Skydark had changed all of that in a few terrible hours. Now the landscape looked more like something out of a geologist's nightmare.

Even since their arrival in this part of the old Midwest—J.B. guessed they were in the middle of the plains state known as Oklahoma—they'd been trying to figure out what had happened here. The more pragmatic members—Ryan, J.B. and Mildred—thought it was left over from the long-ago nuclear bombs that had flown and fallen around the world, irrevocably altering the late-twentieth-century civilization into the twisted remnants that struggled to survive every day.

Doc and Krysty, however, thought that a fault line near what had been the Mississippi River had finally erupted at some point, and that this stark landscape was the result.

Huge shelves of earth rose against one another in massive jagged waves. They weren't high enough to be mountains, nor solid enough to be hills, and they kept falling and reforming all the time, making the nearby ground tremble as they moved. Even now, a patter of falling earth made Ryan look up to see a dusty brown hillock collapse in a cloud of dirt. The phenomenon appeared to be confined to this one valley, which relieved him—he didn't want to have to keep looking over his shoulder to make sure the ground wasn't collapsing behind him when they left this place.

"I'm waiting, lover," Krysty said through gritted teeth.

"Right." Ryan gathered the limply sprawling strands of crimson in his hand again and put the razor-sharp scalpel edge under it about four inches up. Although her hair was relaxed, Ryan easily sensed his lover's tenseness. Without a word of warning, he sliced through the lock in one swift motion.

Krysty hissed with pain. The hair next to the severed strand tried to hide underneath the rest, while two thick tendrils wrapped themselves around Ryan's wrists, attempting to pinion his hands. Fortunately, although Krysty's hair could move, it didn't have a lot of strength, and Ryan was able to complete the rest of his task with relative ease.

Two minutes later it was done. Just in time, too, as

Krysty leaped up the instant he severed the final strand. Ryan was careful to take one step back while she paced back and forth, breathing heavily, her red tresses curled up tight at the base of her skull. "You all right?" he asked cautiously.

"I'll make it…." Krysty said, shuddering as she paced back and forth, calming herself.

Krysty stopped in front of Ryan, then before he knew it, he was falling backward to the ground, with her on top of him.

She leg-swept me, he thought as he crashed to the dry earth, only barely breaking his fall with his arms.

Before he could protest, Krysty was on him, straddling his chest as she kissed him hard, coming up for air after a few seconds. "Want you to take my mind off what just happened, lover. Think you can handle that?"

Ryan's hands were already moving, caressing her lush curves, barely constrained under her modified sleeveless jumpsuit. The front zipper was lowered a few inches, and he arched up and tugged it lower with his teeth while his hand snaked across the back of her neck and brought her face toward his for another hard, luscious kiss before nipping at her neck. Her hair now quivered with excitement, any memory of the torture inflicted on it a minute earlier fading fast.

Krysty's moans were now of pleasure rather than pain, and her fingers were doing their own walking as they unbuckled his belt and began sliding inside his fatigue pants. As they did, another tremor shook the ground around them.

Ryan kept going for a second, cupping her breasts before realizing she wasn't in the moment anymore but was now listening intently to something. And that was when he realized the initial tremor wasn't stopping.

"Earthquake?" he asked.

She shook her head. "This one's different." She rolled off him in a fluid move, crouching and pressing a hand to the ground. Ryan just watched her. He'd known doomies in his time, and the whole group had met empaths more than once, but Krysty's sensing skill was something else entirely. "Not the earth itself shaking… Something shaking it as it moves through it."

Ryan propped himself up on his arms. "You mean underground?"

She nodded. "We better get back to the others—"

Before she could finish, the bone-dry soil erupted around them, spraying the two with dirt. Looming before them was an animal neither had ever seen before.

Rising several feet out of the ground, it looked like a cross between a giant ant and a praying mantis. Its carapace was a mottled green, brown and orange, and covered its entire thorax and abdomen in thick chitin. Its head had a pair of bulbous, copper-colored eyes, and large mandibles easily capable of severing a person's arm that clacked together hungrily. Four arms waved in the air, each one tipped with a serrated, daggerlike claw at the end.

As Ryan went for his blaster, one of those limbs blurred down, aiming right for his crotch!

Chapter Two

Ryan was already scooting backward as the needle-sharp claw spiked into the dirt between his legs, missing his family jewels by a hairbreadth. As it landed, he drew his faithful SIG Sauer P226 blaster and snapped a shot off at the monstrosity's chest.

There was an odd, flat *crack,* and Ryan's eye widened to see the creature still up and full of fight. He hadn't missed—there was no way, not at this range. The 9 mm round wasn't powerful enough to penetrate the chitin.

Still hauling himself backward with his free hand, Ryan aimed more carefully at the big bug's head, or more specifically, its eye, and fired again. This time the bug's limbs thrashed around madly, then the creature flopped to the ground a second later.

"Shoot the head!" he shouted over the sharp report of Krysty's Glock.

"Behind you!" Her answering yell came as another shower of dirt fell on Ryan. He looked up to see one of the nightmares right above him, its daggerlike claws spearing down toward his chest.

He rolled out of the way as three hooks slammed into the ground where he'd been a moment ago. Turning onto his stomach, Ryan put a pair of bullets into the head of his would-be ambusher, then scrambled to his feet to help Krysty.

She stood over another of the wriggling, green mutants, her Glock 18C aimed at its chittering head. The blaster cut loose, and the bug shuddered once and went limp. A second mutie lay near the first, its head also oozing black ichor.

"Is that all of them?" she asked, looking around. Ryan was doing the same while rebuckling his belt when his head snapped around at the sound of more blastershots echoing across the plains.

"Sounds like they found the others. Come on!" Grabbing his Steyr Scout longblaster, he took off toward the camp, with Krysty right behind him.

"Looks like we were all wrong about what was making those hills!" she said in between breaths as they ran.

"Yeah, and I hope it's the last mistake we make here," Ryan replied, his long legs eating up the distance. The blaster shots continued, louder now, making him even more concerned. Ryan's fears were briefly allayed when he and Krysty arrived on a rise overlooking their campsite. Their companions stood back to back around the campfire, which was already dying from lack of fuel. Every person below was shooting into a veritable tide of the green-brown bugs boiling up from the ground all around them. The razor-clawed muties chittered madly as they tried to break through the wall of lead being put up to stop them. At least two dozen bug bodies littered the dirt, with several only a couple of yards away from the defenders' feet.

Even as he tried to figure out how in the hell he was going to get them out of there, Ryan admired how calm his companions were under what would have been overwhelming terror for anyone else. It was obvious that the burrowing insects had been stalking them for at least the past couple of days, and had sprung their ambush well, encircling the group and reinforcing the blockade with more ravenous frontline soldiers.

To defend against the onslaught, Ryan's friends had arranged themselves in a points-of-the-compass formation that gave everyone overlapping fields of fire. Each shooter could be reinforced by at least one other person at all times, which was good, because from what he could see, the huge mob wasn't stopping until the insects sank their claws into warm norm flesh.

On the north point was Doc Tanner, a man who appeared to be some sixty-odd years old by one measure and more than two centuries old by another. Time-traveled a hundred years forward from his home in the late nineteenth century, then from there forward another one hundred years to the Deathlands, his mind often teetered on a razor's edge between lucidity and madness. Hidden within its depths were secrets of the predark technology built by the scientists of that time. He was a staunch friend, and had saved his companions' lives on more than one occasion. Wielding a .44-caliber commemorative LeMat revolver in one hand and a rapier in the other, the old man blocked a pair of questing claws with his blade and put a bullet into his attacker's head, pulping it and dropping the insectoid beast.

Standing near him on the western front was Mildred Wyeth, also a time traveler of a sort, but by very different means. A doctor back in the twentieth century, she was cryogenically frozen when what should have been minor surgery went terribly wrong. Resuscitated a century later by Ryan and his companions, she'd awoken to a world much different from the one she'd known. Now she made her way as part of the group, their friend and healer. It also didn't hurt that she was a crack pistol shot, as good as Ryan himself. This was evidenced by her carefully aimed and placed shots. Every time she squeezed the trigger of her Czech-made ZKR 551 target pistol, something died.

Next to her, guarding the south with his well-used .357 Magnum Colt Python, was Jak Lauren. His shock of white hair and pale skin were almost as blinding as the massive, chrome-plated blaster he clutched in his hand. Whipcord lean, the albino was the shortest of the men in the group, but more than made up for it by being the best hand-to-hand fighter Ryan had ever seen, hands down—and he'd seen a lot of them. Jak was taking down the insectoid invaders on his side, the heavy bullets shattering chests and blowing heads apart.

The fourth member holding the defenses was Ricky Morales. The newest member of their team, he was a few years younger than Jak, and an inch taller. Ricky had joined their group searching for his sister, captured by slavers on their home island of Puerto Rico. He was still looking for her, searching for any scrap of information that might lead him to save his only surviving family member. Like his idol, J.B., Ricky was a weaponsmith and tinkerer, always ready to play with some new bit of tech they might stumble across while exploring a redoubt. He could fix damn near anything, particularly blasters, making him another valuable member of the team. Normally he carried a .45 Webley revolver and a silenced, bolt-action De Lisle carbine. Now, however, he was blasting bugs apart with an automatic shotgun.

Last but not least, on the inner circle of their perimeter was J. B. Dix, Ryan's oldest friend. Nicknamed the Armorer due to his encyclopedic knowledge of weapons and armored vehicles, Dix was the opposite of what most Deathlands people thought a weaponsmith should look like. Mildred had called it during a night of drinks, saying back in her day, people probably would have called him a shorter Ichabod Crane, glasses and all. She'd spent the rest of the night telling everyone the story of the Headless Horseman and other spooky tales from long-lost American folklore.

When he'd heard the comparison, J.B. had just shrugged and hadn't said a word. Slender, bespectacled and sallow skinned, wearing a well-worn grayish-brown leather jacket and a battered but serviceable fedora jammed on his balding head, J.B. would be the first to admit that he didn't look the part of a blaster expert—which suited him just fine. "The more an enemy underestimates me, the more surprised the person is when I do make my move," he'd said during that same night.

During the battle with the bugs, he was backing up whoever needed him, his durable Mini-Uzi, stock extended and snugged to his shoulder, chattering as it spit short bursts of 9 mm slugs. As Ryan watched, the ground beneath the Armorer began to churn and collapse as a bug tried to ambush him from underfoot. As cool and collected as ever, J.B. took one step to the side and brought his submachine gun down. A three-round burst later, the ground stopped churning, with only a pair of clawed arms sticking out aboveground to serve as a crude gravestone for the dead bug.

As he dropped to his stomach on the flat rock plateau, Ryan was figuring out avenues of advance, retreat and flank, all in the name of getting his friends out of what might have been their last stand. They were roughly one hundred and fifty yards away. Normally an easy enough walk, even over the rough terrain, but that was without a mob of kill-crazy mutie bugs attacking from all sides, including from below. Still, Ryan thought he saw a way out. It would require timing, and more than a bit of luck, but if anyone could do it, they could.

"I've got to clear a path for them to get up here," he said as he shrugged off his bandolier of magazines and set it beside him, then snugged the butt of the Steyr Scout longblaster to his shoulder and put his lone eye to the scope. "I need you to spot and reload mags if necessary. Keep an eye on the bugs and let me know if any of them get close to our people."

After giving those instructions, Ryan went to work. Methodically he began picking off the muties coming out of the south area of the ring around J.B., Mildred, Doc and the rest. With his 7.62 mm bullets punching holes through the backs of the attackers, it took all of two seconds for J.B. to see what was going on and immediately organize a fighting retreat toward Ryan's position.

Aided by Ryan picking off the vanguard of the muties with his longblaster, Jak and Ricky led the way, clearing a path with sustained fire. Doc and Mildred came next, the stocky black woman and reedy old man backing up the two teens and also watching their own respective sides. Last came J.B., fighting a rear-guard action that put him in harm's way more than once if not for the timely intervention of Ryan and his Steyr. At one point the one-eyed man shot the head of a burrow-bug off its thorax just as its mandibles were about to close on J.B.'s leg. The bullet shattered the bug's face, and its quivering body was quickly overwhelmed by its brethren, who didn't seem to care that they were carving up one of their own.

The group was making slow but steady time toward the rock plateau that would be their salvation when a high shout echoed off the steep walls of the makeshift ravine.

Ryan was already shifting his longblaster toward the source even as Krysty told him what was going on.

"Doc's down!"

But Ryan could already see that. Doc was sprawled on the ground, his right leg vanished into the soft earth from the knee down. Several sprays of dirt around him signaled the worst was happening.

The creatures had sprung a second ambush—and they'd caught Doc.

Chapter Three

Each member of the group had his or her own quirks and foibles, which sometimes drew teasing from the rest. In J.B.'s case, it was often said that if he wasn't concerned or worried about something, he wasn't happy.

As usual, the phlegmatic Armorer would counter that by saying there was plenty to worry about in the Deathlands every day—he just concentrated on whatever looked most urgent and figured the rest of the group would handle the other, less-pressing matters.

And right now they were in a hell of a mess. There was no helping the ambush—after the past few days here, everyone had gotten used to the minor tremors shaking the ground at all hours, so when the latest one had started, no one had thought anything of it until the bugs had starting bursting out of the ground.

J.B. had seen his share of massed swarm tactics before and knew how to handle that. It usually involved pit traps, a moat and a good, solid, high palisade wall, preferably with sharpened spikes pointing toward the enemy.

But since they didn't have access to such barriers, he'd been forced to improvise. Everything had been going reasonably well—their blastershots had brought Ryan and Krysty back to find out what was going on, and as he'd figured, Ryan had begun creating an escape route, which they were fighting their way through. So far, so good.

Assuming their ammo held out.

J.B. was also often compared to a walking computer, particularly when it came to logistics and supplies. Again, he said that knowing what people had on them was often the difference between life and death every day. He kept a running tally of every bullet each person in the group carried, often knowing more accurately how many an individual had than he or she did. And right now, his computerlike mind was running through the calculations of how many shells they'd expended fighting their way out of this trap, and he wasn't liking what he was coming up with.

It would have been a different story if these burrowbugs had the common sense to retreat when faced with overwhelming firepower. Unfortunately, they didn't seem to have the brains to understand when they should have been running away instead of forward to the slaughter.

But again, that worked only if their ammo held out.

And right now, there didn't seem to be any end to the insect army coming after them. No matter how he figured it, if they didn't reach the safety of that rock ledge, this fight would have only one possible outcome—J.B. and the rest of the group were going to be dinner. Of course, the Armorer had no intention of going down that way. He'd eat the barrel of his Mini-Uzi before things got *that* bad. Right now, he was busy making sure none of the chittering, scuttling, eight-foot-long insects got the drop on any of his friends. You want dinner that bad, he thought, you're going to have to work for it.

But when Doc shouted in surprise as his foot broke

through the ground and he sank awkwardly up to his knee, J.B. had had to give the bugs a grudging bit of respect. After all, they didn't need to get the drop on their next meal—not when they could make it drop in on them.

He lunged forward, grabbing under the shoulders of Doc's ancient frock coat with one arm. He heaved back, but he might as well have been trying to pull the old man out of concrete. J.B. also had to watch his footing, since it was hard to tell where the pit trap began, and if he wasn't careful, he could end up stuck in there with the old man.

Doc's shout had also attracted Mildred's attention, and she'd turned back to help, as well. "Get to the others!" J.B. shouted.

Her answer was to fire a shot that whizzed past his head. J.B. didn't need to turn and check to know a dead bug would be lying on the ground behind him. "Not till you get him out and moving!"

J.B. would have argued, but there was no time. By now, Doc had slipped into the dirt up to his waist. Instead of panicking, he was watching the moving earth below him intently. "I say, John Barrymore, would you be so kind as to hold this for me?" he asked, holding out his LeMat.

"Doc…how in the hell am I supposed to hold that *and* hold you up at the same time?" the Armorer asked through gritted teeth.

"Well, you are not going to like my answer," Doc began as a booming crack echoed across the hills, and J.B. felt something brush his back as it fell.

"Just spit it out, Doc!"

The old man turned to look back at him, his gaze and voice crystal clear. "You are going to let me go."

"If I do, you're dead!"

"Not quite, John Barrymore." Doc held up his other hand, which still held his sword. "I will dispatch the villain attempting to carry me away, and then return—"

Another, closer shot rang out, and this time one of the bugs fell against J.B. as it died. "Whatever you two are going to do, do it fast!" Mildred snapped.

"All right!" Snatching the LeMat out of Doc's hand, J.B. let him go and turned to take out two bugs that had been charging at him from the rear. He heard a shout from Doc—something about eating cold steel—then the man disappeared completely from sight.

"Doc? Doc!" J.B. dropped to his knees at the edge of the collapsed six-foot-deep pit and looked for any sign of the old man.

"Come on, John! These bastards aren't going to stay away forever!" Mildred said as she shot another one through the eye.

"Hang on!" he shouted back, although he knew it was growing more hopeless by the moment. More seconds passed, bullets flying around him, but J.B. kept looking. He was just about to give up hope when he still saw nothing below, but then a wrinkled hand burst up from the dirt, looking for something to latch on to. J.B. leaned down, grabbed it and hauled upward with all his strength.

Emerging from the ground like an old gaunt gopher, Doc spluttered and coughed as dirt cascaded off his face and head. Once he'd sucked in a great, gasping breath, he was able to help by shoving on the sides of the pit with his feet, propelling himself up until they were both lying at the edge of the hole. Doc was still clutching his lion's-head sword, its blade coated in the same thick black gunk that had come out of the other burrow-bugs.

With a mad chitter of rage, a bug exploded out of the pit, its clawed legs feeling about madly for its prey. J.B. aimed Doc's revolver at it and pulled the trigger, hoping the old man hadn't emptied the weapon.

He hadn't. The slug cored the bug's head and sent it falling back into the pit to disappear under the loose dirt. "Let's get the hell out of here," J.B. said.

"Agreed, John Barrymore, much agreed," the other man replied. But when he rose to his feet and tried to take a step forward, he sank to the ground, his face twisted with pain. "I am afraid that one of those buggers may have injured me more than I thought."

"Can you walk at all, Doc?" Mildred asked while J.B. stood over both of them, his Mini-Uzi back online and spitting lead death.

Doc tried to stand again, only to sink back to the ground with a grimace. "I fear not. Mayhap it would be best if you two went on without me. I shall hold the rear to my last breath— I say, whatever are you doing?"

"Saving your skinny ass," Mildred replied as she hoisted him up and slung his arm over her shoulders. "Although I'll be damned if I know why. If I left you here, I wouldn't have to listen to your pontificating anymore. J.B., we're leaving!"

"Yes, ma'am," he replied as he reloaded. "About time too. I'm on my last mag. Move out. I'll cover you."

Mildred still had her blaster in her free hand, and with Doc holding his sword *en guard* to fend off any close encounters, the three headed out again. J.B. estimated they were about fifty yards from the rock shelf, and he saw Ryan, Krysty and Ricky already there. The Puerto Rican teenager was lying next to Ryan, sighting down the barrel of his De Lisle carbine to take out more of the attacking insects. Between Ryan and him, the path to the plateau was opening up—awash in the bodies of dead bugs, but opening up nonetheless. With the two marksmen covering their left and right flanks, J.B. divided his time between guarding their six and making sure neither Mildred nor Doc fell into any other pit traps.

The ground in front of them suddenly dropped away into a pit at least fifteen feet deep. Mildred and Doc skidded to a stop at the edge, breathing hard as they realized just how close to disaster they'd come.

Unfortunately, J.B. had been backing up behind them as he kept an eye on the dozen or so bugs that were tracking the trio about ten paces back. Before Mildred or Doc could tell him to stop or move out of the way, he bumped into them hard enough to overbalance the pair and send them both tumbling into the pit.

Chapter Four

Mildred was more than familiar with the concept of the ant lion, a small, predatory insect whose larva scooped a pit trap in the ground to capture its prey. In her previous life, she'd given a report in the fourth grade about it and other insects of North America. However, she'd never, *ever* expected to find herself in one of those exact traps.

Of course, she'd never expected to awaken in this nightmarish land in the first place, filled with predators on two, four or, like these, six or more legs. But Mildred was a survivor, and had adapted as well as she could to her new, harsh circumstances. It had helped that her revivers were Deathlands natives, able to provide a brutal crash course in living day to day here.

The primary thought on her mind as she tumbled to the bottom in a cascade of sandy dirt was to keep hold of her pistol—if she lost it down there, odds were she wouldn't live long enough to find it again. The secondary goal was to avoid landing wrong and injuring any limbs. It would be difficult enough to climb out of here, and nearly impossible with a busted arm or leg. Bad enough Doc, with his sprained ankle, was also in the trap with her.

Spitting out grit, Mildred scrambled to her feet, aware that the ground was already shifting as the first of the burrow-bugs began emerging to see what they'd captured. She could still hear gunshots above, and knew Ryan and Ricky were keeping the bugs at bay. But that wasn't going to help get Doc and her out of there.

As she began reloading, her fingers ejecting shells and inserting bullets as if they had a mind of their own, Mildred glanced up to see how far up the pit edge was. Her heart sank when she saw it was easily six feet overhead.

"Upon my word, Mildred…that is a ride I would not care to embark upon again." Doc shook his head, sending a shower of dirt pattering around them.

"If you can talk, Doc, you can stand," Mildred said. "We've got to get out of here before we're bug food."

"But of course, dear lady. Never let it be said that Theophilus Algernon Tanner did not come to the aid of a friend in need—"

"Less philosophizing, more stabbing," she replied as she aimed at the bottom of the pit and pulled the trigger of her revolver twice. The dirt there rippled and sprayed around as the insect underneath thrashed and died. However, no sooner had it stopped moving than it was replaced by another one.

"You okay, Doc, Mildred?" J.B.'s head appeared over the edge of the pit.

"Oh, just fine, thank you, except I'm *stuck at the bottom of a pit with huge bugs trying to eat me!*" she yelled back.

"Well, yeah, I meant besides that," J.B. answered. "Here, grab my jacket." He dropped his arm over the edge of the pit, holding the sleeve of his leather jacket. The rest of the garment dangled down the side of the pit, the other sleeve a tantalizing couple of feet away.

A mortal, high-pitched squeal drowned him out as Doc skewered the next bug that appeared, driving the point of his rapier into the armored joint between its head and thorax. With a twist, he withdrew the blade, bringing a trail of the black gunk that served as the insect's blood with it. "They seem to be exhibiting a sort of hive mentality—" he began.

"That's great. You can tell me all about their social structure later. Right now, I'm going to boost you up so you can grab John's jacket. You get out, then the two of you can get me out."

"Are you sure I should go first, Mildred?" Doc asked. "After all—"

"No time for chivalry, Doc!" Mildred said as she put another two slugs into the bottom of the pit. "Your ankle's sprained. That means you go first. Now, shut your yap and step up! Use both hands!"

While the latest bug casualty was being swallowed back up by its brethren, Mildred shoved her blaster into her waistband, then laced her hands together to form a stirrup. Doc tossed his rapier and its sheath up out of the pit, then, grimacing in pain, braced himself with a hand on her shoulder as he put his feet into her improvised step. As he did, she heaved him up with all of her strength.

"Whoa—!" Caught off guard by the move, Doc waved his arms like a particularly ungainly stork, then grabbed hold of the leather sleeve. "Got it! Pull, my good John Barrymore, pull!"

His long legs scrabbled against the side of the pit, sending another shower of dirt into Mildred's face. Shaking her head to clear her eyes, she felt Doc's weight leave her, and drew her blaster and turned just in time to confront the latest abomination coming for her.

"Not today." At less than a yard away, she couldn't miss—and didn't. The .38 bullet entered the bug's eye and punched out the back of its armored head, splattering the pit wall behind it with globs of black goo. The brain-dead bug stood there for a moment, then toppled backward, falling with a *crack* on the next one coming up.

"Okay, anytime you guys want to get me out of here would be fine!" Mildred shouted up.

"Working on it! Sit down and watch my back, Doc!" J.B. replied. "Here it comes, Mildred!"

J.B.'s entire upper body appeared over the pit edge this time as he leaned down so he himself dangled into the hole. The reports of Ryan's longblaster echoed steadily overhead, reassuring Mildred that Doc wasn't left to fend off the bug army alone.

"Be careful, John!" she said.

"Grab the sleeve, and I'll pull you up!"

"I'm getting there, I'm getting there!" Backing up to the far side of the pit, Mildred used the sinking corpse of the burrow-bug as a precarious platform to push off. Running as hard as she could across the shifting dirt, she scrambled up the side of the pit and grabbed the jacket sleeve. "Got it!"

"Okay, just hold on." J.B. was starting to pull her up when the wall next to her exploded. Pelted by dirt clods, her vision obscured, Mildred didn't see what hit her. The next thing she knew, she was knocked backward by a powerful blow that made her lose her grip on the jacket and tumble back down to the bottom.

Something thrashed and writhed on top of her, and Mildred felt a sharp pain stab into her upper chest. Hearing something clacking near her head, she blindly thrust out a hand, ignoring the stabbing ache that coursed through her arm, and grabbed a thick, jagged mandible, cutting her fingers. Realizing a bug had landed on top of her, she jabbed her pistol, still clutched in her other hand, above the shaking bug pincer and squeezed the trigger twice. The bug's body shook spasmodically on top of her, then collapsed and lay still.

"Son of a *bitch!*" Still feeling the dirt quiver and move around her and knowing she couldn't rest, Mildred squirmed out from under the bug carcass, wiping dirt out of her eyes.

"Dark night, that was close! Come on, Millie, let's get you out of there!" J.B. said.

"Amen to that!" Still clutching her pistol, Mildred took a running start again and leaped for the jacket sleeve. This time she used the edge of the hole in the wall for leverage, and was able to get even higher. She grabbed the sleeve with her free hand and pointed her blaster down the black tunnel, hearing faint skittering and chittering noises from inside. "Pull me up!"

J.B. started to do so again, and had almost gotten her to the lip of the pit when Mildred felt a strong tug on her combat boot. She glanced down to see yet another of the bugs with its mandibles firmly clamped around her foot. "Shit! Hang on, John. I have to do a little extermination!"

"Hurry up, for shit's sake!" he said through gritted teeth.

Mildred aimed and squeezed the trigger, but the hammer fell with only a dull *click*. She pulled it again, but with no better result. "Damn it, I know I had one left— misfire!"

"Great!" J.B. said. "Doc, a little help!"

The old man's head appeared over J.B.'s. Apparently he was lying on the Armorer to provide ballast. "Oh, my. One moment…" He stretched out a long arm with his LeMat revolver extending from his hand. His face was caked in dust and dirt, and his eyes were watering profusely, leaving wet tracks down his face and making him resemble some sort of demented, muddy clown. "Do not move, Mildred!"

"Jesus! Can you even see what you're aiming at, Doc?" she shouted back while trying to dig her other foot into the dirt. The burrow-bug increased its pull on her, making Mildred feel as if she was being stretched apart.

"The beast is fairly large—" Doc squeezed the trigger of his LeMat, and the slug buried itself in the bug's head. "That should do it!"

And it did. The bug slumped to the ground—but its mandibles were still locked tight around Mildred's ankle.

"Dammit!" Still holding on to the jacket for dear life, Mildred kicked at the bug's head with her other foot. Slowly it began loosening from her foot.

"Careful, it's starting to tear!" J.B. said. He was right—his jacket had been through a lot already, and the stitches around the shoulder were starting to pop loose.

"Almost got it—off!" With a last hard kick, Mildred freed her foot just as Doc shot another of the tunneling beasts scuttling toward her. Its body slithered back to the bottom, where it disappeared into the tunnel below.

"Can't…hold…on!" she cried. Her bleeding fingers were slippery, and Mildred felt the leather slide through her slick hand. She glanced down to see three of the hungry muties jostling one another to be the first to sink their pincers into her when she fell. Although she squeezed the jacket sleeve with all her strength, she still felt herself slipping. Mildred tried to lift her other hand to support herself, but the injury in her chest flared when she raised her arm higher than her elbow, and she had to let it drop again. Looking back up, she saw more thread tearing away, and the hole between the sleeve itself and the rest of the jacket growing larger. "Please—"

A strong hand suddenly gripped her wrist, and she looked up to see Doc's lined face smiling down at her. "You are so close to being free of this accursed hole, and the world is an infinitely more interesting place with you in it, my dear Dr. Wyeth. Now come with me."

And just like that, with Doc and J.B. helping her, Mildred was free of the pit. J.B. gave her a quick hug, also patting her down for injuries at the same time. "Where are you hurt?"

"Below my shoulder. I can walk," Mildred replied, already rising to her feet. "Let's go."

"No time to reload," J.B. said. The cylinder of Mildred's target pistol didn't swing out for quick reloading— each shell had to be manually ejected with the rod on the side of the gun and bullets inserted one at a time.

He handed her the Mini-Uzi and took up Doc's LeMat. "I'll help Doc, you cover us. Only got about fifteen rounds left. Make each one count."

"Ace on the line with that," she said, switching the fire selector to single shot for more accuracy.

J.B. hoisted Doc's arm over his shoulder, and with the old man's silver stinger ready to repel attackers, the three skirted the large pit and continued on their way toward the large rock plateau.

But they had no sooner gotten around the hole in the ground than they faced a group of the bugs at least three deep and six wide. Aboveground, the bugs were about six feet tall, each one rearing to form an L shape. Eight legs were now visible—the rear four used for balance and movement, the front four for attack and defense.

Mildred glanced back to see more of the armored killers forming to encircle them again. "Damn it, boys, didn't we just leave this situation a few minutes ago?"

"Back in it now…" J.B. began, just as the heads of the first row all opened up as if each one had been hit with a hammer, one after another, spraying black goo over Mildred, J.B. and Doc. Booming reports thundered around them as the entire first row keeled over, dead.

The surprise attack seemed to confuse the second wave of bugs, and they hesitated for a moment. It was all the time Mildred and J.B. needed.

With both the Uzi and the LeMat raised, the three charged forward as fast as Doc's injured ankle would allow, clearing their own path with lead and steel. Six more went down in the first seconds of their charge, five by bullet, one by sword.

Two others stepped into their path and were mowed down by accurate head shots. With a loud, long war cry, Doc impaled another one trying to flank them, pinning the struggling bug with his blade as if he were mounting a particularly large specimen under glass.

The rear guard was charging after them in a wave, and Mildred could feel the animalistic fury at their backs. It just made her go faster, although not fast enough to leave J.B. and Doc behind.

The burrow-bugs were getting closer now, braver. Any that got within three steps died, but Mildred sensed others closing ranks around them. If someone tripped, if an ankle turned on a loose rock, then that'd be all she wrote—the others would have to make the split-second decision to try to help the downed person and risk being torn apart, or keep moving.

J.B.'s Mini-Uzi bucked in Mildred's hand, each shot finding a home in a bug's head. Again, at this range, she couldn't miss, but she also couldn't just shoot indiscriminately either. Only head shots would do.

The bugs were close enough now that they could brush her with their claws if they chose, although Mildred would make sure she was the last thing they touched in their lifetime. She snapped off a shot at one that lunged at her, dropping it in its tracks.

She heard the deafening boom of J.B.'s shotgun and glanced up to see Jak standing like a snow-haired avenger at the edge, blasting away at the bugs behind them. They just might make it....

Doc let out a strangled gasp as his leg buckled. J.B., however, didn't miss a step. He just hauled the taller man with him the last few steps to the rock wall.

"Jump!" Ryan called down, his hand extended to grab the first person coming up.

"Go!" J.B. said to Mildred. Mildred didn't need further urging, and leaped for Ryan's hand. Before she knew it, the powerful man hoisted her up onto the rock shelf, unceremoniously dumping her nearby and leaning down again.

"Hey—" Mildred said, then clamped her mouth shut as she realized he was going back for the others. Doc was next, the old man wheezing as he stumbled away and sank to the ground. Mildred rolled to the edge of the plateau, still firing the Mini-Uzi into the mass of bugs as Ryan hauled J.B. up and onto the plateau. As his combat boots hit the rock floor, the submachine gun clicked on an empty chamber.

"Think you could have cut it any closer?" Ryan asked with the hint of a grin as they watched the bugs surge back and forth below them.

The Armorer shrugged. "Would have been here sooner, except I had to keep stopping for other folks," he replied with his own wry smile.

"'Stopping for other folks?' In case no one happened to notice, Doc and I almost got *killed* down there!" Mildred said.

Both men turned to her, the smiles still on their faces. "We know, Mildred, we know. But we're safe now—"

"No, we're not," Krysty interrupted. She was also standing at the edge of the rock ledge. "If anything, we've just made them madder."

Curious in spite of herself, Mildred got up and joined the red-haired woman at the edge. All she saw was a huge group of the burrow-bugs below them, with more coming out of the tunnels every second. "You can sense their mood?"

Krysty shook her head. "I don't need to sense anything to know how creatures are going to behave. Look there."

She pointed at the bottom of the cliff wall, where a single line of bugs about five wide stood there, as if waiting for orders. Then another line of bugs ran over and stood by the first row. A third line ran over and climbed on top of the row nearest the cliff face, with another row behind that taking a position so that yet another row could climb on top of the second-level row.

"Oh, my God," Mildred said. "They're forming a ramp out of themselves."

"It certainly appears so," Doc said beside her. "And at the rate they are going, it will be high enough to reach us in less than two minutes."

Chapter Five

"Fireblast!" Ryan swore. "Our asses aren't out of the fire just yet."

"We don't have enough ammo to hold them off here," J.B. said. "Have to fight hand to hand."

"So be it." Drawing his panga, Ryan turned to the others. "All right, Jak, Doc, you're with me on bug-repelling duty."

Doc redrew his sword and saluted Ryan with it. *"Sí, mon capitaine!"*

"All right, Doc, save it for the bugs," Ryan replied. "Ricky, Krysty, you take the right flank, Mildred, J.B., you're on the left. We should be able to kill most of the bastards, but if any slip through on either side, you're taking them down. Don't leave your partner to face one of these muties alone."

"Not to argue, Ryan, but are you sure Doc's up to the job?" J.B. asked with a glance at the old man. "No offense, but you did hurt your leg down there."

"None taken, John Barrymore." Doc smiled grimly at the other man, revealing a set of peculiarly white and even teeth. "If I am given the chance to go down while stabbing at these hell spawn, then I will have at them until my blade is ripped from my cold, dead hand."

"Good enough for me," Ryan said. "J.B., we're holding a fixed position and Doc's got the reach with his sword. We need you on a flank."

J.B. nodded. "You got it."

"All right, positions, people. They're almost here!" Ryan called out.

During their brief conversation, the bugs had ascended almost to the lip of the ledge. Those on the bottommost layer, no longer visible, had to have been crushed by the sheer weight of the ones on top, yet the others kept climbing, heedless of their brethren below.

Ryan, Jak and Doc stood a couple of yards apart at the edge of the plateau. "Hit them hard, get them away and move to the next one," Ryan said. "No soliloquies or reciting poetry to them, Doc."

"Never fear, my dear Ryan—Wordsworth or Burns would be wasted on these cretins. Besides, if my Harvard education still serves, most bugs cannot hear anyway, but detect movement and sound by vibration, so my eloquent words would be for naught."

"Damn—Doc takes longer say 'okay' than anyone," Jak muttered.

"Here they come!" Ryan said as the first of the bugs crested the ridge.

In their own unique way, each of the three men was singularly well suited for the task at hand. On the left, Doc had already seen action against the creatures during the battle on the ground, and as such had a good idea of how to face off against them. He was able to parry each bug's attack and either feint to mislead it, then stab, or simply batter its legs aside and skewer it. His rapier darting and stabbing, he spiked every bug that came near him, shoving each carcass off his blade with his

foot and sending it falling back into the charging mass
boiling up from below.

On Ryan's other side, Jak didn't carry a melee weapon
other than his lethally accurate throwing knives. He
didn't need one, since *he* was a melee weapon. His rock-
hard fists and skinny yet powerful arms and legs were
capable of frightening feats of strength. Even against
armored opponents such as these, where an unarmed
warrior would normally be at a disadvantage, Jak was
still in his element. Despite three or four claws coming
at him at once, he evaded every one and delivered dev-
astating counterstrikes. His first blow split the abdomen
chitin of one of the bugs in two, the kinetic shock wave
from the impact pulping its internal organs and killing
it. He soon found their weak spots, the heads and joints
of their legs, and was crushing eyes and skulls and tearing off limbs with abandon.

And what about Ryan, in between them?

At this point in his life, Ryan was near physical per-
fection from a lifetime of survival. Two hundred pounds
of pure, coiled power ready to be unleashed on command. He was the strongest of all of them, and Jak's
equal in dealing death to any opponent.

His fighting style was brutally efficient, and his cho-
sen melee weapon, the panga, was the perfect weapon for
this situation. Its broad, heavy blade was perfect for either cracking armor or pulping bug heads, and Ryan laid
into the surging mass with abandon, his panga, hand,
arm and face soon streaked with black, clotted gore.

They repelled the first tide, but more charged up, with
still more behind them. Although the bugs attempted to
overwhelm the trio, there wasn't enough room for them
to mass a truly overwhelming assault, and each quartet

of insects that gained the top of the ridge was immediately reduced to bleeding, dead bodies and flung off to land on the rest of the swarm below.

That wasn't to say there weren't close calls. More than once, Doc or Jak had to rely on their backup to help out when a particularly ornery knot of the bloodthirsty insects ganged up on them. More often than not Ryan was there, as well. Whether chopping through two limbs on the side of a bug's body with one powerful sweep of his panga or just relieving a bug's body of its head with one powerful swing of his blade, he was death incarnate.

And still they kept coming.

The seconds turned to minutes, the minutes stretched on into who knew how long. Sweat dampened their clothes, and everyone's muscles grew weary with each blow, but the front three, as well as the others, didn't let up for a moment. Everyone knew that it would take only one gap for the bugs to break through and overwhelm them, and if that happened, there would be no hope of stopping the attackers.

By now Ryan had entered a kind of primal killing zone, his conscious mind focusing solely on slaying anything that was green and brown with claws. He swung and bashed, hacked and cleaved, kicked and punched. Everything he touched, whether with fist, boot or steel, died.

The sun was beginning to sink into the west, and they were still at it. Doc had been relieved on the front line by J.B., who was wielding the old man's sword in both hands, lopping off limbs and heads with economical swings of the blade. Jak was also still holding his ground, leaping into the air and kicking a bug's head clean off its body with a vicious roundhouse kick. He punted its body back down the bug ramp and moved on to his next victim, blocking the two limbs that came at him, grabbing them and tearing them off at the joint. Jak drove the animal's own amputated claw into its eye, then made it shriek even louder for a second before he twisted off its head.

For his part, Ryan had lost count of how many bugs he'd killed, or how long he'd been up there. He knew only that the attackers were still coming, and they had to be stopped. A part of him, deep inside, even exulted in the massacre, for that was what it was. He was pure predator now, and there was no shame or dishonor in defending himself and his friends.

Finally, he looked around, but there was nothing left to kill. The whole rock plateau was covered in a half inch of black gore and littered with bug limbs and smashed, broken chitin. Ryan sucked in great gulps of the cooling air, his muscles still tense from the long combat. Wiping his wet forehead, he stared at the mixture of sweat and blood on his skin and realized he had to have taken a flesh wound during the fight. He trudged over to the edge and looked over.

The burrow-bugs were retreating, taking the bodies of their fallen with them. In a few minutes, except for many rapidly drying black stains on the ground and the holes left from their assault, there was no sign of the mob of carnivorous insects.

"Madre de Dios!" Ricky said as he sat down and mopped his forehead. "I never dreamed something like that could exist."

"Determined bastards," Jak said as he examined a shallow cut on the back of his hand, the only injury he'd sustained during the fight.

"Everyone all right?" Ryan asked as he walked into the shade cast by the rock wall on their right.

Krysty and J.B. nodded, although J.B. had a troubled look on his face.

Meanwhile, Mildred was examining Doc's swollen ankle, with the older man stoically trying not to reveal how much her probing fingers were hurting him. "All that swashbuckling didn't do his ankle any good," she said. "Although I have to admit you looked damn impressive up there, Doc."

"I only hope I acquitted myself honorably."

"Absolutely, Doc. You sent a bunch of those bugs straight to hell," Ryan said. "Mildred, what's the word on him walking out of here?"

"If I bind his ankle tight, and we cram it back into his boot, he can probably limp along for a while, but it'll be at half speed at best." She reached for his boot, then hissed in pain and put her free hand to her chest. "Almost forgot one of those eight-legged bastards tagged me, as well."

"Why didn't you say so earlier?" Krysty asked. "Here, let me take a look."

"Sure, just hang on." Rummaging in her pockets, Mildred came up with a small tube of antibiotic ointment.

"Jak, catch," she said as she tossed it to him. "Rub a bit on each cut. The last thing we need out here is infection."

While the two women examined Mildred's wound, and Jak and Ricky treated themselves, J.B. walked over to Ryan. Despite the half dozen instances of near death they'd all encountered in the past hour, he was as calm as ever, but Ryan saw through the placid demeanor of his oldest friend and realized something was seriously wrong.

"How many loaded mags for the Steyr do you have left?" J.B. asked.

"Fireblast, J.B.! I thought I'd take a minute to enjoy still being alive, mebbe wipe the black shit off my face before I did inventory—"

"Hey, I'm as happy as a scavvie in a honey hole that we made it through that, but it doesn't mean our problems are over." The Armorer stepped closer. "How many mags?"

Ryan walked over to where he'd stashed his empties along with the bandolier and blinked at what he found. "One full and one with four bullets left. Damn, blew through more shells than I thought," he said at J.B.'s slow nod. "My SIG has two full mags. What about you?"

"I ran out of 9 mm for the Uzi while getting up here, and there's mebbe a handful of shells left for the shotgun. I haven't checked with the boys yet, but I bet Jak's got one reload for his Colt, and Ricky might have a dozen, mebbe eighteen rounds left. And you know neither Doc nor the women carry a lot of bullets in the first place."

Ryan had already pulled his spare blaster magazine and handed it to J.B., who began pushing bullets out with his thumb and loading one of his empty magazines. "We're low on ammo, is that it?"

The Armorer nodded. "In a nutshell, yeah. I mean, I'm not blaming anyone—we all did what we had to do to get out of there, but now we've got to figure out what comes next, and that involves getting off this rock, and I bet it's going to be some hard running and fighting to get out of here in one piece." He jerked a thumb over his shoulder at the killing ground below. "Those bugs don't seem to be the type to forgive and forget. And with Doc lamed and all of us low on both firepower and supplies, it's going to be a rough, hard trip out of here."

"You thinking those things might come back?" Ryan asked.

"Probably should ask Krysty about that. She seemed to have a pretty good line on them," J.B. replied. "Bottom line is we can't stay here, but we're not sure where we're going, either, except out of this damn valley, I figure."

"Ace on the line," Ryan replied. "Well, we best figure out what we should do sooner rather than later. Come on."

He led J.B. back to the rest of the group and took a minute to explain the situation as the Armorer saw it. "Now, we all kicked some serious ass today. However, there could be another hundred, five hundred or thousand of those bastard bugs down in their hive or lair or whatever. So we should figure on getting out of here while they're still recovering from their ass-whippin'. The more ground we put between them and us, the better."

Nods and murmurs of agreement met his announcement. "A capital idea, my dear Ryan, but where are you suggesting that we go?" Doc asked. "Surely not back to the redoubt."

The redoubt that had brought them here had been cracked open and looted long ago, and their arrival had destroyed its mat-trans unit, as well. Since then, they'd been traveling the dusty plains, with this valley their only encounter with living creatures in the past three days.

Ryan shook his head. "That's a dead end. The important thing is for us to get out of this valley and see where we are, then we can figure out where to go. But that'll mean moving as fast as we can, and with ammo low, we're going to have to be careful how we take care of problems like those bugs, which J.B. and I imagine are going to come after us."

As Ryan spoke, he looked around at the others, seeing exhaustion and pain on everyone's face, even Jak's and J.B.'s. Although part of him wanted to set out right then and there, he knew pushing everyone now would only result in more mistakes later on.

"I figure we should rest for a few hours, then head out at dusk," he continued. "If we travel through the night, we should be free of this place by sunrise. Anyone got any questions or anything else to add?"

Jak spit to the side. "Wonder if bug parts okay eat."

"Only one way to find out," J.B. said.

"But how are you going to cook them?" Ricky asked. "I mean, you're not going to eat it raw, are you?"

Jak shrugged as he walked over to the limbless torso of a bug that had died on the ledge. "Eat worse before." He cracked the thorax, sliced off a piece of the translucent, jellied inside and touched his tongue to it, then spit it out. "Tastes like putrid mutie shit!"

"And you would know that how, Jak?" Mildred asked with a smile.

The weak joke took the edge off the grim mood, and Doc was the first to snort laughter at Mildred's question. Soon everyone was chuckling at the albino, who flipped all of them off with both hands and a narrow grin.

"All right, let's get some rest," Ryan said. "I'll stand

guard for the first hour, then Krysty, then J.B., then Jak. If anyone sees anything, hears anything—bugs, whatever—get everyone up. We move out in four hours."

Chapter Six

Ryan brought his panga down, pulping another of the everlasting horde of burrow-bug's heads with the heavy blade. He whirled, searching for another enemy to kill, but saw none. He was alone, surrounded by hacked and broken insect bodies.

He took a moment to suck cool night air into his starving lungs while checking himself for injury. Blood streamed from several small cuts on his hands, arms and chest, oozing through his torn and ragged T-shirt. Every muscle ached; other than perhaps an hour's rest all told, he'd been running and fighting almost nonstop for the past eight.

He glanced up at the stars but saw no glimmer of sunlight to the east. Not that it mattered—all daylight meant was that it was a bit easier to chill the rad-blasted muties. But just like back at the plateau, for every one he'd killed, two more took its place.

Although Ryan possessed a never-say-die mentality that had served him well through countless encounters with adversity, for the first time in a long time, he was starting to wonder whether he and his companions were going to make it out of this valley of death alive.

They'd eaten a few bites of tough, salty beef jerky—the last of their food—and barely gotten a couple of hours of rest when J.B. had woken everyone, saying he'd heard movement from the holes below. With Jak in the lead, throwing blade in hand, they headed higher into the rocky hills, hoping to lose the burrowing monsters before heading out to escape the valley.

Their attempt had been doomed almost from the beginning. With eight legs, the burrow-bugs were well suited to continue their pursuit, their claws clacking on the rocks as they swarmed up after the group. Ryan was hoping their head start would have been enough to discourage pursuit, but Doc was slowing everyone. It also didn't help that the mutie insects were single-mindedly unstoppable in their quest to kill the intruders.

Traveling through the darkness had turned into a nightmare of running and gunning, trying to cross the broken terrain while constantly keeping an eye out for burrow-bug pursuers behind them and pit ambushes ahead of them. When every step could be the last, it made people hesitant and jumpy. As a result, they were making piss-poor time out of the valley, but it couldn't be helped.

Ryan had issued a no-blasters rule unless there was no other choice, but that edict had been discarded in the face of the odds against them, although to everyone's credit, they tried to conserve their ammo whenever possible. But every so often a bug got too close while someone was fighting another one or two and had to be dispatched with a single shot.

After four hours of a grueling pace, interspersed with several skirmishes, Ryan had called a five-minute break so they could catch their breath. Doc hadn't sat as much as fallen down, his expression nobly stoic, despite the pain he had to be suffering. Leaning heavily on his swordstick, he had staggered through the past hour of travel, and more than once Ryan had thought he was going to have to carry the old man. But Doc hadn't made a sound or said a word about how he felt, just kept up with them as best as he could. But at this point, Ryan wasn't sure how much the old man had left in him.

Ricky and Krysty had also broken out the water bottles only to find more bad news—they were practically empty.

"This trip is getting better and better," Ricky said with a grimace.

"ONE MOUTHFUL EACH. We'll find more when we're out of here."

Ryan walked over to Mildred and kept his voice low. "You got anything that'll keep Doc moving for another couple of hours?"

"You read my mind." She glanced at the tall, thin man, who was drawing his frock coat around him to keep warm in the chilly night air. "He's a stubborn old coot, I'll give him that. But he's also on the edge of exhaustion." She reviewed her small stash of medicine supplies. "I've got a couple of amphetamines that'll keep him going for a few more hours, but when he crashes, it'll be hard."

"As long as it gets him and us out of here, he can sleep for a week afterward, as far as I'm concerned," Ryan replied. "Try to get him to take it now. When we move out, I'll hang back and create a diversion to give you all more time to get out."

"Not to be telling you what to do, Ryan, but you have to be as beat as the rest of us." Mildred held out one of the small capsules. "Take this. Use it only if you think you'll need it. It'll get you through."

Ryan tucked the pill into his pocket. "Thanks, Mildred. Get Doc taken care of, okay?"

As she headed over to the old man, Ryan went to J.B. and filled him in on the plan. The Armorer's only reaction was to raise one eyebrow. "If you think it's best, Ryan, I'm not going to argue. Just make sure you get back to us on one piece, okay?"

Ryan's answering grin was grim. "Trust me, I'd rather not, but if we all stop to fight them, we risk getting surrounded again. Don't worry about me. I'm not planning on catching that last train west just yet. We're almost out of the valley. Just make sure everyone keeps moving, and I'll catch up with you as soon as I can."

"See you out there." J.B. went over to make sure everyone else was ready to move. Ryan went with him.

"How you feeling, Doc?" he asked, checking his face with a small light he carried.

The old man stared back at him with bright eyes. He was breathing a bit faster and had two spots of color high on his cheeks. "Upon my word, Ryan, I am markedly improved from just a few minutes ago. Even my foot does not hurt nearly as much as it had been. That antibiotic Mildred gave me seems to have done the trick."

"Good to hear," Ryan said with a glance at the doctor, who shrugged and rolled her eyes in a "what he doesn't know won't hurt him" gesture. He turned back to Doc. "Everyone get ready to head out. I'll join up with you in a few minutes. I'm going to backtrack and make sure none of those bugs are on our trail."

Krysty rose from her haunches and walked close, her strong hand grabbing Ryan's T-shirt. "Sure hope you weren't going to head out without saying goodbye first—"

Ryan cut her off in midsentence with a long kiss, tasting her sweat and musk, which combined to create a scent that would have made his head spin under different circumstances. "I'm not saying goodbye, just so long for now. Get out of this bastard valley and I'll see you on the other side."

That had been at least an hour ago, and since then Ryan had been engaged in a constant running fight with the bugs. His diversion had worked, all right, but it might have worked a little too well, since it now seemed that every remaining bug in the place was on his ass and his ass alone.

He heard skittering from just about every direction he could go but up. Backed against a sheer rock wall at least fifteen feet high, Ryan drew his SIG Sauer and raised his panga. The bastards weren't going to get him without a fight.

The vanguard of the bugs came into sight, a pair sidling along low to the ground, antennae waving in the air as they tracked their prey. Upon locating him, they paused for a moment, then split up, one coming at him from the left, the other heading right.

Clever little bastards, Ryan thought as he lined up his blaster on the head of the nearest one. A squeeze of the trigger sent a 9 mm bullet deep into the head of the bug on the left, making it collapse to the dirt, legs twitching feebly.

Before Ryan could bring his blaster around, the other burrow-bug rushed in, clawed legs waving. Its two arms beat at his blaster hand, making it impossible to aim and fire. Ryan used his panga to keep the bug's other limbs from stabbing him as well, chopping at them to break or disable them.

Man and mutie strained against each other for a few moments, both seeking to gain the advantage. Then the bug's head darted down, its mandibles seeking Ryan's throat. He twisted out of the way just in time, and the insectile jaws clamped onto his shoulder, serrated teeth shredding his skin and flesh.

Forcing his blaster through the mutie's pummeling legs, Ryan placed its muzzle against the side of the bug's head and squeezed the trigger. The bullet blew the insect's brains out just as its claws stabbed at Ryan's side, opening a long, shallow slash along his ribs.

The bug collapsed on top of him, and Ryan heaved the corpse off with a grunt. He looked all around but didn't see any others. However, his predator's senses were still tingling, and he knew he was still in danger from somewhere.

The scrape of a claw against rock was enough to alert him. Ryan lunged forward as the bug overhead leaped off the rock face. It missed landing on him, but an outstretched claw raked down the back of his leg, making him stagger and fall on his face.

Before he could turn, the bug was on him, claws pinning him to the ground. Ryan heaved and lashed out behind him with his panga, but couldn't connect with the bug's body. His blaster was equally useless. Although he aimed it behind him and fired several times, he didn't hit anything vital. Ryan struggled to the last, trying to fight free, but he could feel the mutie's head coming closer to the back of his neck....

The bug stiffened suddenly, then fell on top of Ryan, crushing him into the dirt. The one-eyed man twisted, rolling the spasming body off him and sitting up. The taped hilt of a throwing knife jutted from the back of the bug's head.

"Jak," Ryan muttered as a white-haired shadow detached itself from the darkness on the outcropping above him and tossed down a rope. Although he wasn't displeased to see the albino, Ryan was concerned about the others getting into trouble with two of the best fighters away from the group.

"Worried you havin' all fun, so came find ya. Hurry up. Bugs not stay away forever," the teen said with a grin. "And get knife before haul ass up."

Sheathing his panga, Ryan jerked the blade out of the insect's head. Wiping the knife clean, he clamped it between his teeth, then reached for the rope and began to climb. But when he put weight on his right arm, his injured shoulder flared with white-hot pain, making him fall back to the ground. Ryan spit the knife out and tucked it into his boot. "Shit! Bastard chewed up my shoulder good. You're going to have to pull me up." Able to hold his blaster in his weak hand, Ryan looped the rope around his left. "Go!"

"Hold on!"

Ryan was jerked off his feet as more bugs swarmed into the area. He took out the nearest two with head shots as three more ran toward him. Ryan brought his legs up just as they lunged at his feet, pushing off the rock face as Jak hauled him up, reaching the top ahead of several more that were already climbing in pursuit.

"Son of a—" Jak had his own blaster in hand and blew two of the ascending insects off the wall, sending them crashing down on the rest. "Time go."

"You've got that right." Ryan dug out his amphetamine pill and swallowed it, then sent a trio of 9 mm slugs down into the mass, killing two more and injuring one so that all it could to was shriek and writhe on the ground, before his blaster's action locked back. "Go, go, go!"

Fortunately, the slash on Ryan's leg was shallow, and he could run with little impairment. He took off after Jak, who was like a white-haired ghost flitting from rock to shadow to rock again.

"Where the…hell're we…going?" Ryan panted as they ran.

"Just follow," Jak replied, not even breathing hard. "Got surprise waitin' for bugs."

Ryan glanced over his shoulder to find the ground behind them covered with bugs as far as he could see. "Better be a damn good one."

Jak flashed a death's-head smile at him. "Is."

The pill kicked in now, reducing Ryan's various aches and pains to dull, faraway throbs. His flagging energy level spiked, and soon he'd drawn abreast of Jak, who skidded to a stop beside him. "Head there."

"There" was a deep, narrow gulch carved out of the rock by wind and water over hundreds of years, snaking up the hill a good sixty or seventy yards. Not waiting for an answer, Jak began to climb, moving so fast up the steep surface he resembled an albino mountain goat.

Ryan followed him, still favoring his injured shoulder. The floor was steep, making the climb difficult, but not impossible. The only question was whether Ryan could reach the top before the burrow-bugs reached him.

It was a close call. Near the summit, the gulch turned almost vertical, making Ryan seek out hand- and footholds to propel himself the last dozen or so feet. Aided by Jak and Ricky, he was half pulled, half dragged onto the top, where he rolled over, breathing heavily.

"You old man," Jak said, still pulling on his arm.

"Watch it, youngblood," Ryan said as he pushed himself to his feet. "What's the plan, hold them off again here?"

"Nope." Ricky's teeth gleamed white in the moonlight. "J.B. planned something way better."

Ryan peeked over the edge to see a large knot of the bugs boiling furiously up the arroyo toward them. "Whatever he's doing, he better do it fast."

"Would, if we off this piece rock," Jak said, dragging him farther back. "Come on!"

Ryan allowed himself to be led away from the edge to the other side of the hilltop, where the rest of the group crouched behind a small outcropping.

"Got Ryan," Jak said.

"Now look who's taking his sweet time," J.B. remarked.

"Yeah, you," Ryan replied. "Those bugs chased Jak and me clear up here and are going to be coming at us any minute now. What?" he asked on seeing the broad smiles on his friends' faces.

"Are they, now?" J.B. asked.

As he said that, Ryan heard a dull *crump* that he felt in the soles of his feet and the pit of his stomach. The ground around them began to shake, and Ryan heard the patter of gravel, followed by the rumble of much larger rocks breaking loose. The noise grew until it was impossible to think, much less talk. A large cloud of dust billowed over everyone, making Ryan and the others cough. After about thirty seconds, the commotion died down, with only scattered falling pebbles and acrid dust hanging in the air left over.

Ryan walked back to the gully's edge, now several feet farther back from where Jak and he had climbed up. J.B.'s controlled blast had brought down the entire cliff face, turning several tons of rock into a lethal landslide. Waving drifting dust away, Ryan squinted through it to look down the hillside. Other than scattered parts of burrow-bugs—a leg here, a smashed thorax there— sticking out of the large pile of jumbled rocks several stories below, there was no living sign of the small insectile army that had been pursuing them.

"Ricky came up with the idea," J.B. said as he came up beside him. "Then it was just a matter of finding the right place to set it off."

"Plus, if fortune smiles on us, the resulting blast should cause no little consternation among those damnably persistent insects," Doc said.

"Yeah, but even that isn't the best news," Krysty said. Taking Ryan's hand, she led him to the far side of the hill, where the sun was just beginning to rise over the eastern horizon. Across a few foothills below them, he looked out onto a barren wasteland that, although sun-parched and desolate, didn't contain any sign of the burrowing horde.

Wiping his face free of blood and bug goo, Ryan smiled. "We're out of the valley."

Chapter Seven

One day later, Ryan would have happily taken on one of those bugs again. He was so thirsty he would have hacked its head off with one swing and gulped down its thick, black blood as if it were fine wine.

His swollen tongue flicked out to try to moisten his parched, split lips, but retreated the moment it touched them. From the arid, cracked ground to the sullen, cloudless, crimson-red sky, everywhere he looked, there wasn't a drop of water to be found. Or plants. Or animals. Once, they heard a long, far-off shriek of some kind of bird, but never saw any sign of it. Doc had grunted that it was staying out of the heat, proving that even a birdbrain was smarter than all of them. Save for the seven people trudging across the bleak landscape, there was no sign of life anywhere—just the endless horizon, wavering and blurry in the relentless heat.

The large lemon-yellow sun beat down mercilessly on them, sapping strength and making it hard to think, much less walk. True to Mildred's prediction, Doc had crashed after the effects of the amphetamine had worn off. He was now being hauled by J.B., who plodded along with the older man's arm slung across his shoulders. Mildred was also favoring her injured arm, bound in a crude sling across her chest. Ryan had also felt the slowness and exhaustion of the pill wearing off, but he powered through it, just as he did every other day of his life. His entire body hurt as if someone had beaten each inch of it with a club, but he walked on, determined not to show any weakness.

Even the normally indefatigable Jak was showing signs of wearing down. "Got find shelter soon…gonna cook, we stay out any longer." His red eyes peered out from the folds of the dingy bright pink T-shirt wrapped around his head and neck, making him look like some kind of demented Bedouin.

"Just…like the…proverbial goose…my milk-haired friend…." Doc wheezed with every limping step.

"Save your strength, Doc," J.B. said. "Need every bit of it to get through this."

Despite her injury, Mildred didn't seem all that affected by the heat, nor did Krysty. In fact, Krysty was scanning all around them, at times lifting her nose almost as if she was scenting the air.

"Something up?" Ryan asked.

"Don't know. The breeze is rising, but it doesn't feel right, somehow." Shading her eyes with her hand, Krysty scanned the horizon all around. "Something's coming. Surely there has to be some kind of shelter somewhere."

"We could dig a hole in the ground, cover up and wait for the bad weather to pass, right?" Ricky offered.

"You take a shot at it, Ricky," J.B. replied. "This hardpan is rock solid. I might be able to blast a hole in it with plas-ex, but it wouldn't be large enough to do us any good."

"Right now I'll settle for any moving air. That breeze should feel good," Mildred said, eyes on the ground in front of her as she walked, her combat boots kicking up small puffs of dirt with every step.

"Mebbe—if it doesn't bring anything with it," Ryan replied, keeping his tone neutral. If a storm blew up here—sand or dust or anything else—they were as good as dead if they couldn't find any cover. Squinting, he tried to pick out anything that might serve as refuge for them from the surrounding wasteland.

"Our real problem is dehydration," Mildred continued. "It's so hot out here that we're losing water but not realizing it because our sweat's evaporating as soon as it comes out."

"Always ready to give us the good news, aren't you, Millie?" J.B. said with a quick smile to let her know he was kidding.

"Nothing funny about it," she replied. "Facts are facts—if we don't find water soon, we're done for."

The breeze was freshening, but even it was deceptive; a hot, dry wind that plucked at their skin and clothes, but provided no relief.

In the end, Ricky spotted their salvation. "There," he said, pointing off to the south. "I think I see a stone building?"

Ryan and J.B. both shaded their eyes. "Hard to tell…" J.B. said. "Out here everything looks like dark smudges against light smudges."

"If it is a building, we'd best get to it," Krysty said, glancing behind them. "A storm's definitely coming our way."

Ryan glanced back as well and saw a dark cloud a few miles away. "Yeah. Best move out double-quick. J.B., I'll spell you with Doc."

"It is not necessary…my dear Ryan.…" Doc whispered. "I just need…to rest…a spell.…"

"Close those lips and move those legs, Doc, and we'll

be safe and sound before you know it," Ryan said as he draped the older man's arm across his shoulders.

The wind was already blowing harder now, ruffling hair, kicking up dust and driving everyone forward with more urgency. As they traveled, the smudge far ahead solidified into what looked like a large, low, stone building.

"What if it's a ruin?" J.B. asked as they went.

"Any shelter'll work to protect us from whatever's coming," Ryan said, leaving the rest of his thought unspoken. Deathlands was home to all sorts of crazy weather, from chem storms to acid—real acid—rain.

"It's gaining on us," Mildred said, casting a glance to their right. "Since we're no longer moving ahead of it, it's going to catch us pretty soon."

"I can see the building now. It's old, but still standing," Ryan replied. "We've just got to get there first. Everybody keep moving."

Somehow, they all managed to quicken their pace. Ten more minutes of trotting and walking brought the companions close enough to see the large, solid stone building in the distance, squat and immovable. And just in time, too, as the storm was almost on them. Visibility was falling rapidly, and everyone was covered in grit from the swirling wind.

"Almost there! Keep your eyes on it—don't look away, or you'll lose it!" Ryan shouted over the now howling wind.

"Everyone join hands!" J.B. said, grabbing Mildred's. If someone got separated or lost, it would be nearly impossible to find the person in the dense cloud.

Staggering through the rising dust storm, the companions pushed on toward their destination. By the time they reached the building, the wind had risen to a deafening howl, and they all were shielding their faces as they fought to stand against the gale. The dust whipped up by the storm was everywhere, caking, blinding, choking.

Ryan was practically carrying Doc along when he reached the old wooden doors. Even in this deserted landscape, they were stuck or locked. "Shit! Won't open!"

"Let me try!" Jak shouted. Ryan hauled Doc away from the entrance while Jak backed up a few steps, then ran forward. When he was a couple of yards away, he leaped into the air and drove his foot into the seam between the two doors. Ryan faintly heard a loud *crack* above the storm. "Again—do it again!" he said between coughs.

Now hacking himself, Jak backed up and ran at the door again. This time his kick broke the doors open, and he fell in the entryway. "C'mon!" he said, holding one of the doors open.

The rest of the group piled inside, and Jak and Ricky struggled to push the doors closed, wedging them shut with pieces of the broken crossbar Jak had smashed through.

"Looks like this might have been some kind of school back in the day," Mildred said as they looked around.

They were standing at the end of a long hallway, with several doors on each side of it. Old gray metal lockers lined the walls between the doors. Lights that hadn't turned on in a century hung from the ceiling, and faded papers hung on the walls, unreadable after all this time. Although it was easier to breathe here, dust could still be seen filtering in through cracks under doors.

"Let's see if we can find someplace as far away from

the dust as possible," Ryan said after trying to bring up enough saliva to spit, but failing. "Bet there's not a drop of water to be found in here either."

"Doubt it," Mildred said. "This place was probably abandoned even in my time. Small town, maybe a mining or oil community once, then the mine closed or the oil dried up, and the town dried up along with it. It happened all the time."

"Lucky for us they didn't tear everything down when they moved on," J.B. said as they walked farther into the hallway. Jak tried opening one of the doors, but a gust of wind and sand blew into his face, and he quickly shut it again while pawing at his eyes.

"Damn dust—hurts like hell!"

Ryan's concern seemed to be well founded. In the center of the building they found a larger room that looked to have been a cafeteria in another lifetime. But when he tried the taps in a large, industrial-size sink in the kitchen, they didn't even move, frozen shut by a century of nonoperation.

"Looks like we made it here, only to die of thirst," Mildred said.

"We're not dead yet, and there's still more to explore. Might find a cache no one knows about," Ryan replied. "Let's keep going."

They reached the end of the corridor and found a stairway behind a wooden door with a wire-reinforced window in it. The stairway led down.

Mildred frowned. "That's weird. I didn't think most buildings in tornado country had storm cellars, although they sure needed them."

"Let's take a look." Ryan grabbed the rusty knob and turned it, opening the door with a scrape across the dusty floor. The moment he did, he froze, except for his blaster arm, which drew his SIG Sauer in a single practiced movement.

Turning back to his friends, he saw they'd all heard what he had once the door was open.

Faint voices from below.

Chapter Eight

Ryan immediately pulled back in case there were any guards nearby. The voices continued talking, echoing down the underground passage. They sounded as if they were fairly far away.

J.B. was beside him in an instant, Mini-Uzi at the ready. "Can you make out what they're saying?"

Ryan shook his head, his reply just as low. "Too much echo. If I had to guess, it sounds like someone arguing over something."

He glanced at Krysty. "You got anything?"

She also shook her head. "The storm is overwhelming everything, and something about this building is blocking my ability. It's like a dead zone in here."

"No tracks on the way in. They must have been here awhile," Mildred said.

"No sign vehicles outside," Jak added. "Caught storm like us?"

"Only one way to find out." Ryan slowly eased the stairwell door open again. "Jak, you're on point. Throwing blades for right now—don't need to cause an alarm if we can avoid it. I want to get the drop on whoever's down there."

Jak had unwrapped the T-shirt from around his head and stowed it while making a knife appear in his other hand as if by magic. "Sneak and peek—fun." He eased through the door, as soundless as a mirage. Ryan gave him a few seconds' lead, then followed, with J.B. a step behind him.

The concrete stairs were covered in a thick layer of dust, also with no footprints on them. "Where the nuke did they come in from?" J.B. muttered.

"Shh," Ryan cautioned, although he'd thought the same thing. They'd already encountered burrowing bugs. The last thing he needed to see was some kind of burrowing humans living in here.

Making no noise on the steps, the companions descended to the lower level, with Jak signaling all clear every few paces. A single light shone from an open doorway at the far end of the hall. They passed a few other doors on both sides of the hallway, most hanging open, revealing empty rooms inside. As they progressed down the dark tunnel, the voices became more distinct.

"—take us to the rest of your people, that's all I'm asking. If she don't get help, she's gonna die!"

"What do you expect us to do? Whatever sickness she's got ain't like nothing I ever seen before!"

"'Sides, it's hard to believe you don't mean us any harm with that blaster pointing at us."

"I'm sorry, but I'm out of patience, and I'm through asking!"

"Look, we can't go anywhere until the storm dies down. And she's right, all we could do is make your friend comfortable until she passes aw—"

A low, loud, bone-chilling moan interrupted the second speaker, the sound of someone in mortal agony. It continued for several seconds, cutting off the argument inside and making Ryan's skin crawl. He exchanged a glance with Mildred, her eyes white and wide against her dark skin, and got a shrug in return as they drew closer.

Jak stepped up to the side of the doorway now and looked at Ryan, who was already handing him a small, polished metal mirror. Jak crouched and carefully extended it past the door frame to get a look into the room. He held it there for a few seconds, angling it around while the discussion of taking the injured woman somewhere continued. Finally Jak pulled his hand back and turned to Ryan, signaling what he'd seen.

Four people inside, all on far side of the room. Hurt one lying down. Two scavvies sitting against the right wall. Man with blaster standing between them and woman.

With a clear picture of the interior and its occupants now, Ryan was ready to take them. He pointed at Jak, then at the left interior wall next to the door. Jak gave him a curt nod, but waited while Ryan detailed what the rest of their strike party was going to do. When everyone was ready, he held up his hand and counted down from three fingers…two…one.

The albino stepped through the door and took up his position on the left side, while Ryan went in and took up a position on the right side. J.B. came next, followed by Mildred and Krysty. Ricky was staying outside with a nearly unconscious Doc.

"Nobody move, and nobody has to die," Ryan said, the muzzle of his blaster dead center on the standing man, who turned his head to look at the newcomers in shock. They stood amid several empty freestanding shelves lining the walls, indicating this had once been a storeroom.

It was the break one of the raggedly dressed people sitting against the wall had been waiting for. He launched himself at the man, barreling into him and sending him staggering across the room. The blaster flew from the man's hand, skittering across the floor to stop in front of J.B., who stooped and picked it up without taking his eyes off the two struggling, cursing figures.

"Fireblast!" Ryan said, striding forward. The scavvie crouched on top of the other man, who was dressed in a relatively clean light blue jumpsuit, and pummeled him with wild, flying fists. The former hostage taker was doing his best to protect his head and face, but his assailant was so pissed that only one out of every three blows was landing.

"All right, enough of that!" Grabbing the one on top by the back of his ragtag jacket, Ryan hauled the short wiry guy, arms still flailing, off the downed man. When the guy tried turning to punch Ryan, he simply lifted him off the floor and held him in midair.

"What're you— Let me go! You gotta kill him before they kill all of us!" the captive yelled in a high-pitched voice. He was dressed in a patchwork combination of what other people would have called rags, but on closer examination, Ryan saw they were stitched with care and fit the guy's small frame well. His pants were a mix of canvas, blue denim and leather, and his shoes were worn construction boots that had been repurposed with what looked like rubber patches on the toe and heels. Ryan turned him around to see his face, revealing short-cropped, dirty blond hair framing a definitely female face now twisted into a combination of rage and fear.

"Look, just calm down, all right? He's unarmed now, and it doesn't look like you're in any real danger."

"You don't understand!" she cried. "They'll—"

Another loud groan interrupted her, and everyone glanced over to see another person lying on the floor, a jacket fashioned into a crude pillow under her head. The woman was dressed in the same kind of jumpsuit as the man, except her abdomen was grossly distended, making the fabric bulge out.

"Just relax, Sammee," the man on the floor said through swelling lips. "Please, help her if you can. That's all I ask.... I'll do whatever you want, just help her."

"You best do what Tully said, kill both of them quick before they come for all of us," the second person sitting against the wall, a lanky black-haired man, said.

"I'm not taking orders from any of you right now," Ryan said. "J.B., Jak, watch these three. Mildred, check her out."

"It's all right, I'm a healer," Mildred said as she crossed the room and knelt by the sweating, ashen-faced woman holding her bloated stomach with both hands. "Do you know how long you've been pregnant?"

The woman shook her head, but broke in as Mildred began asking another question. "Not...pregnant. It's... dying."

Mildred's brow furrowed. "It? What's it?"

Sammee opened her mouth as if to answer, but instead let out a high-pitched scream at the top of her lungs. Mildred placed a hand on her stomach, then drew back. "It's distended and hard...and, oh, my God."

As Ryan and everyone else watched, something stretched out the woman's skin from the inside, creating a small bump as if poking at her, then retreated.

"Do you have a parasite living inside you?" Mildred

asked as she pulled out her small medical kit. "Do you know how long it's been there? Or how you contracted it?"

Sammee shook her head. "Dunno—just know it's killin' me—" Her words turned into another scream of pure pain.

"I'm going to try to cut it out of her!" Mildred selected a scalpel and positioned it at the top of her stomach. But the moment the blade touched the woman's skin, she jackknifed forward, tendons in her neck popping as she strained against something inside her, mouth open in a silent scream, then fell back onto the floor, motionless, her wide eyes staring sightlessly at the ceiling.

Mildred checked her pulse at both the wrist and carotid artery. "She's dead. I'm sorry."

"No! No! No! No!" The other man crawled over to his dead woman and cradled her in his arms. "We were leaving, gonna make a new life…" He looked at the ceiling and screamed, "We were going! We would have left you alone! Why couldn't you just leave us alone?" Mildred was already preparing a small tranquilizer shot, one of the precious few she had, and stabbed it into the man's arm as his screams faded into loud sobs. The man didn't notice, just cried until the drug took effect, and he slumped over into unconsciousness. When he was out, Mildred closed Sammee's eyes, removed the jacket from under her head and covered her with it.

For a moment, no one moved. Then Ryan spoke. "What the hell's going on here?"

"Let me down and I'll tell ya." With both of the jumpsuited people out of commission, the blonde fist fighter had calmed down a bit.

"All right—just remember who has all the blasters."

When she nodded, Ryan carefully lowered her to the floor.

Tully straightened her clothes and walked back to her partner before saying anything. "You know I'm Tully, and this here's Latham." She nodded at her bearded companion. "We're part of a group heading west. We come from south of the Lachan Mountains, but over the past few years the barons over there have been gettin' more and more greedy, putting folks off their land, and killin' them that don't go peaceful. When we had enough, we headed west. Heard of plenty of good land out there, with few people to bother us. We're just lookin' to settle down somewhere and farm and live without any trouble."

Ryan nodded. He'd heard this story many times before. Tales of some sort of fabled Eden were a dime a dozen—and worth just about as much, too. "Go on."

"I will, but first…" Tully rummaged in her pack and pulled out a metal canteen. Opening it, she took a drink, then offered it to Ryan. "You all look pretty dry."

Ryan slowly reached for it, trying not to betray his eagerness. "Thanks." He forced himself to take one mouthful—even though every last inch of him cried out to drain the entire container—then handed it to Krysty. "One swallow each. Jak, have Ricky bring Doc in here."

While he instructed the others, Tully talked quietly with her companion, who grudgingly surrendered his canteen to Ryan and the others. Each of them took a second, precious gulp of the flat, metallic-tasting water, savoring it as if it were the finest predark liquor.

"We'd encountered another dust storm like the one outside a few days ago, and hunkered down in a ville a few miles east of here. That's when we were attacked—"

Tully nodded at the sleeping man and his dead companion "—by these folks."

Jak frowned. "Not seem like much threat. Chill and keep movin'."

The man called Latham snorted. "You wouldn't say that if you saw them in action. These two—" he waved at their prisoner and the corpse "—don't even come close. Can't put them down, not easily.… They take a shitload of damage and just keep comin'." He ran a hand through his thinning hair. "They're…different. They all move and fight together, like…ants or somethin'. I don't know how to explain it. I just know I never seen humans actin' that way before."

"Anyway, they first struck as the storm was dyin', and carried off a half dozen of our people," Tully said. "Came back a few nights later—and our own people were among the force hitting us."

Latham stared at the ground, and Tully paused for a moment as she glanced at him, then shook her head. "I couldn't believe it. We had to—had to chill them that we'd called our own just a couple days earlier…before they did the same to us."

Ryan exchanged a glance with Krysty and J.B. Through their travels, they'd encountered many strange and terrible sights, so this one wasn't that far-fetched. A rogue experiment created by whitecoats, some odd mutation that affected an entire population, or even a strange sect that practiced an unusual form of combat could be behind this new potential threat.

"The elders held a meeting and decided to send parties out to find help. That's what we were doing when we came across this building." Tully spit into a corner. "That fuck got the drop on us, and tried to force us to take him and her back to our people. Then you all showed up, and now here we are."

J.B. had been examining the man's weapon while the two were talking, and now he looked at Ryan while holding up the blaster, a brand-new-looking matte black 9 mm Beretta 92-F. "Wherever he's come from, they got good tech."

"Yeah, they had other weapons, too—longblasters," Latham said. "If it hadn't been for Tully and some of the others, our group wouldn't have survived."

"What do you mean by that?" Krysty asked. "You're not a mercie?" At the other woman's frown, she elucidated. "A hired blaster, coldheart, that sort of thing."

The smaller woman grimaced. "Naw, just got a temper, that's all. Our people don't practice violence.... It's just not our way. But when I saw others bein' carried away or killed, I knew I had to do somethin'. I jumped one of them, got his weapon away and shot him. Shot a bunch more and freed some of the caught ones so we could drive them off."

"But they'll be back," Latham said. "We all know it."

Ryan and J.B. exchanged weary glances at this part. Along with the pipe dream of Eden, a place to live in peace and quiet, right behind that was the idea of not being bothered by any bandits or raiders or anyone, or not having to take up arms to defend what was yours. Ryan and his companions knew that was only wishful thinking on those people's parts, since it was always easier to take than to work, to steal and destroy instead of build and create. There was no shortage of people willing to turn to that kind of life to sustain themselves. It was plain survival in the Deathlands, a way of life. Eventually, the takers would come calling no matter where you were—or how well you thought you'd hidden yourself.

"So keep moving," J.B. said. "If they come and go like you say, they have a base of operations, and once you get out of range, they'll leave you alone."

"A lot of us want to do just that, but the elders don't want to leave family members behind, even ones who've been…changed like these two," Tully said. "If we push on now, we're doomin' them to whatever captivity they're stuck in. If we stay, we risk losing everybody and everything to these people. That was why we were lookin' for help. We got food and water, that's all we can really offer anybody, but that should count for something, right?"

Ryan nodded. "Right." And so does the idea of someone nearby having predark technology and ammunition, he thought. "Why don't we all get some rest while the storm blows itself out, and when it's done, we'll figure out what to do, okay?"

Tully blinked, as if the idea of these new people actually helping them had never occurred to her. "Uh… sure, okay. I mean, we're already in your debt for savin' us from them. The least we can do is feed you before you head out on your way."

"That's very kind of you," Krysty said.

"Don't suppose you have any of that food on you right now?" Ricky asked.

Latham nodded at their bedrolls in a corner. "It won't go very far among all of us, but you're welcome to what we have. We're not too far from the main camp—well, we weren't till you found us—but because you'll be walkin', they're about a day's travel away."

"You got a faster way of traveling?" Ricky asked.

Latham nodded. "Easier to show you than tell you."

"What about them?" Mildred pointed at the other two.

"Didn't seem to have much on them," Tully said. "And they weren't too hungry, either, for some reason. Only took a couple of bites. Don't know why."

"Stress, or whatever parasitic creature was in that woman, may explain part of it," Mildred said. "I wouldn't mind taking a closer look at her if I got the chance."

"Not now," Ryan said. "We're all pretty strung out. We also need to get some rest—" *and talk about what we should do,* he casually signed to the rest "—before figuring out what to do next, okay?"

They shared the scavvie farmers' meager rations— a couple of mouthfuls of relatively fresh bread and dried meat—and used a self-heat tab found on the still-unconscious man to make a cup of watery broth for Doc. Within a few minutes, the two, along with Doc, were fast asleep, leaving the rest of the group free to talk. Even so, Ryan moved them all out into the hallway, finding a vantage point where he could keep an eye on the sleeping scavvies and the jumpsuited man, as well.

The conversation was brief and to the point. "Not a convoy of wags loaded with ammo and trade goods, but it's a damn sight better than nothing," J.B. said.

"Besides, do we have much of a choice?" Krysty asked. "With the mat-trans gone, it could be a couple hundred miles or more to the nearest redoubt. At least if we go with these people, we have a shot at finding wherever the others are coming from, mebbe even locate a redoubt of their own. Solve a couple problems at once."

"Exactly," Ryan replied. "Our low ammo and supplies are major problems, so we might as well stick with these folks and see what we can see. At the very least we'll get fed, and if things go our way, we could get a hold of a lot more than that."

"Maybe when he wakes up in a few hours, we can ask him about where he came from." Mildred yawned. "Don't know about you folks, but I'm dead on my feet. I'm going to take advantage of the relative peace and quiet here and sack out."

"Works for me," J.B. said. "Watches?"

Although tempted to let everyone get some shut-eye, Ryan knew all too well the potential folly of trusting folks they'd just met. "Two-hour spans. I'll take the first, Jak second, Krysty third, Ricky fourth." He nodded at the three sleepers in the next room. "They shouldn't give any trouble, but even so, don't get too close. Everybody get some rest while you can. Jak, I'll wake you when your turn comes."

Chapter Nine

Though surrounded by the hot, baking plains and the searing dust storm, for some reason Jak dreamed of his home, deep in the swamps of what had been Louisiana long, long ago.

It wasn't a true dream, just a series of disjointed images and sounds…trickling water…a snake slithering through the deep forest…and perhaps a slaughtered animal being dragged toward a ville for butchering.

It was this last sound that caused the albino's eyes to pop open and blink to see Ryan standing over him. "Time, huh?"

The black-haired man nodded. "Heard some scuttling earlier—there may be a rat around here. Keep your eyes open."

Jak rolled his eyes. "No shit. Why not teach me suck eggs, too."

As the albino got up and stretched, Ryan walked over to Krysty, curled around her protectively and was asleep in seconds.

Jak watched the sleeping couple for a moment, wistfulness passing over his scarred features. The land they were traveling through reminded him of the area around the farm he'd stayed on for a few months with his wife, Christina, after leaving the companions. Those had been good times—until she and their baby girl had been killed and the homestead contaminated by a bunch of rad-blasted crazies. With the life he'd built in ashes, Jak had rejoined the companions, and been with them ever since.

But that didn't mean he didn't mourn the loss of his wife or daughter, or envy those in the group who had found love. Granted, he was happy for them, but at the same time, he wondered if he'd ever get the chance to know real love again, like what he'd had with Christina.

A slight rustle in the dark room, near the body of the dead woman, attracted Jak's attention, and he glanced over at her. Night had fallen outside, rendering the room and outer hallway so dark that they'd left a small flash-light on for visibility. It was dim, but more than enough for Jak to see the entire room as if it were high noon.

As he looked more closely at the woman's body, he saw the jacket Mildred had placed over her head and chest had slid off. Something gleamed wetly in the light, and the albino walked over to check it out.

Her stomach had deflated over the past few hours, and now the corpse looked like any other normal dead woman. Well, not quite. Jak leaned closer to see what looked like some kind of shiny mucus ringing her mouth. "What…" He leaned over to see the trail of thick slime dripping down the side of her dead face and onto the floor…as if something had come out of her mouth and left it behind.

A throwing blade appeared in Jak's hand as he looked along the glistening trail to the nearest person—the still-sleeping guy who had taken the scavvies hostage.

But as Jak peered closer at the man, he realized he wasn't just sleeping—his entire body was twitching, as if he was being shaken or something. As the albino took a step closer, he realized that the trail ran not only to the man's body, but whatever had come out of the dead woman had actually slithered *onto* him. Jak wrinkled his nose at the thought, even as he leaned down for a closer look at the sleeping man.

That was when his eyes snapped open.

At the same time, his hand shot up and grabbed Jak around the throat—or tried to. Jak, however, had been fighting since he could walk, and evaded the clumsy grab with ease. His blade flicked out in return, and the man drew back three bleeding fingers.

The albino took a step back as the man sat up, then rose to his feet. All trace of his earlier hysteria was gone, replaced by an intense stare at the white-haired teenager.

Jak stared back at him. "Best sit, if know what good for ya."

The man cocked his head as he regarded Jak. "Current subject appears to be result of massive mutations in parents, resulting in abnormal skin, hair and eye appearance. Given the typical genetic weaknesses inherent in offspring of mutations, subject is deemed not suitable for implantation. Recommend rejoining the rest of the primary group for debriefing and complete physical examination." He flexed his fingers, which had already stopped bleeding.

"What say 'bout me?" Jak asked. The man didn't answer, but stepped to the side, apparently intending to go around him. The albino moved over to block his path. "Not goin' anywhere—"

This time the man moved fast—so fast that even Jak was caught off guard. He slammed an open palm into the smaller man's chest, knocking him back several steps. Hitting the wall, Jak rebounded and came at him again, cutting him off before he reached the door. "Fucker!"

"What's going on, Jak?" Ryan asked.

"Slime trail from dead woman," Jak replied, not taking his eyes off his opponent. "Went this guy. Tried grab me. Said nonsense, now tryin' leave. 'Bout show him that's bad idea."

Blaster in hand, Ryan had also risen to his feet during Jak's speech, and now pointed the weapon casually at the man's midsection. "Best stand down before the Jak puts a world of hurt on you."

The man regarded Ryan with that same flat stare. "New subject acquired. Initial scan shows excellent physical health, with only detractor a missing left eye. Subject otherwise suitable for implantation. Move to acquire if possible before returning to primary group."

The man stepped toward Ryan, but was stopped again by Jak, who raised his fists. "Said get back, fucker!" He flicked out a fist whip fast, snapping the man's head back and loosing a trickle of blood from his nose.

The man stopped, now looking at Jak again. "Re-evaluating initial observation of mutant. Reflexes and strength both demonstrated at abnormally high levels. Suggest obtaining him as well before departure. Resetting adrenaline levels in anticipation of possible conflict during subdual." Oddly, his nose, like his fingers earlier, had already stopped bleeding.

"What the hell, Ryan! Are we setting up pit fights now?" J.B. asked from his corner.

"Got a weird situation," Ryan replied. "Jumpsuit here's trying to leave, but he keeps spouting stuff about Jak and me."

He nodded to the albino. "Take him down, but make sure you keep him alive. We're going to get some questions answered afterward."

A thin, feral smile creasing his features, Jak nodded and started advancing on the man, who stood motionless as he approached. "Not go anywhere," he said,
then immediately lashed out with a right fist, aiming
for the guy's cheek to stun him before moving in to finish him off.

Only that wasn't what happened.

Instead, Jak missed.

The man moved his head aside just enough so that
Jak's callused hand grazed his ear. While he did that, his
left hand shot up to try to grab Jak's wrist, while his right
hand pistoned forward into Jak's stomach. The combination of dodge and riposte were so fast they blurred
together into one single action, faster than Jak, Ryan or
J.B. had ever seen.

Even so, Jak managed to move out of the way of the
punch so the man's fist glanced off his ribs. "Son of a—"
He backed off a step, dancing on his feet, bobbing and
weaving back and forth. Two angry spots of pink col-
ored his high, pale cheeks. "Done playin'!"

"Don't kill him, Jak," Ryan warned.

The albino shook his head, making his snow-white
hair sway back and forth. "Won't—just put him down
hard."

He came in fast this time, a blur of motion. Feint-
ing high to draw the man's attention, Jak dropped into
a crouch and swung his leg out in a roundhouse sweep,
intending to knock the man off his feet, then take him
out with a punch to the face.

But again he was thwarted. Committed to his sweep,
his feral look of glee turned to disappointment as the
man stepped over his swinging leg even as he leaned
down to hook it with his arm. Using Jak's momentum

against him, he brought the leg up and pushed it back, sending the skinny kid over onto his buttocks.

Kicking free, Jak kept rolling, turning the takedown into a somersault so he could land on his feet. That was good, because the man wasn't stopping either. He advanced on his smaller opponent and tried to grab him again, this time at the scruff of the neck. Jak batted the incoming arm away with a swat and followed that up with a ram's-head punch to the man's shoulder, staggering him.

"Shouldn't we help him?" Mildred, who had been awakened by the commotion, asked.

"Ninety-nine times out of a hundred, Jak doesn't need any," J.B. replied.

"What about the hundredth?" she asked.

"Still waiting to see it," he replied. "Although this guy's giving him a decent run for his money."

Jak darted close to the man and fired several short punches into the right side of his rib cage. The blows had to have hurt—Jak heard the snap of at least one rib in the flurry—but the injury didn't seem to slow the man in the least. He swept Jak's fist aside and followed that up with a front kick to his chest that knocked Jak off his feet and sent him skidding across the floor and into the two scavvies.

"What the fuck—?" Tully asked.

"Stay down!" Wincing, Jak got up again, moving a bit slower now.

"You still got him?" Ryan asked.

"Damn right!" Fixing the man with a venomous stare, Jak took two steps forward and leaped into the air, his combat boot–shod feet lancing out to crush the man's sternum.

The man grabbed Jak's feet with both hands and started to pull him to the floor. That, however, was exactly what Jak wanted him to do. The moment those fingers closed around his ankles, he jackknifed forward and reached out to slam his cupped hands against the man's ears.

The painful twin blows rocked his opponent, and he released Jak's feet, letting him fall to the floor as he clapped his hands to his head and swayed on his feet. Jak scooted forward, hooked the guy's legs with his own and swept them out from under him, sending him crashing to the floor, his head bouncing off the concrete. Just like that, the fight was over.

"How hard did you hit him?" Ryan asked.

"Enough make him let go," Jak replied. "Mebbe burst eardrum, too." He grinned at Ryan's wince. "Hey, stopped bastard?"

"Yeah…just hope you didn't kill him. Mildred, check him out."

"Sure." She got up, grabbed the flashlight and went to the semiconscious man, thumbing back his eyelids and shining the light into them. "Pupil response is good. Better observe him for the next couple of hours, though… ugh, what's this?" She wiped her fingers on her pants leg. "He's got some kind of slime all over his mouth."

"Same stuff saw on dead woman." Jak pointed at the dead body.

Mildred straightened and walked over to take a look. "What is this?" She followed the drying trail to where the other man had been sleeping. "It's like a giant snail came out of her and into him…which means whatever was inside the dead woman was still alive after she died."

Chapter Ten

"Sure you want to do this, Mildred?" J.B. asked.

She nodded. "Look, if some kind of parasite is running around here, we could all be at risk." She glanced at the woman's body, which was beginning to smell, lying on the counter. "If I can find out what happened to her, maybe I can get a better handle on what this thing is."

Mildred stood in the abandoned cafeteria, along with Ryan, J.B. and Krysty. Doc was still sleeping, and Jak and Ricky were guarding their prisoner. The dust storm had abated somewhat, but was still kicking up enough dirt that it was dangerous to go outside.

"Makes sense, it's just…" Ryan shook his head as he stared at the body they stood in front of. "I've spent enough time putting people in the dirt. I'm not too keen on doing much poking around in them afterward."

"Well, it's a good thing you have me here," Mildred replied. "All right, you all will probably want to stand back before I make the first incision. She's probably not going to smell any better once I open her up."

Ryan and the others did as she suggested. Once they were at a relatively safe distance, Mildred selected her sharpest scalpel and made a Y-shaped incision, cutting down from each shoulder to the middle of the chest, then straight down from there to the waist. Then she peeled back the skin and flesh to reveal the chest cavity. True to her word, there was a release of noxious gases that made the rest of them turn away and cover their noses and mouths.

"I warned you." Without pausing, she began examining the body's organs.

"What are you looking for?" Krysty asked as she edged closer.

"I'm not quite sure," Mildred replied. "But I'll know it when I see it." Grabbing the breastbone, she wrenched apart the rib cage with a sharp *crack!* "So far, nothing out of the ordinary." She glanced at the others. "You guys don't have to watch this if you don't want to."

"No, I'm good," Ryan replied. "It's not so bad once you get used to the smell."

J.B. just nodded in agreement.

"All right, then." Mildred picked up her scalpel again. "Krysty, if you don't mind, I'm going to begin removing organs and handing them to you. Just set them aside on the table, if you would."

"Should I be looking for anything in particular?" the red-haired woman asked. "Back in Harmony, Mother Sonja taught me a good deal about human anatomy."

"If you see anything you think is odd, sing out," Mildred replied. With that, she efficiently cut out and removed the lungs, heart, stomach, liver, pancreas, gallbladder, kidneys and large and small intestines—the last one taking the efforts of both women to remove.

"Anything yet?" Ryan asked.

"Not really, except that all of these organs are in really good shape—not what I'd expect from your typical Deathlands dweller. Even if a person lived in a redoubt for most of his or her life, there can be vitamin deficiencies, organ malfunction, things like that. But these look like they're at the peak of health."

"Mildred, what's all this?" Krysty had set down the slimy loops of small intestine and was peering into the chest cavity. "That doesn't look familiar to me at all."

"No, it sure doesn't…." Mildred took one of her scalpels and reached inside the body to cut something off.

Ryan and J.B. walked closer to get a look at what was on her knife blade. "Any idea what that is?" Ryan asked as he looked at the tiny strands of what looked like white filaments.

"I have no idea, but they're everywhere on the back of her," Mildred said. "Have a look."

The others all gathered around and looked inside the now empty chest cavity. A fine network of the tiny white lines ran all through the woman's back, along her spine and perhaps even farther.

"It'll take me a while to cut into the back of the head so I can see if this goes into the brain, but I'm pretty sure it will," Mildred said. "It looks like whatever was in her had extended some kind of nerve fibers to her organs, her spine and probably her nervous system, as well."

"To what end?" J.B. asked.

"Hard to say," Mildred replied. "Typically parasites are content to simply feed off their host. They don't seek to control them, except in very specific instances. There are, however, many instances of parasitic insects laying their eggs in a host, and when the eggs hatch, they use the host for food or protection. There's even a barnacle, genus *Sacculina,* that not only sterilizes its crab host, but forces the crab to gestate the barnacle's young, even to the extent of altering a male's hormones to make it more feminine, and better able to birth the young."

"Okay, as fascinating as all this is, what's it got to do with her?" Ryan nodded at the body.

"Well, from what I'm seeing, this sort of invasive system goes far beyond simple feeding or protection. It looks like the parasite is actively seeking to control the host in some way. That could explain the improved fighting ability and resistance to physical injury. If the parasite is able to control the nervous system, it can block off the nerve impulses transmitting pain from limbs or injuries, control blood flow…pretty much do whatever it wants to the host."

"He did say something about 'resetting adrenaline level' when fighting Jak. Could that be part of it?" Ryan asked.

Mildred nodded. "Sure. An advanced enough organism could control any bodily system, down to a person's smallest aspect." She shuddered. "Don't ever want to see one of those coming my way, thank you."

J.B. had been taking in all of this without saying a word. "Is this anything like what went on in Heaven Falls?" The four of them exchanged glances as they recalled that encounter. Heaven Falls had been a utopian ville with a dark secret—its inhabitants had been brainwashed by irradiated honey that had transformed them into superhuman beings with a hive mentality. When Ryan and the others had encountered them—and almost fallen prey to their seductive lifestyle—they had been forced to destroy the entire place in order to prevent the "queen" from spreading her influence throughout the Deathlands.

"Yes and no," Mildred replied. "For example, it looks like these two were escaping from wherever they came from, so they obviously had retained or regained some free will at some point."

"Yeah…" J.B. rubbed his chin. "I don't know about the rest of you, but I've got no desire to be facing anything like that again."

Ryan chose his answer carefully; their time in Heaven Falls had nearly torn the group apart. "I hear you, except these two didn't seem to be *that* dangerous. Also, we still need supplies if we're going to get to another redoubt, so I think they're our best bet. We all just have to stay on guard, and not take anything for granted this time."

J.B. nodded. "Sound advice."

"Wait a minute. Something's still bothering me about this woman." Krysty looked up from where she had been staring at the autopsied body. "Mildred, you said the organs all looked to be in good shape, right?" At Mildred's nod, she asked, "Then what killed her?"

"I wouldn't be able to tell without running far more detailed tests," Mildred replied. "However, depending on the level of control this thing had over her, if there was ever a contest to maintain dominance, it's possible the parasite might have inadvertently killed her while trying to incapacitate her as a last-ditch effort to survive. Of course, it would then have to find a different host."

"Mebbe…" J.B. said. "All I really know is that the guy spoke a lot different when he didn't have that thing in him than when he did."

"Yeah, what about him?" Krysty asked. "They both obviously came from the same place, yet he didn't seem affected by these things, but she was. Did he have one previously? What happened to it?"

Mildred held up her hands. "Hey, hey folks, I'm not Quincy." She looked around the three blank stares she was getting. "It was a television show—never mind. Anyway, best thing to do now would be to head back down and talk to that guy, see what answers we can get out of him—"

She was interrupted by the sound of boots pounding the floor as someone ran toward them. A moment later, Ricky skidded to a stop in the doorway.

"There's a…problem…with the…prisoner," he panted.

Ryan and the others took off at a run back downstairs. They all entered the room to find the man slumped against the wall, his eyes wide in death, with Jak standing a few feet away, blaster drawn and pointed at the body. A trail of slime led from the man's mouth to what looked like a smashed piece of raw, black meat on the floor.

"What happened?" Ryan asked.

"Was sleeping, then started to convulse," Jak said. "Before we could do anything, *that*—" he pointed at the lump of whatever-it-was with the muzzle of his blaster "—came out him. Crushed it before could get anyone, and sent Ricky up get you all."

Glancing at Tully and Latham, Ryan saw them both nod to affirm Jak's story. Doc was still asleep, snoring softly.

"You didn't do anything to him?" Mildred asked as she knelt by the dead man.

"Never touched," Jak replied.

"He was twitching for about five minutes before he started trembling all over," Ricky said.

"Based on all that—and it's an incomplete diagnosis at best—he most likely died of an acute subdural hematoma," Mildred said as she felt the back of his skull. "I think there's some blood pooled here, but I'd have to cut him open to be sure, and I've done enough of that already for one day."

"But shouldn't we find out if that thing was trying to control him?" Krysty asked. "Cut him open to see if there're more of those white nerve things inside?"

"I could, but I bet it'd look a lot like the woman," Mildred said. "My guess is that the brain injury was too much to handle, so it had to eject, so to speak." She rose and walked over to look at the crushed lump of flesh and slime on the floor. "What I wouldn't give for an electron microscope or a CAT scanner right now."

"Think Doc might know anything about this?" J.B. asked Ryan.

"Only one way to find out." Ryan walked over and nudged the sleeping man curled up on the floor. "Doc? Wake up, Doc."

The old man stirred but didn't rouse immediately. "Hmm...are we in Sacramento already, my dear? Yes, I could go for a light repast once we're in the city proper."

Ryan nudged him a bit harder. "Doc!"

With a startled snort, the silver-haired old man awakened, sitting up and looking around with wide eyes. "What—where?" Blinking owlishly, he peered up at Ryan while wiping his mouth on the sleeve of his frock coat. "Oh, it is you all...and I was in the middle of the loveliest dream, too."

"Sorry to take you away from all that, but we need that brain of yours." Ryan filled him in on everything that had happened since they'd arrived at the old school building, ending with "Do you know if the whitecoats ever worked on something like this?"

By now Doc was up and standing over the thing that had come out of the jumpsuited man, poking at it with the end of his swordstick. "I do not recall a project of the Totality Concept experimenting with symbiotic organisms that would be implanted into a human host, but that certainly sounds like something they would do, if they could. Mind you, I am sure I was not privy to all files that focused on all projects.

"Imagine making anyone dance like a puppet on a string…" Doc's voice turned soft and dreamy, and he suddenly turned away from Ryan and the others with his left arm held out as if curled around a lady's waist, and his right as if he was holding his invisible partner's other hand as he twirled and spun around the floor.

"He sure talks funny," Tully remarked to Ryan. "He all right?"

"Yeah…he's from the South. They have different… customs than other folk."

"Like dancing with no one on his arm?" Latham asked.

"Look, there's nothing wrong with him, he's just a bit…" Ryan searched for the right word.

"Addle-pated?" Tully supplied. At Ryan's questioning look, she added, "Not right in the head sometimes."

"Good way put it," Jak said.

"Jak!" Mildred scolded.

"Yeah, he's a bit…addle-pated," Ryan replied. "But Doc'll be back to himself in no time."

"So…what's all this mean?" Tully asked, waving at the dead man and what was left of whatever had come out of him.

"It means we're going with you to meet the rest of your people," Ryan said. "See if there's anything that can be done about—" he toed the stiffening lump of flesh with his combat boot "—this."

Chapter Eleven

The scavvies stripped the bodies of their clothes, boots and personal items, then the corpses were buried. It was time to head out, and the group headed back to the school building to retrieve their packs. "Perfect day for sailin'," Tully said as she climbed a utility staircase at the far end of a corridor and opened two heavy steel storm doors to step outside. Her comment earned her puzzled stares from everyone but Latham. As the companions joined the couple outside, they showed them what she meant.

Both land craft were interesting vehicles, and familiar to the companions. Only Ricky was curious, as they were unlike anything he had ever seen. "*Santa Maria!* Would you look at that!"

The land craft consisted of two rough seats mounted on a flat wooden cross made out of two poles that connected two small wheels in back with a single wheel in the front. But there was a third post that rose from the beam into the air a few feet ahead of the seats, with another pole making an L shape sticking out of that one. Various lines and cords ran everywhere, all leading back to the seats.

The two scavvies pulled out a bundle of cloth, unrolled it and swiftly attached it to various rings and loops of fabric on the vertical and horizontal poles. When Tully pulled on a white cord, the cloth rose along the vertical pole, forming—

"A sail! Of course, a land yacht!" Doc put a hand to his forehead. "We encountered a group of people called tech-nomads who used such vehicles. Quite the ingenious construction."

Tully beamed. "Thanks. We call 'em windriders and started puttin' them together after we crossed the Missip and saw all those plains. We got some oxen for pulling the heavy stuff, but the wind blows all the time out here, so we started foolin' around with it to see what we could do, and it works pretty well."

Once they had the sail rigged, they started working on Latham's sailer. "We're about twenty miles due east of here," he said as he checked the joints and tires of his ride. "We can head out ahead of you all, and send a wag back, or we could take two of the lighter folks in with us, and come back around for the others."

"I'll go," Jak volunteered before the other man finished talking.

"Me, too," Ricky said almost at the same time.

"Hold on, now. I'm sure everyone'll get their chance," Ryan said, "However, I'm going to suggest that Jak and J.B. take the first ride in, and the rest of us can get picked up a bit later."

Sure about this? J.B. signed to him.

It's fine, Ryan signed back. *Go on, and make sure Jak doesn't get into any trouble.*

Okay. J.B.'s expression, however, didn't look as if he was convinced, although he was impressed with the design of the land vehicles.

With help from the others, they wheeled the sailers away from the building onto the open hardpan. The brisk wind blowing from the west filled the sails and made them flap back and forth, already pushing the crude yachts forward.

"Hey, Ryan, do me a favor and hold it back till we're ready to go, will ya?" Tully asked.

"Sure." Ryan reached down and grabbed the crossbar, surprised at how strongly the wind was tugging at the vehicle. "How fast can it go?"

"Never measured it, but we keep up with the animals out here," Tully replied. "Hey, Jak, why don't you ride with me?"

"Sure." He scrambled over and sat in the hard, black metal chair. "Already hot."

"Yeah, the sun beats on it something fierce," she replied as she wrapped a dirty, light green scarf around her head and pulled on a pair of dark green goggles. "Won't be so bad once we get movin'. Sorry I don't have goggles for you. Best cover your face as much as possible."

Pulling out the bright pink T-shirt, Jak quickly wrapped it around his head, leaving only his eyes uncovered. "Ready."

"You ready?" she called to Latham, who was getting J.B. squared away. He nodded and gave her a thumbs-up.

"Let 'er go!" Tully said.

Ryan released the back end of her windrider, and Ricky and Doc let go of Latham's. The wind grabbed them immediately, and the jury-rigged transports took off, rapidly gaining speed until they were only specks on the horizon in a couple of minutes.

"Mierde..." Shading his eyes, Ricky watched them go until they vanished from sight. "How come you didn't let me go first, Ryan?"

"Don't take it the wrong way, Ricky, but if there's any

kind of trouble with these people, those two will be sure to come out of it alive," Ryan replied. "Don't worry, we got a long way to go before we reach them, and if they come back, you'll go next."

He checked the barren prairie all around them, then took a step forward. "Let's get moving."

"Yee-haaaaw!"

Jak couldn't help himself. The shout of pleasure burst from his throat to be whipped away by the wind pushing them forward faster than he'd ever gone before.

They'd accelerated more quickly than he thought possible, until they were skimming along the ground, leaving the building and the rest of his companions behind in a couple of minutes. Their shadows chased them across the blurry, packed dirt, rippling and wavering in the heat. The wind, hot and oppressive a minute ago, was now cool and refreshing as it rippled over his head and arms.

"What do you think?" Tully called, her smile evident in her voice.

"Awesome!" Jak shouted back.

The short girl glanced back to check on how far Latham and J.B. were behind them. "We should be there in about ten minutes."

"Take long as want. This great!" Jak said.

"Glad you said that—hang on!"

The sailer slewed over to pick up on a large dust trail off to their right. Jak glanced back to see the pilot of the other windrider also changing course. "What happening?"

"Might have spotted some food. Up to doing some hunting?" She nudged a bound bundle of crude spears lying on the crossbar.

Jak pulled out his .357 instead, the sunlight winking off the chrome barrel. "Just get me close enough and I'll drop plenty!"

Distant words carried to them on the wind from the other windrider, but neither Jak nor Tully could make out what J.B. or Latham was saying. Instead, they concentrated on getting closer to whatever was running across the baked plains.

Finally, they pulled within sight to find what people would have called a herd of antelope a hundred years ago. These animals, however, bore only a passing resemblance, primarily in their tan-and-white fur. Twice as tall at the shoulder as their twenty-first-century ancestors, they now sported two extra legs to run even faster. They were also well armed for defense, having not just one, but two pairs of four-foot-long horns spiraling out of each forehead. The noise from the impact of their hooves on the ground was deafening, creating a vibration Jak could feel in his teeth.

Tully pulled up behind the antelope. She stayed in their draft for a few seconds, trying to see if she could cut one or two from the main group. For his part, Jak squinted through the blowing dust, trying to select which one he'd shoot first.

"Can't split them up!" Tully shouted. "Shoot whenever you're ready!"

Needing no further urging, Jak extended his arm to aim at the nearest one, a young buck as tall as him at the shoulder. He squeezed the trigger, the Colt Python boomed and the antelope faltered and went down in a cloud of dust.

"Nice shooting!" Tully shouted. The roar of a shotgun could also be heard, and Jak looked over to see that

Latham and J.B. were doing the same thing, with the Armorer taking down two runners in quick succession.

"Let's keep going!" Jak shouted.

Nodding, Tully adjusted the trim of the sail to pull even closer. Jak steadied his hand again and pulled the trigger just as the herd suddenly turned ninety degrees and charged due south.

"Why they change direct—" he began, when the answer to his question burst out of the dust cloud and dived right at him!

A huge bird, its dark blue feathered wings easily thirty feet across, and its breast and underbelly covered with tiny overlapping scales, shrieked as it passed just a few yards from the top of the windrider. It was close enough that Jak caught a glimpse of its large orange beak, which could have easily snapped his head off in one bite, and its pair of huge talons, each of which could have easily grabbed him. He wasn't sure if the flying predator could carry him off, but he sure as hell didn't want to find out either. He aimed his blaster at the beast, but it was already climbing out of range, possibly coming back around for another pass.

"Holy shit! What was *that?*" Tully shouted.

"No clue. Just lots feathers and claws!" Jak replied. "Let's get meat. Birds scavenge if can."

"Right! Keep an eye out for it!" Tully pulled on the cords and the windrider changed direction again. Instead of moving directly with the wind, she now used the sail to move diagonally to the breeze from the west. They would sail that way for a few hundred yards, then Tully would move the sail and steer across the wind at a forty-five-degree angle to their first run, and keep going. It wasn't as fast as sailing with the wind, but they did keep moving fairly quickly, definitely much faster than a person could run.

Jak kept turning, scanning the skies for the huge bird. It took a moment, but he saw it shadowing them high overhead. "He's following us!"

"We might have confused him!" Tully shouted. "Mebbe he doesn't know what we are!"

"Not good!" Jak had dealt with plenty of large raptors. He knew the one thing birds of prey weren't was timid. "If thinks we're threat—"

As if it heard him, the bird suddenly starting to dive toward them. The bird rapidly grew larger in his vision. Gripping the seat with his legs, Jak braced the wrist of his blaster hand with his other one to steady it. "Come on… Just a little closer…"

"Shoot, Jak!" Tully screamed, as the bird was now only about a hundred yards away. But just as he was about to pull the trigger, the bird suddenly put on the brakes and flared out its wings. At the same time, it puffed out its chest, and the scales there suddenly flashed as they reflected the bright sunlight—right into Jak's eyes!

"Shit! Fucker blinded me!"

Chapter Twelve

Latham didn't talk much, which was fine by J.B. He did, however, have an extra pair of goggles, which J.B. accepted after stowing his precious spectacles in the inside pocket of his leather jacket. He also tucked away his fedora, knowing there was no way it would stay on his head once they got moving.

As rides went, this one wasn't too bad. It was nice and quiet, and what it lacked in amenities—his seat was unforgivingly hard, and pressed uncomfortably into the small of his back—it made up for in speed. The ground was flat and smooth, and the rubber tires absorbed most of the small bumps as they sailed across the flat landscape.

Then Tully and Jak spotted the antelopes, and things started going to hell.

There wasn't any question about going after them. Food was food, and they had the means both to keep up with the stampeding animals and to bring them down. J.B. had attempted to tell Jak to conserve his ammo, and that the M-4000 shotgun was a much better choice for hunting, but the kid either hadn't heard or ignored him.

"Damn! He's going to waste bullets trying to take one of them down," he muttered as they kept an eye on the lead windrider closing in on the galloping animals. A few seconds later, they heard a loud *boom,* even above the thunder of the herd, and passed the still-twitching body of an antelope as it skidded to stop in the dust.

Latham grunted. "Mebbe your boy's a better shot than you thought."

J.B. was man enough to admit when he was wrong. "Guess so. But why don't we show them what we can do?"

"You got it." Latham caught more wind in his sail, and soon the windrider was almost flying across the prairie as it passed the other one. It went so fast that the right wheel next to J.B. rose off the ground, so they were skimming along on two.

"What should I do?" he asked calmly, as unflappable as ever.

"Don't panic, and lean toward the wheel!" Latham shouted as he leaned in that direction, as well. Gradually the errant wheel settled back down to the earth with a *thump* and they kept going.

"Get ready!" the pilot said as they drew closer to the lead antelope, a magnificent creature easily a full head higher than the rest, and with a set of horns twice as large as any of the other bucks.

Feed us for a couple days at least, J.B. thought as he aimed and fired. The cloud of double O buckshot smashed into the chests and legs of the two lead animals, sending them collapsing into the dirt in a tangle of hooves and horns. "Keep trailing them. We'll come back for the meat!"

"Not too much longer. It won't last long in this heat!" Latham called back.

"Right, just want to try to get one more— Whoa!" J.B. had also seen the herd suddenly change direction. The move caught Latham off guard, and by the time he readjusted his sail to pursue, Tully and Jak were cutting across to head into the dust cloud—right when the huge raptor flew by.

"Dark night!" J.B. said, turning to keep an eye on the gigantic bird of prey. "I've seen few birds that large before!"

"Damn! It's going after Tully," Latham said while hauling on the lines to turn his windrider around. "Best get after them, see if we can catch it from behind."

Latham knew how to pilot his craft, but beating into the wind made for slow going. J.B. kept tracking the bird while the rangy scavvie kept his gaze on the far-off sailer. They were still at least five hundred yards away, however, when the bird folded its wings and plummeted toward the speeding vehicle. Glancing down, J.B. saw sunlight glint off the barrel of Jak's blaster, and held his breath as he watched the giant bird scream toward its prey. "Not yet...not yet... Just one second more..."

Then the bird abruptly spread its wings and slowed. "What the hell—" J.B. began. At the same time, Jak threw his blaster arm over his face as the bird's forward momentum carried it into the top of the sail. The impact was strong enough to tip the vehicle, spilling both occupants into the dirt.

"Get us over there!" J.B. said, settling the M-4000 against his shoulder. "I can take it out at a hundred yards!"

"I'm tryin'!" Latham struggled to get the sailer over there, but had to tack back and forth to do it. Meanwhile, the raptor circled again and came in for a landing, its huge talons thudding into the dry earth. Watching the two nearby humans with quick, jerky movements of its head, it began stalking them.

"Almost there!" Latham began. "Hang on—"

"Shut up!" J.B. hissed when he saw Jak throw out a warning hand to Tully, who was scooting back under the overturned sailer.

"What're you doin'? It's gonna kill them!" Latham said.

"No, it's not," J.B. told him. "Trust me. Jak knows what he's doing."

"That kid can't take that thing on. It'll tear him to ribbons!"

"Just get us closer, but stay quiet," J.B. ordered, still sighting down the barrel of the automatic shotgun. He could have taken a shot at the bird's head, but it would still be a long one at that range, and Jak was close enough to the animal that he didn't want to risk hitting him with stray buckshot. Besides, if he knew Jak, that bird was as good as dead—it just didn't know it yet.

Oddly, however, Jak wasn't being his normal, aggressive self. While he was leading the predator away from the upended windrider, he was holding both arms out in front of him and stepping very cautiously. Did he get blinded by the dust? J.B. wondered.

The bird hopped forward and darted its head toward Jak, who skipped aside while lashing out with his right hand. The bird shrieked and recoiled while a small cluster of blue feathers drifted down to the dirt.

"Holy—" Latham began.

"You haven't seen anything yet," J.B. said.

True to his word, the incensed bird lashed down with its head again, leading with its beak and intent on stabbing the large point into Jak's head. This time, however, the skinny teen waited for the bird to come at him. When it looked as if he was about to be impaled, he sidestepped just enough so the beak smacked into the ground.

As the bird's head went down, Jak leaped up, twisting in midair to land on the back of the bird's neck. Squawking in alarm, the raptor tried taking off, but Jak was heavy enough to keep it grounded. It settled back down, taking a few ungainly steps to try to get enough velocity to launch, before it suddenly flopped on the ground with such force that Jak was pitched off. He kept rolling, moving out of reach of that large beak. The mutie bird flapped its wings once and snapped weakly at him, then settled back on the ground, its eyes glazing over.

By this time Latham's sailer was close enough for J.B. to get out and run over. He made sure the bird was truly dead, then turned to Jak, who was covered in dust from head to foot. The albino sat up and shook his head, then blinked and tried to wipe the dust off his face and profusely watering eyes. In his right hand was a bloody throwing knife.

"Black dust, kid, took you long enough to chill that buzzard," J.B. said with a smile.

Jak glared at him. "Didn't see you helping."

"Had him in my sights, but I figured you had it under control. Where's your blaster?"

"Dropped when feathered fuck blinded me—"

"What? What do you mean 'blinded you'?"

Jak pointed at the dead body. "Had reflective scales on chest. Thought was attackin', then pulled up and got right in face with sunlight. Had fight blind."

"Wait a minute—you took that thing on without being able to see?"

Jak shrugged. "Not that bad. Could see movement. Big splotch of blue. Heard him, too. Fucker wasn't quiet."

"Still, that's pretty damn gutsy," J.B. said as he slung his shotgun over a shoulder. "Nice job."

"What expect?" Jak stared at the huge bird. "Fucker gonna tear heads off if I not chill."

"Ace on the line with that," J.B. said, holding out a hand to the youth. "Well, come on, we've got to get to those carcasses and bleed them before they spoil."

Jak took the hand, and J.B. hauled him to his feet. "Damn right. Good to get a full belly after all fuckin' around."

"By the way," J.B. said, patting the barrel of his shotgun. "Next time we go hunting, let the guy with the big blaster take the lead."

Jak snorted. "Get out there first and I will. Took so long herd woulda been in Mex Gulf before you shot."

Chapter Thirteen

The sun was setting when the group finally came within sight of the small ville where Tully and Latham's people were holed up.

Prepping the animals for transport was much more time-consuming than they'd figured. Luckily, Tully's windrider wasn't damaged in the crash, so after they had gotten all of the antelope carcasses in one place, they had her go back and start ferrying the rest of the party from the school building to join them. Meanwhile, Latham and J.B. rigged a framework from which to hang the gutted antelope to drain them, while Jak kept an eye out for more birds or any other kind of trouble.

It was hot, sticky work, but by the time the party was reunited, the four antelope were ready for transport. The hindquarters of each animal were cut out and distributed equally among the group. The rest was tied to the front of the sailers, along with a trophy from the raptor for Jak. At last, the entire group, dusty and sticky with blood and sweat, set off to cover what Tully and Latham estimated was about five miles to town.

An exhausting two hours later, they trudged toward the end of what looked to have once been one of hundreds of thousands of small towns across America— back when there had still been an America. It was a classic Main Street setup, with two rows of buildings facing each other and a wide road running down the middle of it. Where the main drag might have once been chockablock with buildings, the wooden ones had surrendered to the harsh environment long ago, leaving empty gaps in the three-block-long skyline. Oddly, there were also some signs of recent construction, including hastily erected scaffolding on one building that looked as if it was being dismantled. Any signs or identifying features on the stone and brick buildings were long gone, along with their windows, leaving empty, gaping holes behind.

They stopped at the skeletal remains of what had been a gas station, its pumps and small building drained of fuel and supplies long ago. It was agreed that Tully would go ahead and let the rest of the folks know whom and what they had brought back with them, while Latham would stay with the group to show there was no ill will on either side. The silence while they waited was absolute, broken only by the lowing of a cow somewhere deeper in town.

When the slim young woman appeared at the far end of the street and gave the signal, Ryan and his group slowly walked in, with him, Krysty and Doc on the left flank of Latham's windrider, and J.B., Mildred, Jak and Ricky on the right. As they came in, Ryan saw no sign of Tully's vehicle, and assumed it was parked somewhere out of sight.

They faced a group of about forty people, ranging from kids as young as five years to weathered elders who could have been anywhere from fifty to seventy years old. A few obvious families stood together, but there was also a fair number of single people both young and old. Expressions were grim, with the stress of their situation weighing heavily on each face.

The men were all bearded, with many divided into two braids forking down over their chests. Hairstyles were oddly short for both women and men, with several shaved heads among both sexes. They all looked relatively healthy, all things considered—no obvious mutations or rad sores from contamination, just the majority of them aged beyond their physical years by enduring a hardscrabble life in the Deathlands.

Their clothes were all similar to Tully and Latham's patchwork garments, although Ryan spotted the two recovered jumpsuits clutched in the hands of the women in two separate families who both looked as if they needed them. As he studied the people around him more closely, he saw light blue patches of cloth from what had to be other recovered jumpsuits mending other garments, and in several cases, forming sleeves and pants for several of the townspeople alongside tanned hides, leather and cloth of every type. Several of the men sported cloth bandages, and one had his arm bound in a sling. Also, and not surprisingly, given Tully's description of their group, while Ryan saw several staves and canes used by the elderly, and many men wore knives on their leather belts, he didn't spot a single firearm among the lot of them.

As Latham brought his heavily laden windrider to a stop, several teenagers silently came forward, untied the two antelope carcasses from its front and disappeared back into the crowd. Others took the hindquarters from each of the walkers, the ones hefting Krysty's and Mildred's loads obviously surprised by the weight each woman carried.

As usual, Jak's appearance drew stares and mutters,

mostly from the children, but no one stepped forward to accuse him of being a demon or an evil mutie. Of course, it was still early—anything could happen in the next few hours. One person whom Ryan noticed couldn't seem to take her eyes off the albino was Tully. She tried to look as if she was observing the entire group, but her gaze always settled back on him. Ryan made a mental note to keep an eye on both teens—they hadn't come this far just to be cast out, or even worse stoned to death, or watch Jak get a particular part of his anatomy cut off just because he couldn't keep it in his pants.

A suntanned man who looked to be in his fifties, but with a straight back and steady gaze, stepped forward, regarding the companions from under a faded, stained trucker's cap with the words *Libertarian Party* barely readable on it.

"Greetings, travelers. I am Elder Mattias Bough, one of the leaders in council of this collective. Sister Tully has told us of Brother Latham's and her good fortune in meeting you folks when they did, and of the assistance you twice bore them during the journey back here, including the bounty that you have seen fit to grace our table with this evening. Is this true?"

Ryan cleared his throat. "Yeah, thank you." He took a moment to introduce himself and the rest of the group. "Regarding the hunt, that was more of a cooperative thing. We wouldn't have been able to get close enough to the herd without their windriders. As for what happened in the school building, it just seemed like they were in a spot of trouble, and we thought we might lend a hand."

"And they have apprised you of the trouble we are facing?" Elder Bough asked with the barest hint of hesitation in his voice.

"Yeah, and we thought we might be of some assistance with that, as well," Ryan replied. "We've dealt with this kind of thing before."

That caused a fresh round of muttering and whispers to break out among the assembly. Elder Bough raised his hands for silence. "Still your tongues for now, people. Perhaps our prayers have been answered, but now is not the time to speak of it."

He turned back to the party. "We will discuss that at the council later this evening. For now, the collective of Silvertide bids you all welcome as our honored guests. What is ours is yours. You will dine with us tonight, and share in the goodness that you have blessed us with."

"It would be our pleasure," Ryan said.

Elder Bough turned to the group behind them and raised his hands. "Let us pray."

Every eye around them closed, every head dropped. Many clasped their hands to their chests, or crossed them and covered their hearts. Ryan casually signaled his group to follow their lead. As long as they looked as if they were going through the motions, there shouldn't be any trouble.

"O Lord, we thank you for the blessings that you have seen fit to bestow on us this day," Elder Bough began. "First, with the joyous return of Sister Tully and Brother Latham from the treacherous plains, and for the removal of two of the devil's own plague that seeks to undermine us and tear us apart. Thank you, O Lord, for the generous strangers whose paths you saw fit to cross with our children, and whom were saved by your everlasting mercy. We hope that they may hold our salvation from the vexing invasion we are afflicted with. And finally, thank you for the newcomers' skill at the hunt, that they have so generously afforded us this bounty, of which we will make sure no part goes to waste. In Jaysoos's name, amen."

"In Jaysoos's name, amen," the rest of the congregation intoned.

"Come, you must be tired and hungry," Elder Bough said. "I know this place doesn't look like much, but you may be surprised what we've been able to do in the few days we've been here."

"Your hospitality is much appreciated," Krysty said.

"Elder Teale will take you to your quarters for the evening, and to the bathing area," Elder Bough said. A middle-aged woman stepped forward with three daughters in tow, ranging in age from late teens to early twenties.

Mildred blinked. "I'm sorry. I must have too much dirt in my ears. Did you say 'bathing area'?"

Elder Bough nodded. "Yes, it is one of our most treasured inventions. Elder Teale will explain it to you."

The three girls hid smiles as their mother waved the group over. "This way. We also have clothes that you can borrow while we clean and repair yours."

"That's very kind, but there's really—" Ryan was interrupted by a sharp elbow from Krysty.

"That would be heavenly," she interrupted. While the collective women walked ahead, she whispered, "Mebbe you like smelling like you've slept on the ground for a month, but I don't. I also don't think it's too much to ask for cleaning and repairs to our clothes and a good, hot meal."

"Hear, hear," Mildred chimed in.

"All right, all right, I'm sure they'll find plenty to fix

on my clothes, as well," Ryan said. "Even so, no one surrenders their blasters."

"Course not," J.B. said, with nods and agreement all around. "I'm hoping we get a chance to see what Tully picked up from those guys—hopefully something we can reload our weapons with, if not use ourselves."

They were escorted down a side street to a two-story, L-shaped building that might have actually been a motel long ago. Elder Teale and her daughters brought the group up to three rooms on the second floor and showed them inside.

"With the water machine, we're able to have running water in these rooms, so you can wash up." She indicated three doors next to each other. "These are the washing rooms."

"You have no idea how wonderful that sounds," Mildred said. "I think every square inch of me's covered in dust and dirt."

"What is the water machine?" Ricky asked.

"It's a sun-powered condenser that produces—" one of the younger sisters began before receiving an elbow in the ribs from her older sibling that made her clap her hands over her mouth.

"You know we're not supposed to talk about it to outsiders!" the older one hissed. Flustered, the girl stared at the floor.

Ricky smiled. "It's okay, we're not going to steal it or anything. I'm just always interested in new machines." He looked around at everyone, all of them now looking at him. "Um…I think I'll go to my room now," he said with flaming-red cheeks before turning and heading down to the farthest door.

"Girls, stand to collect our guests' clothes when

they're prepared." Each daughter stationed herself at one of the three doorways. Elder Teale shook her head, her smile growing a bit strained. "Children—forever speaking before thinking."

"Well, like Ricky said, we don't mean any harm," Ryan said. "I'd rather not see the girl punished for what she said."

"Marijah's always been headstrong. Since she broke one of the collective's rules, I'm afraid that's up to the elders—but I thank you for your words." Her gaze flicked to the roof of the building. "Due to the limits of how much water we can produce, we only ask that you keep your washing as brief as possible."

"Don't you worry about that. I'll be in and out faster than a jackrabbit on a blacktop highway in August," Mildred said. Her comment also brought blank stares from the others. "Okay…guess it's time to go change, too."

The others filed into their rooms as well, with Ryan and Krysty taking one, J.B. and Mildred taking the next, and Doc, Jak and Ricky sharing the last one.

Inside was mostly empty. An oddly new-looking cardboard box by the door was the only obvious place to set their clothes. The window glass was long gone, and the empty frame was now covered by wooden boards.

Closing the door, Ryan put his ear against it to see if anyone was planning on listening to their conversation. Hearing nothing, he turned to Kristy, who had already shucked her boots and was peeling off her dusty, sweat-stained jumpsuit. "Gaia! It smells like a cross between a dirt-floor outhouse and low-end gaudy house," she said, wrinkling her nose.

Kicking off his own boots, Ryan stripped as he padded toward her. "Lucky for you I like my women to smell…earthy."

"Women? *Women?* Best change that to the singular, unless there's something you want to tell me." Ryan's grin was infectious, and Krysty stripped off her own T-shirt and threw it at his head. "You like how I smell so much, well, how about now?"

Ryan took a moment to breath in the mingled scents of sweat, musk and that indefinable aroma of the only woman for him. "Smells just as good to me as the day we met."

It had been that way between them since they'd first seen each other. Ryan was with the Trader, who had come to the pest-hole ville of Mocsin, only to find himself in the middle of a power struggle between its baron, a sad sack of mutie shit named Jordan Teague, and his lieutenant and head of his sec force, a cold-eyed bastard named Cort Strasser. After saving Krysty from a mutie assault, they had grown close in the days after, and had soon become lovers. Now, he couldn't even imagine a day without her by his side, and knew she felt the same.

"Flatterer." Wearing only panties and a bra, Krysty shook her hand back and forth, narrowing her gaze at the small cloud of dust that drifted out of it. "Ugh! You want first wash?"

"Nope." Ryan took her hand and led her toward the smaller secondary room. "Since we have to conserve water, I know the best way to do it."

Krysty cocked her head as they walked into the smaller bathroom, her eyebrows raised in disbelief. "You aren't serious?"

"Why wouldn't I be? We haven't had a moment to ourselves since the redoubt, and besides—" his strong fingers cupped her breast, while his other hand drifted lower, making her gasp with mingled surprise and pleasure "—you still owe me for cutting your hair back on the plains."

"I owe you, huh?" Krysty's hands were moving as well, splayed across Ryan's tight stomach and unbuckling his pants. "I suppose a quickie wouldn't hurt. There's just one problem."

"What's that?"

She grinned wickedly as she stripped off her bra and panties and stepped into the dingy, grimy bathtub. "I don't think you *can* finish in a minute."

Ryan's grin was just as sly. "Never have yet. Guess we'll just have to turn the water off during—"

Krysty's mouth found his as she turned the tepid water on, and Ryan quit talking and got very busy doing.

EVEN WITHOUT THEIR other activities, the shower was heavenly. The sun-warmed water sluiced the dirt and dust from their skin, running dark brown toward the drain at first, then clearing up. The collective made its own soap, fragrant with clover and lavender, which pleased Krysty almost as much as the shower itself. As requested, they used as little water as possible, but made sure every inch of each other was very, very clean by the time they were finished.

The hardest part had been keeping quiet, so as not to arouse suspicion from their hosts. Ryan now sported a deep red bite mark where Krysty had sunk her teeth into his uninjured shoulder to stifle her cries of pleasure. They figured they'd been mostly successful, and Ryan said he'd just claim that his other shoulder injury was acting up if anyone did ask.

"Yeah, because that's *exactly* the noise you make when you're hurt," Krysty said as they dressed in the assortment of clothes that had been left for them. Their own had vanished, but all of their weapons were still where they'd put them. Even Ryan's panga and the web belt it was on had been removed from his old fatigue pants.

"Could be—after all, you haven't heard *all* the noises I make," Ryan replied. Overall, his replacement outfit was a decent fit, with the long sleeves on the shirt just an inch short, which he solved by rolling them up to his elbows. The patchwork pants were also a trifle snug in the crotch and short around the ankles, too, but he figured he'd just tuck the ends into his boots and grin and bear the rest. "Besides, I'm pretty sure I heard other sounds from next door, as well," he said as he repositioned his knife at his back.

Krysty rolled her eyes as she pulled her shirt on. "Oh, please."

"Hey, I'm just saying we weren't the only ones taking advantage of the situation." Ryan pulled his boots on. "You just watch. Mildred will have that 'cat who just drank the cream' look on her face when they come out."

She smacked him on the chest. "You're terrible."

"You look at her when we go back out there and tell me I'm wrong."

"All right, all right—anything to get you to stop talking." Krysty was still grinning, although Ryan couldn't tell if that was because of what they were talking about or what they'd just done. "What do you think about Tully? You know she's got her eye on Jak."

"Yeah…" Ryan watched for Krysty's reaction while

lowering his voice. "Let's keep an eye on that situation, okay? No sense riling up the natives if we can avoid it."

"You and I probably can, but from the way she was sizing him up during our meeting earlier, I think he's in trouble and doesn't realize it yet. Besides, he makes his own decisions, you know that."

"I know. I just don't want the rest of us to pay for it, that's all. Besides, usually we're in a superior position in a place like this—not that I expect we're going to have to fight our way out," he said quickly upon seeing her shocked look.

"They all seem on the up-and-up to me," she replied. "Have you seen anything that tells you otherwise?"

Ryan shook his head. "Nope, at least not yet. But those raiders are still around, and we're low on ammo and just went through a few days of hell out there, so none of us are at our best right now. I just want to make sure nothing comes to a head while we're here, that's all."

"Well, I know one head I didn't mind seeing a few minutes ago," Krysty said, which made Ryan's jaw drop. She didn't usually make those sorts of jokes, considering them coarse and demeaning, since the majority of them were often directed at women. She reached over and closed his jaw. "Thought I'd help you before the flies got in. Shall we go to dinner?"

Chapter Fourteen

"Okay, you were right." Krysty's whisper made Ryan smile.

Escorted by Elder Teale and her eldest daughter, they were walking with J.B. and Mildred. The moment they'd come out of their room, Mildred had stretched out her arms and taken a deep breath of the cooling evening air.

"I hope the wash was agreeable?" Elder Teale asked. "Some of you seemed to take longer than others. Your friends are already with the rest of the collective at the common area."

"It was wonderful, thank you," Krysty replied. "You'll have to forgive us. We don't get the chance at running water too often, but we kept it as quick as we could."

Mildred nodded, as well. "I don't know about you all, but I feel a thousand times better—what?" she asked Ryan. "Just exactly what're you smiling about?"

Ryan quickly wiped the smile off his face. "Nothing at all. It just feels good to be clean again, like you said."

"Yeah…except I didn't say that, exactly." She glanced at J.B., who was his usual inscrutable self.

Ryan noticed a glimmer of firelight through a gap between two buildings at the same time that he caught the delectable scent of roasting meat on the breeze. "Forget it. That meat smells great."

"They put a haunch on to roast as soon as they got them, but I doubt it will be done in time," Elder Teale said. "However, the cuts from the hindquarters should feed everyone quite nicely."

"Looking forward to that," J.B. said. "It's been a few days too long without a real meal." As they drew closer, he could hear several people talking over the crackling fire. Long-ingrained habits made him glance around, noticing the moving shadows of people standing sentry duty on rooftops under the clear night sky. Even if a person was on every roof in the area, which was impossible, as there were still more buildings than people to man them, there were still plenty of ways to slip out of the former ghost town.

And that was the real problem, since it meant there were plenty of ways to slip into the town, as well.

They emerged from the alley between two buildings and into what had probably been the backyard of some long-dead business, maybe a restaurant a hundred years ago. Now the large flagstone patio was filled with tables and benches arranged in a three-sided U shape, all piled high with platters of food. What Ryan could see—loaves of fresh-baked bread, larger ceramic bowls of vegetables, even some kind of salad greens featuring dandelion leaves, along with sweating clay pitchers of water—made his mouth water even more. A large fire roared in the middle of the arrangement, warding off the night chill, with a pile of old, weathered boards salvaged from a nearby building ready to be used to keep it going.

Apparently everyone not on guard duty was in attendance; children helped carry plates or minded the younger ones while young women bustled in and out of the empty doorway of the nearby stone building, making sure everything was ready. When Krysty nudged him, Ryan noticed Tully, all cleaned up and in what had to be her best clothes—an ankle-length skirt and sleeve-less button-down blouse, both composed of mostly the same light blue muslin, with mother-of-pearl buttons that gleamed in the firelight. She was helping to prepare the eating area, but every time she appeared, her gaze strayed to a particular group of men—and the white-haired speaker in the middle of them.

"Looks like Jak isn't the only one attracting atten-tion," Krysty said with a nod of her chin as Ryan set his longblaster next to his bench. He and J.B. had discussed leaving the weapons back in the bathrooms or hiding them somewhere in town, but in the end had decided to keep them at their sides, just in case. Ryan straightened and looked over to where she was pointing.

Off to the side, and flanked by Ricky and Doc, Jak regaled a group of men with his adventure against the mutie bird, the farmers hanging on his every word. "—not see clear, but saw it movin', so knew had to wait for it make first move. Then came at me—"

"Better watch out," J.B. muttered. "They'll be calling him the hero of Silvertide before this is over."

Ryan nodded. "Yeah. Let's make sure Jak keeps his ego in check."

"That's not all. Just about every girl here is watching both of them, too," Krysty said.

Ryan casually glanced around to find his lover was right. The teenage girls there alternated between doing whatever chore they had been assigned and staring in Jak's and Ricky's direction. "Great. They're going to be on those two like stickies on a bonfire—"

"Brother Ryan, Brother John, Brother Theophilus,

Brother Jak, Brother Ricky, Sister Krysty and Sister Mildred, welcome to our table," Elder Bough said as he emerged from the same building, carrying a platter heaped high with thick cuts of antelope meat. "Please, as our honored guests, sit, sit!"

Bringing the platter to the head table nearest their kitchen and setting it down, he indicated the seats near him. Ryan and the others took their places and were joined by everyone else in the area.

While people were getting settled, Ryan made sure he sat next to Jak. "Quite the tale you were spinning over there."

Jak had already filled his glass with water, and was busy draining it. He caught Ryan's tone, however, and turned to him after wiping his mouth on his sleeve. "What? Always tellin' me be polite. Was being polite. Asked what happened, and told 'em. That's all."

"Was it? Sure you weren't stretching the truth even a little?" Ryan asked.

Jak surprised him by shaking his head. "Fuck, no. Had correct 'em on couple points—thought chilled damn bird with bare hands." He grinned. "Not that crazy."

"Where'd they get an idea like that?" Ryan asked, although he was pretty sure he already knew the answer.

Jak looked around before answering. "Guess Tully's been tellin' everyone what saw." Although he tried to contain it, Ryan saw the teen's chest puff up a bit. "Not my fault mostly tellin' truth."

"Just don't go around telling stories you can't back up. Right now, us and them—" he pointed with his chin at the rest of the people around them "—are on fairly equal terms, and I'd like to keep it that way."

"No funny business?" Jak asked.

"It's not my place to tell you what you should or shouldn't do—you make your own decisions," Ryan replied. "Just be aware that a lot of choices carry the fates of others with them, whether that's the rest of us, or these people. I'm just suggesting that you to think before you act, that's all. And pass that message on to Ricky, okay?"

Jak nodded. "Got it."

"Brothers, sisters, come, be seated, and let us rejoice in this bounty that God has seen fit to grace our table with." Heads bowed again, and Elder Bough delivered a similar prayer to the one he had used when the group had arrived, although this one was blessedly shorter. Amens were muttered around the group, and then everyone dug in.

The meal was simple, but savory. The steaks had been done to a variety of tastes, and although a bit stringy, were still very good. Sides consisted of large pots of boiled potatoes in butter, asparagus and cooked beets. As often found with rural farming communities, the fresh-baked bread was superb—crusty outside, warm and tender inside, and served with fresh-churned butter and honey. Pitchers of water and milk accompanied the meal.

Conversation was sparse, mainly because everyone had their mouths full. Ryan and his companions took their cues from their hosts, and kept their comments limited to requests for more food and drink at first. Seeing as how everyone was putting away very good helpings—instead of giving their guests the best of what they had, and taking lesser portions for themselves—Ryan signaled his people to relax and enjoy the meal, which all of them were doing anyway.

He watched their hosts, in particular the table of elders—Bough, Teale and three others he hadn't been introduced to. All of them were variations on the same physical theme—lean, strong middle-aged men and women. He was surprised to find that this obviously theocratic society allowed women at its highest level, as the typical religious cults usually had one gender in charge—usually the males, although they had come across their share of female-controlled villes during their travels, as well.

Once second helpings had been put away, the women cleared the tables and brought out several varieties of fruit pie. The thick slabs were served with even thicker cream, and everyone dug in again.

"If those raiders were smart, they'd hit us now, when we're all too stuffed to move," J.B. observed while letting his belt out a notch. Ryan just nodded, fearing if he took too large a breath to answer, he'd bust the wooden button right off his pants.

At length, Elder Bough pushed his chair back and rose from his table across from Ryan and the others. "If starts pontificatin', gonna fall asleep right here," Jak whispered to Ryan.

"And I'll be damn sure to wake you back up, too," the one-eyed man replied. "Stay alert. I'm sure our names are going to come up pretty soon."

"First, I want to thank the kitchen sisters for that wonderful meal," Elder Bough began, extending a hand to the various women, who were still moving around the tables, taking platters and dishes. "Truly, they are doing the Lord's work every day, and we thank them for it."

Nods and murmurs of appreciation were heard and seen around the tables. "Before we open the floor to our most pressing issue at hand, is there any other matter that the elders should pronounce judgment on?"

Everyone looked around, and then the young girl whom Ricky had talked to stepped forward out of the bustle of women around the kitchen. "Yes, Elders, there is."

"Step forward, Marijah, and share with us," Elder Bough said.

Head down, the girl toed the dirt in front of her as she replied. "While we were escorting the visitors to the bath rooms, I spoke of the water machine—"

"It was my fault." Ricky's voice carried to everyone in the area. Ryan looked over to see him standing up at the end of their table, with all heads turning toward him, as well. The girl, however, kept her eyes on the ground. "I was just interested in the machine, that's all. I asked about it, and she started to answer, but one of her sisters cut her off before she could tell me anything." He took a deep breath. "I didn't mean to cause any harm, and I don't think the *señorita* should suffer for what she said."

"Is there anyone else who wishes to speak on this matter?" Bough asked.

Ryan raised his hand and levered himself up from his bench. "I just want to say that Ricky's story is how it went down—all of us were there to see it. If it was up to me, I'd class it as a harmless mistake."

The elders looked at one another, then back at Marijah. "Well spoken, Brothers Ricky and Ryan. Does the transgressor have anything to say on her behalf?"

She looked up now, on the verge of tears. "Only that I'm very sorry, and that I promise never to do it again."

Everyone appeared moved by her contrition, and even

Elder Bough cleared his throat before continuing, "Now, now, child, it will be all right."

He raised his voice to carry to the assembly. "Since the transgressor willingly came forward and confessed her misdeed, and taking into consideration the testimony on her behalf from our visitors, the punishment shall be light.

"Sister Marijah, you will go without food tomorrow from sunrise to sunset. During that time, you will carry out all of your duties while reflecting on the error of your ways, and bookend that meditation with hunger. The elders have spoken, so let it be done. Amen."

The assembly all nodded and said amen as well, and Ryan let out a small sigh of relief as he sat down again. As punishments went, that one was light. He had seen much worse done to people for much less elsewhere.

"If there are no more new matters at hand, we will therefore open the floor for discussion of our primary problem—the continued assault of our collective by these people who wish to capture us and turn our brethren against us." His voice trembled with anger, and Elder Bough accepted the cup of water pressed into his hand by Elder Teale. He emptied the cup and set it back down. "Thank you, sister."

"We have prayed long and hard for a solution to this obstacle. Truly, the Lord has said, 'Ask, and it shall be given you, seek, and ye shall find.' And so we did, sending forth our people to find help in our hour of need.

"Now it would seem that our prayers have been answered. We have been blessed with travelers who have arrived in our midst, men and women who have proved themselves adept in defending themselves and others when necessary."

Along with the head of every other person there, Elder Bough turned to Ryan and his group. "What say you, Brother Ryan and friends? Will you help us now, in our time of need?"

Chapter Fifteen

Ryan stood again and looked at the people seated around the tables, every last one of them staring at him with hope shining on their faces. He glanced over at his companions, all of whom would follow whatever course of action he set in his next few words.

"Elder Bough, Elder Teale, members of the collective. You've shown us hospitality, and for that we're grateful. It seems like our paths have crossed for a purpose, and we'll do what we can to help you fight your enemy."

There was a sudden knocking on wood, and Ryan looked over to see Tully rapping on the tabletop in front of her. It quickly spread, until all of the seated men and women were tapping their knuckles on their tabletops, including the elders.

"Then it is settled," Elder Bough said with a nod. "And all of us thank you, travelers. As stated when you first came to our ville, what is ours is yours. Food, drink, shelter, all of it is at your disposal. You merely have to ask."

"Much obliged," Ryan replied. "But since we're all getting down to brass tacks here, mebbe you should tell us more about the situation, so we can all figure out the best course of action."

"You speak with wisdom, Brother Ryan," Bough said. "Well, let's just say I've had enough people trying to put me in the dirt over the years that I believe in getting as much information about my enemy as I can," Ryan replied. "We got some of the story from Latham, but why don't you tell us what happened the first time these raiders hit you?"

Bough nodded slowly, as if weighing his words before starting. "Whoever they are, they're cunning. It began about three days ago, with what seemed like a minor incident. We lost one of our scouts, a good man named Belthus. He just disappeared like he never existed. We searched for him the rest of the day and into the night, but found no trace, no sign of his passing. We had searched this place while looking for him, and, finding it suitable, made camp, intending to continue looking for him the next day.

"He returned that same night—leading a group looking to claim more of our collective. Belthus was able to get close to a family, and he and the others nabbed Japeth, his wife and their son. The younger daughter was left alone, for what reason we cannot fathom.

"All of them returned the next night, but this time we were ready. However, they were well armed, and killed two of ours, and wounded several while taking four more of our people away. If not for the bravery of a few—" he nodded at Tully, who sat stone-faced on her bench at the far part of the U "—who, despite breaking one of our most sacred laws, took up arms to drive off the attackers. However, it is the general consensus that these people will return again and again, until they have gathered us all under their insidious will."

"Right," Ryan said. "From what Latham said, these people don't seem...normal?"

"That is correct," Bough replied. "They move and

react as one group, as if they are all connected in some unknown way. One of them is a match for two of our strongest men, and they absorb punishment that should kill a normal person, but remain standing."

"I can shed some light on that," Mildred said as she pushed her bench back and rose to her feet. "I'm a healer, and I know a great deal about the human body. I don't know what, if anything, Latham or Tully told you, but we encountered two of those people, a man and a woman, when we found your two scouts. The woman was very sick, and she died shortly after we got there. The man was heartbroken, practically hysterical, and had to be sedated. We all rested, but when the man woke up, he was...different. He attacked my friends, and they subdued him. I then decided to examine the woman's body further, as I had seen what looked like evidence of a parasite living inside her. Further examination revealed that I was right, but that the parasite had left her body and traveled to the man. We found out the man was also dying, and when he was gone, the parasite had left his body, and was then killed by one of us."

Mildred looked around at the shocked looks and gasps from her audience. "The point of my long-winded explanation is that these parasites seem to be able to control their human hosts to the tiniest degree. They seem able to block pain, and most likely regulate bodily functions to make those hosts stronger and faster than they were before."

"What about...what about their minds?" a woman asked in a quavering voice. "Are they still themselves?"

"That, I don't know," Mildred said. "I would need to observe a living subject with one of these things inside him to be able to tell. But if you're really asking if those that were taken might be saved…" The woman nodded emphatically, and Mildred hid her quick grimace. "Unfortunately, my answer is the same—I don't know."

The collective members muttered to one another until Bough rapped his water cup on the table. "It would seem that two choices lie before us. We can attempt to locate our brethren and save them from this pernicious evil that has not only befallen them but seeks to ensnare the rest of us as well, or we accept that some of our own have fallen to the dangers that stalk these lands and press on in the hope of saving the rest of us from a similar fate."

"You would leave my Joseph in the hands of these— these monsters!" the woman who had spoken before now said, her voice rising. "How could you—"

"Calm yourself, Sister Saea," Bough replied without rancor. "It's not my will that we will follow, it's the will of the collective."

"The will of the collective," every other person— including the woman who had just spoken—said in unison. Ryan exchanged a wary look with Krysty and J.B. They hadn't seemed like cultists, at least not until the past few seconds.

"Sister Saea, although it would seem that you have made your view on this matter very plain, is there anything else you wish to say on the matter?"

She looked around at everyone with wide, frightened eyes. "You all know what happened to my family. Baron killed my husband, Reth, when he wouldn't turn over his land. They burned the house with my little girl still inside…." She took a deep breath and wiped her eyes. "When we all voted to leave, I was with you all, because with Joseph by my side, I could face anything. But now, thinking of him in the hands of those monsters…" She buried her face in her hands. "I—I dream of him…calling for me…from somewhere cold, and white…and I can't go to him…." She collapsed back on her bench, sobbing.

"Thank you for your words, Sister Saea, and the collective grieves with you," Bough said. "Does anyone else have anything to say on the matter?"

Other members rose to tell their stories, either of loved ones lost to the invaders, or how the other missing members shouldn't be forgotten. There was almost no mention of pushing on without their people.

Finally, Bough turned to Ryan and the rest of the companions. "Is there anything else any of you would like to say?"

"Yeah." Ryan rose from his bench again. "We're not going say what we think you should do. This is your decision about your people, and it wouldn't be right to try to influence you all one way or another. But I want to say that if you decide to go ahead and try to rescue your people, you should be aware that there's a good chance it'll cost you other folks in the end. You've already paid the price with some, and I'm just saying that you all should weigh the risk carefully before charging into something that might cost a whole lot more before it's finished."

"Thank you, Brother Ryan." Bough turned to the rest of the assembly. "People of the collective, you have heard our situation, and of the two paths open to us. Who among us believes that we should stay and try to find our missing brethren?"

All the members raised their hands, including the other elders at the table. Bough looked around with quiet satisfaction before raising his own. "The vote is unanimous, and with the count from those on guard duty, not a single person of the collective opposes trying to find our missing members. Truly, you are all a kind and benevolent people."

"That's 'cause everyone here knows we'd do the same for them," Tully remarked in the silence afterward.

Bough nodded. "Quite true."

He turned to Ryan. "We place ourselves in your hands now. What would you have us do?"

Ryan had already given that some thought. "The most important thing right now is to keep everyone together so the group is harder to attack. If you haven't already done that, people need to leave any outlying buildings and all plan on sleeping in one place—probably the building with the bathrooms—which can be guarded more easily. Also, we'll need to change up the guard positions and rotation, since any males who were taken probably know the schedule, and therefore when to strike. From this point on, no one is to go anywhere by themselves. I'm sure these people will be just as happy picking off a lone man or woman if they can't get to the main group." He looked over at Tully. "We'd also like to get a look at those weapons that were taken, and get an idea of what we might be going up against when they come here again."

"So we're staying put for now?" one of the other elders, an even thinner man with gray-white hair, asked.

Ryan shook his head. "Only for tonight. Right now it's far too easy for a small group to slip into the ville and be among us before we know it. Pass the word, pack up whatever you can tonight and prep the water machine and whatever else you've got so we can move out early tomorrow. They've had the advantage when they came at you before, so we're going to try to remove that and face them on more even terms."

"What about finding our own?" Saea asked. "How are you going to do that?"

"One step at a time," Ryan replied, not wanting to reveal his plan for finding the redoubt yet if he could avoid it. That was going to be trickier, and he needed them on his side as much as possible before that could happen. "We need to make sure everyone left is secure, then we go about looking for the lost."

Ryan turned to the group's leader. "Elder Bough, am I right that the bath building should be able to hold everyone?" At the other man's nod, he continued, "Then I suggest you all pack up your things and move into that building. It may be a bit cramped, but it's only for one night, and besides, it's better than the alternative."

Talking among themselves, the collective members rose and began heading back to their various shelters. Ryan's companions clustered around him, with Doc clapping him on the shoulder.

"My, my, dear Ryan, it seems to me that you missed your calling. Perhaps a career in what they called 'crisis management' would have suited you in another time."

"Sure, Doc, as long as the job allowed me to chill anyone who got in my way," Ryan replied. "Just telling these people what's going to happen, that's all. Too much rests on their shoulders at the moment, and that's what worries me."

"Still, we're giving them something that's been in short supply recently—hope," Krysty said.

"Yeah, but that only goes so far," Ryan replied. "If people keep getting snatched and we can't stop that, or we can't find the redoubt, that well's going to dry up pretty quick."

"Locating the redoubt shouldn't be hard, if I know what you're thinking," J.B. said, then looked around Ryan's shoulder. "Head man's eyeing us. We'll talk about it later."

Ryan turned to see Bough leave the other elders and walk toward them. "Brother Ryan, I just wanted to thank you again for agreeing to help us during these most dire times. I know my words are paltry recompense for what you and yours are undertaking, but the feeling behind them is true."

"Understood and appreciated," Ryan said as he reached down to retrieve his longblaster. "But we've all got a long way to go before we can put this behind us, Elder, and if you don't mind, I'd like to get started by taking a look at those recovered weapons tonight."

"Absolutely." He glanced at Tully, who had been standing a few feet away, hands clasped behind her back. "Sister Tully and I will take you to where they're being stored. If you'll follow me."

They all followed the older man and young woman to a small cinder-block building that was probably more than a century old, although it looked as if it had been built a few years ago, and would still be standing a century after everyone here was dead and buried. The door was made of faded tin, with a hand-machined hasp and a gleaming, mass-produced, predark padlock on it.

"Water-pump room," Mildred said.

"Whatever was inside, any machines there were stolen or destroyed long ago," Bough said, pulling a silver key on a chain from under his shirt. "However, the building itself is strong enough to be sure that no one—

from our group or otherwise—would be able to get their hands on these instruments of destruction."

Unlocking the padlock, he slipped it off and flipped the hasp open, then opened the door. "No light inside, I'm afraid."

"No worries, we've got our own." Ryan took out his small pocket light and turned it on as he entered the room.

The inside was as plain and bare as the outside, and consisted of a packed-dirt floor with a hole in the corner. Two short-barreled automatic longblasters and two handblasters had been set in the corner, with the longblasters leaning up against the wall. Web belts holding several magazines sat on the floor next to them. Ryan noticed one of the longblasters had what looked like blood and maybe a bit of hair on its buttstock.

"M4 carbines." J.B. shouldered past Ryan and headed straight for them. "It has a 14.5-inch barrel, collapsible shoulder stock, 5.56 mm with thirty-round magazines—" picking one up, he pulled the cocking handle back and took a look at the chamber, then eased it back into position "—and both are practically brand-new." He glanced down at the other weapons. "Handblasters are 9 mm Berettas, also just out of the box." He looked up at Ryan, the question—and excitement—on his face unmistakable.

"Well, this is a big help," Ryan said. "The more weapons we can field against your enemies, the better we can stop them. We'd like to break these out, if you don't mind."

Bough nodded. "As you wish."

"What of training?" Tully asked with a glance at the elder. "Since I've already broken our laws, and there's no telling how many of them might come this time. We'll need all of the longblasters working that we can get."

"Although I wish you would choose to lay down the weapons and submit to purification, if the travelers allow it, I will not stand in your way." Bough looked at Ryan. "I also leave this matter in your hands, Brother Ryan."

Ryan glanced from the defiant-looking Tully to the resigned elder. "I think we'll start you off on one of the handblasters and go from there, all right?"

"All right." She tried but failed to hide the growing smile on her face.

"But we'll start tomorrow," Ryan said. "Right now, get some rest. It's going to be a very long day."

Chapter Sixteen

Ricky tossed and turned on his folded blanket, unable to sleep.

He should have been exhausted after everything they'd done that day, and to be fair, he was physically, but even so, his racing mind wouldn't let him fall asleep yet. Mainly because he was thinking about all those girls.

It had been something else to stand with Jak while he'd distracted the men with his story about the giant bird and all that. It had been more intoxicating when he had been served dinner by several attractive young women, all of whom seemed just as enamored of him as he was of them. Ricky had tried not to stare too much, but it had been a while since they'd seen *any* young women, and now, to have this many this close... Well, it was almost more than he could stand.

Even Ryan's warning, relayed by Jak, didn't dampen his enthusiasm. Of course, Ricky knew all about the birds and the bees—he'd been told of those things back home in Puerto Rico. And while he had no intention of getting involved with any of the young women, if the opportunity came to speak to them away from their parents, then who was he to not take advantage of it?

Rolling over, he glanced at the other two sleeping figures in the room. Doc slept with his back to them, his stentorian snores piercing the quiet night. Jak, on the other hand, slept on his back, hands folded over his chest, which rose and fell almost imperceptibly.

Ricky licked his dry lips. They should have been here by now.... "Jak...Jak?"

"What?" the albino said without opening his eyes.

"They're still coming, right?"

Jak twitched a shoulder. "Tully said so. Said let us know when here. Nothing do but wait."

"Feels like we've been waiting forever," Ricky replied.

"Couple more minutes not hurt," Jak said, just as they both heard someone rap on their boarded-up front window. Jak opened his eyes, his pupils huge in the gloom. "Come on."

It was dead quiet. Jak checked the outside hallway to make sure no one was up and about, then waved Ricky forward to the window at the end of the corridor. A knotted rope dangled off the roof, and Ricky looked up to see Tully, along with three other girls, looking down at them.

"Well, are you just gonna stand there, or are you coming up?" Tully whispered.

Jak clapped Ricky on the shoulder. "Go."

Hand over hand, he shinnied up the rope in a flash, swinging his leg over the edge to roll onto the roof. One of the girls reached out and grabbed his shoulder to help him, and he flashed her a quick smile. "Thank you," he whispered.

Jak popped up next to him. "Tully, sure not seen?"

Tully nudged him. "Relax. All of the guards on this watch are our relatives, and we convinced them to trade places with us for an hour. It's fine."

Below them, the entire Silvertide collective had crammed themselves into all of the motel rooms, with several also sleeping in what had been the former lobby. Out of respect to Jak and his group, they had been allowed to keep their rooms as originally assigned. Ryan had also set up guards on the buildings around the motel. Most of those were one story, while the motel itself was two stories, so the group wouldn't be seen as long as they didn't go too close to the edges.

Tully drew everyone close. "Okay, Jak and Ricky, this is Jael, Helah, Michal and Tamar."

Like the elders, the girls were more or less of a kind. All somewhere in their late teens, they were lean and browned from the sun. Jael was a dirty blonde, like Tully. Helah and Michal were redheaded twins, and Tamar was even duskier skinned than the others, with long, raven-black hair that hung in a single braid down her back. Standing this close to all of them, Ricky felt a little light-headed, but he clenched his teeth and steeled himself, determined not to show any weakness or embarrass himself in front of the girls.

Apparently, Tamar was also the group troublemaker. "I snuck us out a little something, too." She produced a clear glass jar three-quarters full of a clear liquid.

The other girls' eyes widened and their mouths fell open in shock. Tully recovered first. "You didn't!"

"Try some and see." She held the jar out to everyone.

"Tamar, you are so bad!" Helah said with a giggle.

The girls shied away, but Jak took it from her. "What is it, skullpop?" Ricky also looked on with interest, a grin spreading across his lips as he saw the other side of the Silvertide collective—and their rebellious daughters.

"Let's just say what Marijah got as punishment for just mentioning the water machine is nothing compared with what would happen if we got caught with this,"

Tamar said. "It's our real trade good. We're forbidden to have any. They save every drop for using to get what we need at villes along the way."

"How'd you get this out?" Tully asked. "Your dad watches every drop like a hawk."

"He's finally teaching me how to work the machines," Tamar replied. "I just took the opportunity to siphon off a bit when I had the chance. This is from the last of the corn crop. It's pretty raw, so it's gonna kick like a mule."

While she was talking, Jak had unscrewed the top and sniffed it, blinking at the vapors that drifted out. He took a healthy swallow and coughed loudly, turning away and trying to cover his mouth. Jak was no stranger to shine, but this stuff packed a powerful wallop.

"Jeez, Whitey, be quiet, will ya?" Tamar said. "I'll be shoveling ox shit for a month on bread and water if they find us up here."

"Tastes like poured gas down throat, then ate lit match!" Jak handed the bottle to Ricky. "Your turn."

Ricky also sniffed the concoction, finding it to be as he'd suspected, pure distilled alcohol. "Back home, we would usually mix something this strong with something like coconut milk or fermented pineapple juice." He took a cautious sip. It burned the roof of his mouth and the back of his throat, but not as bad as he had feared, and cleared his sinuses at the same time. "It's not bad, although I wouldn't drink too much too quickly."

"Lemme try." Tamar grabbed the jar back and brought it to her mouth, making sure everyone was watching. She tipped it back, taking a mouthful, then her eyes widened as the alcohol's burn hit her. Ricky carefully relieved her of the bottle as she looked at all of them with her mouth full.

"In or out, it has to go somewhere," he said.

Eyes watering, she swallowed it and sucked in a breath, then let it out with a faint squeak while fanning at her mouth. "It's…good…" she managed to choke out.

The other girls clamored to try, and each had similar reactions, with one of the twins—Michal, Ricky thought—almost throwing up her mouthful. After that, no one was willing to go for a second round, so Ricky suggested they take a few minutes, then try it again later, and asked about his original goal—besides seeing the girls, of course. "So the water machine is on this roof, yes?"

"Sure, though I don't know why you still care about that thing," Tully replied. "But if you wanna see it, come on."

She led them down to the far end of the building, where a large cube, half again as high as Ricky and twice as wide, sat on the roof. A large white pipe ran from it into what looked like some kind of main water pipe a few feet away. "Stay on this side, away from the other buildings."

"What is it?" Ricky asked. "Marijah said something about it being sun powered."

"It is. Let me see that jar." Tully took another swig. "Not so bad the second time."

"It's a solar-powered water-condensing system," Jael said. "My brother works on it from time to time. When the elders found it, they thought it was supposed to purify water, but it actually creates it instead. It's good for drinking, of course, and also supplies the water for the shine."

"Fascinating," Ricky said, which was the absolute truth. He found machines of all kinds, whether they were vehicles, weapons or tools for survival, intensely interesting. "Can you tell me where you found it?"

The girls exchanged a conspiratorial glance. "The elders never said exactly how they got it," Tamar said after another swig of liquor. "All I know is that they brought it back with them from a trade trip a couple months before we set out west."

The twins had another go at the jar, and then Jak and Ricky took a second pull, as well.

Meanwhile, Tully had carefully maneuvered herself to be standing right next to Jak. "Ryan said I'd be learning how to shoot a handblaster tomorrow." She stared into his eyes. "Mebbe you could teach me a few things."

Jak stared back at her for a moment. He opened his mouth as if to reply, then quickly began closing it, but not before a loud belch escaped.

The teenagers all stared at one another, then Tully was the first to dissolve into a fit of giggles. The twins were next, turning away from the group in an attempt to stifle their mirth, followed by Ricky, then Tamar, then Jael, with Jak grinning sheepishly.

"All right, all right, damn it, keep your voices down!" Tully said when she had finally regained control of herself. "And give me that jar." After a third healthy swallow, she fixed her gaze on Jak. "So whaddaya say?"

"Sure, teach how shoot," he replied.

"Not *that*...jeez." Tully came back over to Jak and threw her arms around him. Before he knew what was happening, she planted a long, wet kiss on his mouth. Jak stood there for a moment, then brought his arms up and around her as he returned the favor.

Ricky watched in amazement until he realized he was staring, and quickly looked away. He caught Tamar's gaze as she lowered the shine jar again, and she sidled toward him. "Been wonderin' if you kiss as good as you look, Ricky. Think it's time I found out."

Ricky was torn between staying where he was and saying or doing something to deflect the very intent-looking girl. Only a step away now, she was stretching out a well-muscled arm to snake around his shoulders, her lips coming closer and closer, until they alighted on his.

For Ricky, the sensation blew the fire of the moon-shine away. It was kind of like being electrocuted; his body felt tingly and numb at the same time. Her mouth was soft and wet, her warm breath redolent with the shine's sharp tang. He was acutely aware of her arms clutching his back, and her body molding itself to his, the press of her breasts against his chest. Belatedly, he brought up his own arms to wrap around her, as well. At the same time, he was also conscious of a particular part of his anatomy swelling in response to the girl in front of him, and he shifted his hips so it didn't press into her.

But even through the sexual fog that enveloped him, Ricky's combat reflexes were sharp enough to still maintain awareness of his surroundings. So when he heard the odd noise in the distance, he had enough presence of mind to come up for air and look to the north, toward where he thought the sound had come from.

"What's wrong?" Tamar sounded disappointed.

"I heard something," he said, straining to listen.

"Probably just an open door swinging in the breeze," she said as she grabbed his chin and tried to move his mouth back to hers. "C'mere."

"There's not enough wind to move a door." Even with his suspicion, Ricky was on the verge of giving in when he heard it again—like something scraping against a wall. Whatever it was, it didn't sound natural. Gently twisting his face out of her grasp, he looked in that direction, noticing that Jak was, as well.

"You see anything, Jak?"

"No—that's problem. Not see guard on building."

"When's changeover?" Ricky squinted, trying to see through the moonlit night, but his night vision wasn't as good as Jak's.

"Not 'nother hour."

"Should we check it out?"

The albino was already moving toward the edge of the roof. "Yup."

"Wait—where're you going?" Tully asked.

"Guard's missing," Jak replied. "Mebbe takin' a piss, or mebbe the people-stealers coming back. Gonna go see."

"We gotta come with, then," she said. "You all don't know who's who, and if people from our ville are there, we wanna catch them alive."

At the roof's edge, rope in hand, Jak paused. "Not guarantee can do that, but try. Better come, Tully. Rest stay here and watch that building. If see us come out and wave arms or you hear shots, wake everyone, Ryan first."

"Won't the shots do that anyway?" Jael asked with a pout of tipsy confusion.

"Yeah, but you'll tell them what's going on," Ricky said. "And get them moving in that direction."

"Wastin' time—come on!" Jak climbed down with hardly a sound. Ricky had Tully go next, then climbed down after her. Doc was still snoring in their room.

"What about a blaster for me?" Tully whispered.

Ricky and Jak exchanged glances. "Wait here," Ricky said. He slipped back into his room, picked up his De Lisle carbine and chambered a round. Coming back out, he drew his Webley revolver and offered the butt to the girl. "Six shots. No need to cock it, just point and pull the trigger." He paused. "*Por favor,* don't shoot either of us."

She glared at him. "Well, I'll try not to shoot Jak, at least." She turned away from him and waved Jak forward. "Let's go."

The albino trotted to the end of their sleeping quarters, where a concrete stairway led to the ground. Blaster in hand, he crept down and headed toward the building in question, hugging the wall and checking around corners before flitting across a narrow alley choked with dirt and mummified garbage.

Knowing Jak had the front covered, Ricky divided his attention between Tully ahead of him and checking behind them every few steps.

The target building had been an automotive garage long ago, with a pair of large doors covering the vehicle bays. A row of glassless windows revealed pitch darkness inside. A smaller, boarded-up door stood next to the two big doors. There was no sign of any guards out front, and Ricky couldn't see anyone looking down from the roof either.

"Stay close," Jak whispered to the other two. "Move when I do." He checked right and left one last time, then ran to the smaller door and put his back to the wall next to it.

To her credit, Tully knew how to move. She gave Jak a two-step lead, then followed him, taking a position behind him, blaster held in both hands in front of her. Ricky brought up the rear again, putting himself behind

Tully. Jak signaled him to look through the garage window, which Ricky did, but he saw only darkness.

Ready? Jak mouthed to Ricky, who nodded. The albino reached for the steel door handle, eased it open a few inches at a time and slipped inside. Tully followed him, with Ricky entering after a last glance around, carefully pulling the door shut behind him.

This part of the garage had been divided by thin slabs of drywall into a small office. A doorless entryway on the back wall led to what had to be the main garage area. The remains of a shattered counter were strewed over the floor, with the laminated counter leaning against the wall. On the other one was a calendar faded to near illegibility. Ricky could just make out what looked like a small green lizard under the word *Sinclair,* which had faded from bright red to a dusty rose. The displayed month, with the bottom two weeks torn away, was November 2000. It was completely silent inside.

Jak hissed to get Ricky's attention. On the floor were boot tracks heading into the bigger room inside—new boot tracks, complete with a clear tread pattern. The albino leaned over, studying them for a moment, then straightened and signed to the other teen with one hand: *three or four inside.* His other hand now held a throwing blade.

Ghosting over the dirty, littered ground, Jak crept to the empty doorway at the back of the room, putting his back to the wall on the left side. Fingers white on the Webley's butt, Tully walked to the other side. Ricky stayed by the door they'd come in for the moment, his De Lisle held at the ready.

Jak poked his head through the door whip-quick, then pulled it back. He shook his head at Ricky, indicating he didn't see anyone inside. Ricky nodded. Jak held up a hand to Tully in a clear message—*stay here*—then stepped through the door, blade held at his side to throw underhand.

The moment he disappeared, Ricky crossed the room to Jak's previous position and rested his back against the wall. Through the doorway, he could make out a portion of the rest of the old garage, including two large wag lifts, both raised, in the bays. He strained to hear any sounds, catching what he thought was the scrape of Jak's boot on the stained concrete. A bit of drywall dust trickled down onto Ricky's shoulder, making him glance at the ceiling, but he didn't see anything unusual there. His blood pounded in his ears, and even with everything that was going on, he could still taste the faint flavor of Tamar's lips on his.

A soft whistle made Ricky peek in to see Jak standing by a wooden staircase, waving him over. Ricky nodded at Tully. "Go," he whispered just loud enough for her to hear.

She entered the larger room, crossing the open space to Jak in a half dozen steps. When the albino waved him over, Ricky took two steps before he was suddenly bowled over by a heavy weight crashing down on his head and shoulders.

The carbine flew out of his hands, skittering across the floor with a clatter as he went down. Stunned but not out, Ricky rolled over to see a grim-faced woman in a black jumpsuit standing over him, aiming an equally deadly looking blaster at his heart.

Chapter Seventeen

Hearing noises from the far side of the garage, Ricky glanced over just long enough to see two more jump-suited assailants drop from their hiding places atop the wag lifts. They both landed at the exact same time and straightened, longblasters aimed at the three.

Ricky then looked at Jak in time to watch him shift his body just enough to hide his throwing knife. The two exchanged a glance that carried an entire conversation about what they needed to do.

"Do not try to shoot any of us, or we will be forced to kill you," a blond-haired man said to Tully, who had turned and was aiming Ricky's blaster in their general direction. "Set the weapon down and step away from it." At Jak's nod, she did so, then stepped closer to him. "You too, White-hair. Remove the weapon from your belt and set it on the ground. Any resistance will be met with force."

With a frown, Jak did so. "Any collective members?" he asked Tully.

"I can't tell. It's too dark in here," she said. "He doesn't sound like one, though. She doesn't neither."

The intruders, however, didn't seem to have any problem seeing in the darkness. All of them were examining the teenagers with interest.

"Subject verified as first located by Kenneth approximately seventeen point seven miles south-southwest of this location is now here," the first man said as he and his partner both stepped toward the three, moving in lockstep while sighting them down the barrel of their carbines. "Probability of error in confirming identity one point eight percent. Assimilation potential high. Subject is top capture priority."

"You talkin' me?" Jak said, then spit into the corner. "Not goin' with you!"

"All three appear to be suitable subjects for joining us," the woman stated. "Together with the one we have already secured, this trip is rated successful. Let us secure these and depart."

"Wait! Don't take me!" Ricky said. "I can get you more than just us—lots more!"

"Ricky, no!" Tully said.

"I'll take you to all of them! Just let me go, and I'll leave here and never come back!" Ricky's terrified whine wasn't entirely made up, but he was still in control of himself. Any way he could give the other two a chance to either run for help or get to weapons to take these people out, he'd do whatever he had to, including appearing to sell out the collective to save his own skin.

The woman cocked her head as she regarded him. "Subject's voice stress level indicates probability that he is telling the truth is approximately fifty-eight point seven percent. Percentage is not enough to trust that he will do as he claims. We will secure them all and leave now." Blaster still trained on Ricky, she reached down to grab the front of his shirt with her free hand.

"Tania—" one of the others started to warn even as silver flashed in front of Ricky's eyes, and suddenly the back of Tania's hand sprouted a thin steel knife handle.

Her fingers popped open, and she dropped her blaster into Ricky's waiting hand. However, her other hand had grabbed his shirt, and she straightened, hauling him to his feet. Before he could get the muzzle aimed at her, she pivoted and threw him against the office wall hard enough to put a huge crack in the drywall.

Ricky's right shoulder slammed into a wooden stud, sending a sharp pain down his arm and through his chest as he fell to the ground again. The second rap to his head made stars burst in his vision as he brought up the blaster—still clutched in his hand, although he had no idea how he'd managed to hold on to it—and aimed it at the woman. He heard footsteps pounding on the stairs, but wasn't sure if someone was coming or going. That was followed by the *boom* of Jak's Colt Python, its muzzle flash lighting up the dark room, revealing the two men frozen in time for a second as they took evasive action. Oddly, neither of the two men returned fire, but Ricky figured he knew the reason for that. They still want to take us alive…

Not while any of them could fight back, though. Ricky aimed the blaster at the woman running toward him and squeezed the trigger. She jerked, half turning, and Ricky thought he'd hit her, but she turned back to face him as she kept advancing, and he was shocked to find no dark stain of blood spreading across her chest.

He'd missed—from less than three yards away.

She'd *dodged* the bullet was the only thought he could muster even as she was on him. He squeezed the trigger again just as she swept in, batting the blaster aside with a blurred arm even as it went off. Again, the muzzle flash illuminated his enemy's face, which was as calm as if she was helping a friend who had just slipped and fallen on the ground. She showed no rage, no fear, no pleasure—no emotion of any kind.

At the same time, Ricky became aware of a stabbing pain in the forearm of his blaster hand. His gaze flicked over to see the haft of Jak's throwing blade sticking out of his arm just as the albino's Magnum blaster boomed again.

His attacker had stabbed him! Not only that, but she was also picking him up again. Gritting his teeth against the pain in his arm, Ricky tried to bring the blaster into firing position, but she brought her head down as she lifted him up, and smashed her forehead into the bridge of his nose.

The pain Ricky had suffered from the previous blow to his head and getting thrown around like a rag doll was nothing compared with this. It shot through his skull, making his eyes water and his nose ache as if he'd just inhaled a handful of dried habanero pepper. Blood gushed from his nose, and his head lolled on his shoulders as he felt the blaster being stripped from his hand, causing another bolt of pain to lance through him. He clung to consciousness, aware that if he passed out, he was as good as theirs. But it was getting difficult to hold his head up. Where are Ryan and the others? he wondered.

The woman suddenly left him alone. His vision clearing, Ricky looked around to see what was going on.

The woman and two men were trying to capture Jak, who was a white-haired blur in the darkness. Normally the skinny fighter would have no problem facing these three, but they were able to either evade his blows or take the worst of what he could dish out and come back for more. As Ricky watched through half-closed eyes,

Jak leaped high into the air and lashed out with his foot, the roundhouse kick catching one of the men on the side. Normally he'd be either unconscious or dead, but this guy simply picked himself up off the floor, ignoring the gashed, bloody flap of skin now hanging off his cheek, and came back at the fighting teenager.

They also moved in near perfect synchronicity. A couple of years ago Ricky's uncle Benito had been hired by a local baron to fix an old machine that displayed moving pictures on a small glass screen. When Benito and Ricky had gotten the device working again, they had both sat in awed silence watching the tiny figures on the screen as they leaped, punched and kicked at each other in what could only be called an incredible dance of combat. When Ricky had asked what they were watching, Benito had carefully removed the large black plastic cartridge that still had the words *Loaf of Kung Fu* visible. Ricky and Benito had never figured out what that meant, but he'd always remembered how those warriors had moved, using each other as barriers, launching platforms and even weapons.

The three arrayed against Jak now moved in much the same manner, utilizing one another almost as props to fight the agile, fast-moving teen. Jak was doing everything he could to avoid getting caught by the men or woman. He leaped up again to deliver another flying kick, but this time one of the men picked up the woman and literally tossed her at the teenager. The two bodies collided in midair and fell to the ground, both of them rolling with the impact and coming up on their feet again. However, the other two had figured out where Jak would land, and had moved to encircle him. When he came up, he was surrounded by the trio.

"Surrender, and you do not have to die here," the woman said.

"Fuck off!" Jak replied, turning in place to try to watch all of them at once.

Spotting his carbine a few yards away, Ricky crawled toward it, trying to ignore the blinding flashes of pain that bloomed every few seconds in his head. It felt like an hour, but was probably only a few seconds before his hand curled around the cool wooden grip of the De Lisle. Ricky rolled back over and aimed his weapon at the combatants on the other side of the room.

Bracing his longblaster with his good arm, Ricky sighted down the barrel and squeezed the trigger. The muffled crack of his De Lisle signaled its discharge, and one of the men fell to one knee, dark blood spattering on the concrete.

Shouts and footsteps could be heard outside, making the attackers' heads turn toward the noise, then back to look at one another.

"Too many coming," the woman said. "Take what we have and go. For the Mind."

"For the Mind," all three said at once. They nodded once, curtly, and quickly drew their blasters, aiming them at Jak.

"Ricky! Jak!" Ryan shouted from outside. The noise distracted their enemies enough for Jak to leap up, grab the wag lift and pull himself on top of it. The woman fired a couple of shots at him while the two men turned their blasters on the office door and walls, peppering it with bullets.

"In here, Ryan!" Ricky struggled to chamber another bullet with his one good arm. He was also praying that neither of the two men turned their blasters his way. As he rammed the De Lisle's bolt home, the woman materialized above him, the butt of her blaster slashing across his face.

Ricky saw one last blinding burst of light, then nothing....

Chapter Eighteen

Ryan had awakened instantly at the first shot fired.

The familiar report of Jak's Colt had him up and out of the makeshift bed with his SIG Sauer in hand.

"Blastershots. Jak?" Krysty asked in the darkness.

"Yeah. I'm going to see what's up," he replied. Hearing a babble of voices and footsteps pounding down the outside corridor, he grabbed his Scout longblaster and ran to the door, opening it in time to see three teenage girls running toward him, all talking at once.

"—Jak and Ricky—"

"—couldn't see the guard—"

"—Tully went, too—"

"—all at the north building—"

Ryan raised his hand with the SIG Sauer in it, cutting off all of them. "Show me!"

They turned and ran back toward the end of the covered hallway. Ryan followed, meeting J.B., armed with one of the M4 carbines, as he passed their door. Mildred stood behind him also dressed and armed.

"Stay here in case they get by us," Ryan said. "You and Krysty rouse everyone and get them into the main room downstairs." Mildred started heading back toward Ryan's room.

As they pounded down the corridor, other sleep-bleary faces peeked out of the rooms. "What's happening? What's going on?"

"Get everyone up and go to the main room on the bottom floor," Ryan answered to each query.

At the stairs, the girls pointed to a building about fifty yards away just as another shot roared from inside. "You all get to the main room below!" Ryan said as he and J.B. ran down the stairway.

Normally the two men would have approached more cautiously, using available cover and watching each other's back as they moved. But not knowing exactly what was happening inside the building, and with no shots coming at them, they risked their lives on a mad dash to the front door, Ryan on the right, J.B. on the left. At a nod from the Armorer, Ryan yanked the door open and J.B. covered the inside, just as they both heard the familiar muffled sound of Ricky's silenced carbine.

"Ricky? Jak?" Ryan shouted as both men headed inside and swept the small room.

"In here, Ryan!" Ricky's answering shout was close, but at the same time, blasterfire began perforating the room, making both men hit the floor.

J.B. returned fire, his heavier bullets punching larger holes through the thin walls. He spaced his shots so as to have a decent chance of hitting someone on the other side, careful to avoid the area where they'd heard Ricky.

Meanwhile, Ryan had crawled to the doorway and peeked around its edge, trying to see anything inside. A flurry of movement near the back made him extend his handblaster and fire three times in that direction. A burst of return fire made him duck behind the wall as bullets stitched the drywall panels above his head, showering him with fragments and dust. Something else fell on his head, and Ryan brushed away a sheaf of brittle, flaking papers with a bullet hole through the middle.

"That's no handblaster!" he said.

"They brought their M4s, too," J.B. said from the corner. "Where's Ricky?"

Ryan shook his head. "Didn't see him."

"They took!" Jak shouted from inside the large room. "Up—" A flurry of shots cut him off, too.

"Dark night!" the Armorer replied. "Can't let them have him!"

"They won't have him long," Ryan replied. "At least Jak's still here." He raised his voice. "Jak, you all right?"

"Yeah." More shots interrupted him. "Fucker got me trapped!"

"Just hang tight," Ryan called back.

"Spot where the shooter is, J.B." The one-eyed man stuck his SIG Sauer around the doorway and fired two shots, receiving another burst of bullets in return.

"On the stairway, mostly covered by the railing and the upper floor," J.B. said as he rolled over past Ryan to the other side of the doorway and came up in a kneeling position. "Keep his head down for a few seconds."

Ryan complied, emptying his magazine in the shooter's direction. While he did, J.B. rested his elbow on his knee and sighted in on the man. He fired three short bursts, then ducked behind the wall, the smoke from their weapons thick in the air.

Silence reigned for several seconds. "Think you got him?" Ryan asked as he changed the spent magazine in his blaster for a fresh one.

"Stick your head out and find out," J.B. replied.

"No, thanks." Instead, Ryan stuck his blaster out and

fired a round. No return fire answered him. "Looks good."

"Or he's playing possum," J.B. whispered. "If these people have the parasites, they take a lot of pain and can still be dangerous."

"That's why I'm not going to rush up those stairs," Ryan replied. "Let's go, nice and slow."

The two men ran toward the staircase without taking a single shot. On the way, Ryan spotted Ricky's De Lisle lying near the far wall, and detoured to snatch it off the floor.

Jak joined them there, the front of his sleeveless jumpsuit covered in dirt and stains. "Empty," he whispered. Ryan tossed the silenced carbine to him. Jak checked the load and nodded.

Ryan pointed up the staircase, then to himself, then to J.B., then Jak. Getting nods from the other two, he raised his blaster as he crept to the first few steps.

The staircase went straight up and toward the back wall for three steps, then opened onto a small landing before turning left ninety degrees and continuing up to the roof. Stepping on the far edge of the stairs to minimize creaking, Ryan climbed two of them, leading with his blaster. He felt J.B. right behind him and knew the shorter man was finding his own avenue of fire even while Ryan was in front of him. One more step, and Ryan would be visible to the shooter on the stairs. Steeling himself, he stepped out onto the landing.

The man lay on his stomach, sightless eyes still open, carbine still gripped in his fingers. A large pool of blood beneath him dripped down the stairs. Ryan didn't lower his weapon, however, but kept it trained on the body as he began climbing, staying to the right of the staircase.

When he was three steps away, the body moved.

Swiveling his head to look at Ryan, he raised the M4 even as Ryan, J.B. and Jak all unloaded on the man. The bullets pulped his head, tearing off his lower jaw and killing him before he could squeeze the trigger.

"Shit, look that!" Jak said as he worked the De Lisle's bolt action.

Something was moving in the dead man's mouth. His throat bulged as a slimy, slug-like creature emerged from the esophagus. Night black and glistening, it had no eyes, but waved two antennae as it began oozing onto the stair.

"Ugly bastard," Ryan said as he steadied his blaster and pulled the trigger.

"No, wait!" J.B. said, but it was too late. The 9 mm bullet tore through the squishy mass, almost tearing it in two. The parasite writhed once, and all three men clutched their heads as a strange shriek reverberated inside their brains, like the grating noise of overstressed metal being torn apart.

"What fuck that?" Jak asked when it had died away. "Other one not do that."

"No idea," Ryan replied. "Come on, let's get Ricky." He stepped over to the body and pulled the M4 out of the corpse's hands. "Bullet hole in the stock, and the receiver took one, as well. It's junk now." He tossed the mangled weapon aside. "Let's go."

The top of the stairs ended in a trapdoor. Ryan tried opening it, but it was stuck or locked. "I'm going to shoot it."

"Wait—if it's steel, the bullet could ricochet and plug one of us instead." J.B. squeezed past him enough to reach up and push up on the hatch. "Got some give— probably tin. Go for it."

"Stand back." Ryan put two bursts into the handle, the reports making his ears ring in the enclosed space. When he tried shoving the door up this time, it opened.

"Slow," J.B. whispered.

"I know, dammit!" Ryan eased the trapdoor open just enough to peek out. From his vantage point, the roof appeared empty, but he knew how deceiving that could be. "Sure wish I had a stun gren."

"Wish had rocket launcher, but don't," Jak whispered. "Goin' out, or me?"

"Hold on, Jak. Are you trying to get yourself killed?" Ryan whispered back. "On three, J.B. One...two... three!"

Shoulder blades tensing in anticipation of receiving a bullet, Ryan shoved the door open and dived out onto the hot, sticky roof. At the same time, J.B. came up and covered the side opposite the hatch with his M4. Jak served as cleanup, covering the left and right sides as he emerged from below.

At the far end of the garage roof, three moving forms were visible in the moonlight, each carrying another person over his or her shoulder.

"Hold it!" Ryan shouted even as the invaders extended their blasters at the three.

Ryan, Jak and J.B. hit the roof as the invaders opened fire, but they couldn't shoot back for fear of hitting the hostages. Steel blurred through the air, however, and one of the kidnappers dropped his hostage and fell to his knees, clutching at his suddenly fountaining throat. The freed captive managed to roll away, even with arms and legs bound.

Hauling the last hostage up in front of her as a human shield, the woman unslung her longblaster and sat down, covering her companion with aimed shots as he began lowering the other captive off the side of the building.

"I can't get a clear shot!" Ryan said. "We have to flank them!"

"I'm open to suggestions as to how!" J.B. replied from where he was lying behind the hatch, the only cover on the roof. "She's going to walk rounds right on top of us if we don't do something!"

"Fuck that! Take out!" Jak said, rising on his elbows enough to aim at the other man. He triggered a shot, making his target jerk as the round hit him in the back, but the guy stayed on his task. Jak yanked the bolt back and chambered another round, but three shots from the woman made him hug the roof before he could shoot again.

"Can you get her with the Steyr?" J.B. asked.

"I'll try." Holstering his SIG Sauer, Ryan brought around the Scout longblaster and snugged it into his shoulder. The range was far shorter than how he normally shot, but what he really needed was the magnification provided by the 2.5x scope. The woman's face leaped into focus, appearing to be only a few yards away. She was scooting backward, hauling her unconscious hostage—Ricky, Ryan noticed with a grimace—toward the edge of the roof while keeping the M4 tight to her shoulder and firing single shots at the three men. One-handed.

He had only another second or two to get a shot off before she disappeared over the side with Ricky. Taking a deep breath to steady himself, Ryan settled behind the crosshairs and aimed for the only visible part of the woman—her head. When it came into sight again as she leaned out to glance over the side, he squeezed the trigger.

The shot boomed out, and the 7.62 mm bullet impacted the side of her head, sending a spray of blood and bone arcing into the night. Already leaning over, the woman fell off the side, leaving Ricky on the roof.

"Let's get him. Cover!" Ryan said as he got up and approached the prone form of their friend. Jak and J.B. were right next to him as they ran forward, but even as they did, two dark objects clattered onto the roof from the far side and rolled toward them.

"Grens! Hit the deck!" One came close enough to Ryan for him to kick it off, but the other one was too far away. Again, the three men dived to the roof, covering their ears and closing their eyes as the bomb went off in a series of flashes so bright Ryan could see them even through his eyelids. They were accompanied by a series of deafening booms that buffeted his body and left a sharp ringing in his ears.

Shaking his head to try to dispel the gren's effects, Ryan got up and staggered to the edge of the building. Below were the man and the woman, each still moving—even her, with a large chunk of her skull missing—and both carrying a captive over their shoulders. As if knowing they were being watched, the pair turned and raised their blasters while walking backward.

Ryan threw himself back as bullets flew all around him. Rolling to the far edge, he slung his longblaster and lowered himself by his one good arm. When he had extended himself down as far as he could, Ryan shrugged off his Steyr Scout and let it drop, then let go of the roof, hitting the ground and rolling backward to somersault onto his feet again. He grabbed the Steyr and ran to the corner to peek around it. Chattering from J.B.'s M4 above told him his friend was trying to keep the kidnappers busy enough so Ryan could hopefully get the drop on them.

Ryan saw them disappear around the corner of a half-demolished ruin of a house, and began trotting toward it. Halfway down, he heard boots hit the ground behind him, and glanced back to see J.B. running toward him, M4 held in both hands.

"Where's Jak?" Ryan asked.

The Armorer nodded back at the roof. "Tully escaped back there. Told him to make sure she was all right. Come on."

The two men ran to the corner and peeked around it. They were on the north end of the ville now, and the buildings were sparser, with the few scattered ones giving way to the endless plains beyond them.

"Movement." Ryan pointed at a building with an attached, listing carport on the side. The two survivors were putting their cargo into the back of some kind of all-terrain wag they'd hidden there. "Would help if we could get that wag, too."

"I can take one now," J.B. said, raising the M4 to his shoulder. As he did, bright halogen lights burst into life atop the truck, illuminating the two men's position.

"I can't see!" J.B. pulled back while shots were fired at them, forcing both men to withdraw a few more feet from the corner.

"They're going to get away!" Ryan said. "Can't let them take Ricky! Fireblast!" Dropping his longblaster, he ran back to the corner in time to see the high-clearance, six-wheeled truck pull out of the carport and begin to accelerate, making hardly any noise as it sped up. A head appeared from the passenger window, aiming an M4 at him.

"Go!" J.B. shouted from behind him as he opened up with his own carbine, aiming at the shooter first to force him back undercover, then dropping his muzzle to the front tire. The bullets chewed into it, making it deflate with a loud hiss, but the truck kept moving. It was, however, significantly slowed, allowing Ryan to gain on it.

Putting on a burst of speed, Ryan grabbed for the top of the tailgate, getting his fingers on it just as the truck shifted gears and surged ahead, pulling him off his feet!

Chapter Nineteen

As he held on by one hand, Ryan's combat boots bounced and dragged against the hardpan as the truck accelerated even faster into the scrubby plains. The two blown tires didn't seem to be slowing it all that much.

Gritting his teeth, Ryan reached up with his other arm, which still throbbed unmercifully from his still-healing burrower injury. Shooting with it hadn't been bad, but lifting it over his head was another story. Ignoring the pain, he grabbed onto the side of the truck bed and pulled himself up to fall inside it. Even as he hit, Ryan rolled forward, aware that the people inside probably knew someone had caught up with them.

Sure enough, a head emerged from the passenger-side window again. It was the woman, her face covered in blood, and she was pointing a blaster at Ryan, who ducked out of the way. The next thing he heard was footsteps right overhead. Glancing up, he saw the woman standing on the roof of the truck cab, the muzzle of her blaster tracking toward him.

Ryan grabbed her feet and yanked them toward him as the weapon fired close enough for him to feel the brief blast of flame on his scalp. The woman slammed down hard enough on the passenger compartment to leave a large dent in the metal. Still holding on to her, Ryan stepped backward, dragging her off the cab. She managed to get an arm underneath to break her fall, but her blaster pitched from her hand and fell into a corner of the truck bed.

Even seriously injured and flat on her back, the woman was dangerous. She wrenched a foot out of his grasp and immediately pistoned it back into his stomach. The air whooshed out of Ryan's lungs, leaving him stunned just long enough so that he was unable to block a second kick that tore her other foot from his grasp and sent him staggering back toward the tailgate. He stopped only when the back of his knees hit the metal, and for a moment he teetered on the edge, a hairbreadth away from falling out of the truck.

Regaining his balance, Ryan sucked in a breath and stepped forward to find himself facing the woman, who was now standing up. Although the bullet had plowed through her skull and a good portion of her brain, she was still moving as if she hadn't been injured at all. Even in the bed of the fast-moving truck, she easily kept her balance as she watched him.

Ryan's hand shot to the butt of his SIG Sauer and pulled it from his hip holster. But even as he brought it up, she leaped forward, a hard hand gripping his wrist and wrenching the weapon away from him. Clenching her other hand into a fist, she launched it at his jaw, but Ryan grabbed that one in his other hand.

For a moment, he strained against her, their muscles flexing as each combatant tried to get an advantage on the other. Ryan was shocked at the woman's strength, especially since she was several inches shorter than him, and at least sixty pounds lighter. Her grip, however, was crushing, and trying to move her was like pushing against a granite wall.

The truck hit a patch of rougher terrain, the jouncing bed making it more difficult to keep their balance. Even so, she brought up a leg and tried to kick Ryan in the crotch, using their locked arms as brace points to help keep her balance. Ryan saw the move coming, however, and twisted his hips to take the blow on his thigh. He kept turning, using her force against her and pulling her off balance. While she staggered to try to stay on her feet, he pulled her all the way around and let go of her wrist while twisting his other wrist out of her grasp, intending to let her go flying into the tailgate and out of the truck as he almost had a few seconds ago.

At least that was what was supposed to happen.

Unfortunately, he didn't break her hold on his wrist. Instead, she leaped into the air and drove her elbow down toward his face. Ryan saw it in time to duck his head and take the blow on the top of his skull. Even so, he saw a bright white flash for a moment, and he countered by driving his free hand into her nose, crushing it. The blow snapped her head back and made her entire body recoil, but she still didn't let go of his blaster arm.

Now they had switched places, with Ryan facing away from the cab. He shoved her toward the tailgate, the punch stunning her enough so that he could use his superior weight to force her back. He had just gotten her up to it when the truck swerved violently to the right, catching them by surprise and knocking both Ryan and the woman off their feet.

He fell into the side of the bed, painfully banging his elbow and ribs. She slid into the side with her head and shoulder, but again, didn't seem affected by it at all. Ryan grabbed his blaster arm with his other hand to try to force it over to her head. He had moved it about six inches when the truck swerved to the left, making them slide across the cargo area to slam into the other side.

Ryan pulled his arm close to him, bringing her with it. At the same time, he arched forward to slam his forehead into her face, pulping her already broken nose even more. Her head snapped back again, then she brought it forward to smash her forehead into *his* face.

Pain exploded on his cheekbone, and the world turned to red and white stars for a moment. Furious, Ryan blinked away the tears caused by the shot and moved his head out of the way just in time to avoid another forehead butt.

"That's *it!*" Tossing his blaster to his left hand, he jammed it into her rib cage and fired repeatedly. The cluster of bullets plowed through her body, shattering her sternum and sending jagged fragments of bone through her chest cavity to shred her heart and lungs. And all this on top of the damage the bullets themselves caused, which included tearing out her spinal column, as well.

And *still* the woman didn't stop coming after Ryan. Bleeding profusely and with her legs now useless, she nonetheless tried to climb on him, her still-powerful arms and hands clawing at his face or throat. Her movements took on a frenzied quality, as if the thing inside her knew it was in trouble.

"Dammit, bitch, get...the fuck...away from me!" Ryan dropped his empty blaster and shoved her off him. Standing up, he grabbed her by the throat and leg and picked her up off the bed, holding her far enough away to avoid her other flailing arm. He started hoisting her up to pitch her over the side when the truck lurched again, tipping him off balance and sending him crashing on his butt, only this time with her on top of him.

Feeling fingers scrabbling at his throat, Ryan threw up a forearm to block them while reaching for the panga at his hip. Drawing it, he got his leg between her and him and pushed her away. She rolled to the front of the bed and turned over, then began crawling back toward him, dragging her useless legs behind her.

"That's right…. Come here," Ryan said, rising in a crouch and waiting for her. When she was close enough, he stood, planted a foot on her back and crushed her to the truck bed. She tried to lever herself up, but Ryan brought the panga down in a savage blow that laid her neck open and severed her jugular vein. Dark blood dribbled out as he pulled the blade free and brought it down, removing the woman's head from her body. It rolled into a corner, covered with dirt and blood, while the body spasmed under his foot.

Ryan watched the stump of the neck carefully, and when the disgusting slug-creature came out, he was ready. He chopped it into two with a single blow of his panga, wincing at the psychic scream of pain that pierced his skull. Just to make sure the thing was dead, he chopped each half into two pieces, as well. He was satisfied only when all the pieces stopped moving.

Dropping to his knees, he sat back on his haunches and took several deep breaths, not caring that all he could smell was blood, sweat and dirt. Just about every part of him hurt from the knocking around he had taken in the past few minutes.

Glancing at the cab, he noticed that the truck was slowing. Ryan looked around for his blaster and found it in another corner of the cargo bed, spattered with blood. He searched through his pockets for a full mag but came up empty.

By now the truck had come to a full stop. Ryan kept his bloody panga close while searching for the woman's Beretta. He found it in another corner of the bed, picked it up and checked the chamber. It had a round in it. Picking up his panga, Ryan got up and trudged to the front left corner of the bed, ready for the truck to take off again at any moment.

As he did, he noticed the driver's window was starred, as if a bullet had passed through it. He reached out to tap on the glass, and the whole thing shattered into hundreds of tiny fragments, which spilled to the ground. A faint tendril of smoke wafted out from inside. The truck had been turned off, and only the ticking of its cooling engine could be heard in the silent night.

"Ricky?" Ryan asked. "You in there?"

"Yes. Ryan? Is that you?"

"Yeah." Still holding both of his weapons, Ryan threw his leg over the side and slowly, painfully climbed to the ground. "Are you okay?"

"I…think so."

Stepping to the driver's door, Ryan reached for the handle with his blaster hand. He pulled it open and covered the very dead driver with the Beretta.

Still belted into his seat, his head tipped back, the man looked as if he had been mauled by a bear or some other wild animal. His entire chest was covered in blood, with a drying pool of it puddled in his crotch. The cause was obvious—his throat had been messily torn open, the resulting large hole spilling his life's fluid everywhere.

Beside him crouched Ricky, breathing heavily while he worked on something in his lap. With a pleased grunt, he lifted his hands and removed the cut zip tie that had bound his hands, massaging life back into his white, swollen fingers. He stared at Ryan with wide eyes, looking much like the animal that had killed the man. The lower half of his face and his shirt were both covered with blood, so much of it that Ryan had no trouble figuring out exactly how the teen had opened up the man's throat.

"You sure you're okay?"

Ricky nodded at the driver's corpse. "Better than him." He grinned, revealing bloodstained teeth, then suddenly whirled, leaned over the passenger-side door and threw up.

"At least you had the presence of mind to do that outside," Ryan said when he had finished. "Come on, let's get this guy out of here and head back to the ville." He sheathed his panga and moved to unbuckle the man from the driver's seat when he heard a strange, rattling hiss from the dead body.

Ryan threw himself backward just as a slug creature burst from the corpse's ruined throat and lunged at his mouth. Having missed with its initial attack, the creature hung half in, half out of the dead man's neck, writhing around as its antennae tried to home in on its next target.

"Bastard!" Ryan drew the flensing knife from where it was sheathed at the back of his neck and stabbed the creature through its middle, pinning it to the chest of the body. The slug squealed and struggled, then went limp as it oozed black ichor down the front of the body to mix with the drying blood.

"Ricky, get his seat belt off."

The kid did so, and Ryan hauled the body out and dumped it on the grass chest up. Drawing his panga, he retrieved his flensing knife, cleaned it and put it away.

Then he hacked the slug into four pieces with his panga for good measure.

Once that was done, he went to the back and dumped the headless body of the woman out of the bed, kicking her head out, as well. He then got down and climbed into the driver's seat, wincing at the sticky wetness he had to sit on. "Let's head back."

Ricky nodded, still staring at him with wide eyes. "Thanks for coming after me."

Ryan grunted as he familiarized himself with the truck's controls. "Sure as hell wasn't going to leave you with these bastards."

Chapter Twenty

Several hours later, Ryan stood on the second-floor balcony of the motel, watching as the members of the Silvertide collective finished their preparations to leave the ville and keep heading west.

He and Ricky had returned to find the people already packing up their wagons. J.B. and the others had apparently informed them of what had happened, and the good folk had taken it upon themselves to pack up and get the hell out of Dodge. Even the large water machine had been moved off the roof, aided by the use of an ingenious block-and-tackle system that enabled three men to move it with ease. It rested on a wagon now, covered by a thick tarp.

Ryan and Ricky had gotten a chance to clean up using a couple of buckets of water, and Mildred had set Ricky's nose, which he said hurt like hell. His face around his eyes was turning several shades of black and blue, his voice had a muffled, clogged aspect to it and he had a pounding headache from the shot he'd taken to the chops, but he was otherwise all right.

However, Ricky wasn't sure what had been worse—getting treated by Mildred, or getting grilled by her about the attackers and having to repeat everything he had gone through at least twice, not to mention answering her follow-up questions. By the time she was finished with him, Ricky swore he had at least two kinds of headache, and not just from his broken nose either.

Other than being sore all over, Ryan was also okay. When he'd returned, J.B. hadn't said a word, just shook his head. Ryan figured they'd be having a conversation about their enemy soon enough. Meanwhile, Mildred was concerned about the blow on his cheekbone, which was turning a brilliant shade of purple, but gentle probing revealed nothing had been broken. "Doubtless your hard head saved you again," she muttered.

"You don't see me complaining," he'd replied, then winced as she started to apply alcohol to his various scrapes and cuts.

Tully had also been recovered safely, and the third kidnapping victim, one of her cousins, had been recovered safe and sound from the rear passenger area of the truck. Except for a bump on the head and a splitting headache, he'd come to without any other problems.

There had been one spare tire on the truck, which Ryan and J.B. had used to replace the more chewed-up tire on the front driver's side. The rear one, although run flat, they thought would be a loss until Elder Bough had put a few of the scavvies on the job. Within an hour, they'd presented Ryan with the patched and filled tire. It was much heavier now, as it had been filled with sand to retain its shape. It had taken both of them to mount it again, but once on, it did its job pretty well. Perhaps not as responsive as the air-filled ones, but given that the vehicle was drivable, they certainly weren't going to complain.

J.B. had been particularly impressed with the truck. "The good news is that we don't need any gas for it," he said while showing it to Ryan. "See these?" He tapped the hood and top of the cab, both of which were covered in what looked like hundreds of small plastic squares embedded under a layer of clear Plexiglas.

"Yeah," Ryan said. "What are they, solar panels?"

If J.B. was disappointed that Ryan had guessed the answer, he didn't show it. "That's right. Even the dent in the side only knocked out a couple of them. They charge up the electric engine quick and store it in batteries under the seats and cargo bed. Even at night, these things have a range of about two hundred miles. It's exactly what we need to get around out here."

The truck was the fastest thing they had, next to the windriders. The rest of the convoy consisted of oxen-drawn wagons, complete with canvas covers over the back, that looked straight out of the nineteenth century. The only difference was the rubber tires instead of wooden ones. Doc had even commented with pleasant surprise when he'd first seen them. "Upon my soul, these look familiar. Mayhap I could spell someone once we are under way, as I did know my way around a pair of reins back in the day." Fortunately, everyone else was too busy tending to tasks to ask him what he meant by that.

Spotting the elders clustered around the lead wagon, Ryan and the rest of his group headed down to let them know what would happen from this point on. Startled stares greeted his battered appearance, but Ryan ignored that and got straight to business.

"All right, since everyone is ready, we'll head out now and put as much distance between us and the ville as possible. We'll stop around midday for a couple of hours to eat and rest—no sense traveling during the hottest part of the day—and then push on again until dark."

He turned to Tully and Latham. "The windriders will

be about a half mile out from the main convoy at all times. Stay within sight of us, and we'll do the same. Either of you see anything odd, you come back and report it, got that? No investigation, no heading over just to get a closer look, just come on back. Once you report what you saw, J.B. and I will make the call as to what, if anything, we do about it."

He glanced at Ricky and Jak, both of whom were outfitted in a similar fully covering outfit of the windrider pilots. Each young man also carried an M4 carbine. "Since we may encounter more of those body-snatchers at some point, armed riders will go with each of you."

He eyed Ricky. "You sure you're up for this after last night?"

The Puerto Rican nodded. "Yes, Ryan, I'm fine."

"All right."

Ryan looked at the Latham. "Keep an eye on him, will you?"

"Ryan!" the teenager protested. "I'm fine. Really!"

"So you say. Even so, I'll feel better if he watches out for you, that's all." Ryan looked at everyone. "J.B. and I will take the truck for the first day. Elder Bough, I'd like to have Krysty ride with you. Mildred, you and Doc will be in the last wagon." He made sure he had everyone's attention before continuing, "That warning I gave the scouts goes the same for everyone else. If you see anything, sing out and pass the message up the train to us. We'll decide what to do about it. Above all, do not leave the train, no matter what. I do not care if you see your great-aunt Matilda standing out on the plains waving at you, no one leaves the train. Splitting up will most likely be the death of you and us. Doc? Doc!"

Ryan was about to snap his fingers in front of the old

man, who, although he appeared to have been listening, had a peculiar, far-off expression on his face, as if he had been daydreaming. But at his raised voice, Doc blinked and looked at him with utmost attention.

"Eh, what, Ryan? Yes, I was paying attention, Mildred and I are to join those at the rear of the wagon train and watch for hostile Native Ameri…I mean, danger," he amended upon receiving an elbow in the ribs from Mildred. "I stand ready to do my part, of course."

His brow furrowed, Ryan stared at him for a few seconds before continuing. "Okay. Are there any questions?"

Everyone looked around at one another, but no one spoke. Then Elder Bough stepped forward. "Elders, let us pray."

The five leaders bowed their heads, and Bough uttered a brief prayer for swift and peaceful travel through these lands. Even Ryan nodded and said "amen" with the others once he finished.

"Okay, let's move out," Ryan said. As the others scattered to their positions, he stopped Mildred and Krysty. "I need a word with both of you."

"Sure, Ryan, what's up?" Mildred asked.

"In your opinion, Mildred, has Doc been acting… well, odder than usual?"

The healer mulled his question over for a few seconds. "You do realize the term 'odder than usual' is always relative when referring to him, right?"

Ryan's smile at her answer was brief. "Yeah, but on the whole, we usually know what to expect from him. Over the past day or so I've been less and less sure."

"Well, along with the rest of us, he's been through

a lot," Krysty pointed out. "There was the whole bug battle—"

"Culminating in you, Jak and him reenacting the Last Stand at the Alamo," Mildred said, frowning at their confused stares. "It's a historical thing.... I'll explain it later."

"And then we got little sleep, ran away from the rest of those bugs the rest of the night and walked around under the hot sun for a day before almost getting buried alive in a sandstorm." Krysty glanced at the gaunt old man walking jauntily away with his swordstick. "Frankly, I'm surprised he's doing as well as he is."

Mildred shrugged. "On the whole, I agree with Krysty. We all took a beating these past couple of days. You know that sometimes Doc just takes longer to recover than the rest of us. I think this is one of those times, that's all."

"All right." Ryan had also been watching the silver-haired man head down the line of a dozen wagons to the rearmost one. "With J.B. and me in the truck and Ricky and Jak scouting, that leaves you three—" he nodded at the two women "—which sort of means you two will be overseeing the train if there's trouble. Keep an eye on Doc while you're doing that?"

"As usual." Mildred rolled her eyes. "I'm going to need you to spell me at some point, Krysty. I like the old guy well enough, but some days..."

"You take the morning, I'll take the afternoon," the flame-haired woman replied. "We'll handle him, just like always."

"Yeah." Mildred cast a wistful glance at the truck. "I better get back there before he gets into some kind of trouble." She headed toward where Doc was, leaving Krysty and Ryan alone, more or less, in the throng of quickly packing scavvies.

Krysty slipped her arms around him. "I definitely like you better after you've cleaned up, lover."

Ryan grinned. "What, are you saying I wasn't appealing covered in blood, dirt and slime?"

"Not in the least. By the way, I may have to baby-sit Doc during the day, but I'm still all yours at night."

"What the hell are we waiting for, then?" Ryan asked. "Let's get going!"

THE FIRST HALF of the day passed uneventfully. The land was still, with the hot sun rising to blaze overhead. There was no wind, and only a few wispy clouds in the magenta sky. Even the large birds, which J.B. had warned Ryan about, weren't out hunting that day, although they kept a wary eye overhead, just in case. The air was filled with the creak of harness and tack, and an occasional low bellow from an ox as they plodded relentlessly forward, hauling the wagons behind them.

In the newly cleaned truck, Ryan and J.B. rode outrider around the train, each watching all around for any sign of trouble.

J.B. broke the silence in the second hour of their patrol. "Least with all this flat land out here, it'd be really hard for anyone to sneak up on you."

"Yeah," Ryan murmured. "Unless there's more of those blasted burrow-bugs around."

"True." J.B. glanced behind them at the wagon train slowly trailing the truck. "That plan of yours to find the redoubt."

Ryan didn't pause in his methodical sweep of the desolate landscape. "Yeah?"

"I figure it relied on having these kidnappers make a successful hit, and then following them back to wherever they're holed up." J.B. looked sidelong at him. "That about right?"

Ryan rubbed his chin. "That was the size of it."

"Any reason why we didn't follow through with it last night?"

"Because we weren't ready," Ryan replied. "You know as well as I do that something like that takes time to set up proper."

"I'm well aware of the logistics," J.B. replied. "That the only reason?"

Ryan grunted. "Only one that counts."

His oldest friend turned to look back out at the scrub prairie surrounding them. "You're a good tactician, Ryan. Always have been. Good at adapting to things on the fly, too. Hell, been lots of times where you and I've always been on the same page regarding a scenario with hardly a word exchanged, even when it went to hell."

"So what about it?" Ryan's brow furrowed as he tried to figure out the other man's point. "Fireblast, J.B., you got something you want to say, just spit it out."

J.B. paused for a few seconds, as if weighing his next words carefully. "It just seems that you might have been more inclined to run with the plan when it was just the collective members that got grabbed." He turned back to regard Ryan soberly. "But Ricky getting snatched changed the whole thing, didn't it?"

"Don't forget our intel was shit, too. Until last night we didn't know how they were getting their victims away from the ville either. We wouldn't have been able to follow them fast enough to do anything."

"Tires leave tracks, even out here," J.B. replied quietly. "But you haven't answered my question yet."

"Well, shit—course it matters!" Ryan replied. "You've gotten a close-up look at what happens when one of those things gets inside someone. Is that what you want for Ricky? Or Doc? Or Mildred?"

"Course not," J.B. replied. "I don't want that happening to anyone, least of all anyone I care about. Look, I'm not saying you made the wrong choice. I'd probably have done the same thing, too. Just worried that we may have lost a decent chance to locate their base."

"And you think that's worth risking Ricky's life for?" Ryan asked.

"Nope. I'd prefer to figure out a way to find them without risking anybody." J.B. sucked air through his teeth. "But I also don't think we should be so dismissive about these people that we're supposed to be trying to help either."

Ryan felt the beginnings of that slow burn of anger he usually got when he thought someone was talking down to him, but he also knew J.B. was the last person who would do that. He took a breath as well, letting it hiss out his nose as he thought. "I don't think I was exactly dismissive about them. I mean, we got them all back, didn't we?"

"Yup, and a good thing, too. But let's face it. If it had been Ricky who had gotten away clean on the roof, you and I would have probably been less concerned about who got taken and more concerned about tracking the takers back to where they live."

"I don't know about that," Ryan said. "The way Jak was itching to jump out there and start blasting away made me wonder who he was more worried about."

"Yeah, but I'm pretty sure he was all for saving Ricky, too," J.B. said. "Still, didn't you wonder how they happened to be out there in the first place?"

"Yeah, so much so that I asked Ricky on the way back," Ryan said. "He told me the good people of Silvertide are making moonshine to trade along the way, and that the girls—plural—they snuck out to meet last night brought along a jarful."

"Well, if that don't beat all," J.B. said. "Truth be told, I was wondering how these people were going to survive on what we've seen of their stuff so far. Good for them. You know, people used to make a decent shine with corn liquor and fermented apples back in Cripple Creek. Wonder if theirs even comes close."

"Let's finish this little talk before you go swapping recipes," Ryan said. "I was about to say, 'any plan that works even halfway is a good plan.'"

"You seriously quoting Trader at me?" J.B. asked.

Ryan grinned. "Yeah. Since it's still the plan I aim to use, you best let me know if you have a problem with it. I already know it's going to require some sacrifice— you heard what I told 'em at the vote—but we'll try to make sure none of the collective gets hurt or killed. But look out there." He waved his arm at the endless yellow-and-brown land on all sides. "We're surrounded by who knows how many square miles of land with no chance of searching even a fraction of it in the time we have. The best bet is to make them come to us, and then follow them home."

"No argument there," J.B. said. "But if it comes down to a choice between saving some and saving all, we're still going try to save all if we can, right?"

Ryan nodded. "Right."

"Figured as much." With that, the Armorer and Ryan both returned to watching the landscape for any sign of trouble. After a few moments, J.B. broke the silence again. "I just hope we aren't biting off more than we can chew."

Ryan grunted. "Hey, they bleed and they die. There's nothing else we have to know about them."

"Yeah, except that we're not trying to kill *all* of them, remember?" J.B. asked.

"Yeah, I know—fireblast, you're getting to be more and more like an old woman every day, J.B."

"Just trying to make sure we all come through this in one piece, that's all," J.B. grumped as he looked back out the window. "I said this could be dangerous, that I didn't want to get mixed up in anything like Heaven Falls again, yet here we are."

"I know. Look, that wasn't right for me to say, okay?" Ryan answered. "But like we all agreed, we're helping these people, and once we get a handle on where the redoubt is, we'll clean it up, and that'll be that."

"If you say so, Ryan," J.B. replied in a tone that made it clear he didn't agree with the other man's simple assessment at all.

"Of course it will be," Ryan said. "You'll see." Just then his bruised cheekbone flared with pain, and he opened and closed his jaw, trying not to wince. "It'll be fine."

Chapter Twenty-One

Just before the hottest part of the day, one of the wind-riders came back to the lead wagon. Ryan spotted the sail as they came up on the right side of the train while finishing their latest pass.

He pulled up alongside the lead wagon as Elder Bough reined his team to a stop. One of his family members stood on the back of his wagon and waved a red flag, signaling that the entire train was to halt. The land sailer swerved to a stop in front of both of them, and Ricky got out and ran over.

"Got a strange pit ahead, thought you might want to check it out."

"Strange how?" J.B. asked.

"It's not naturally made and looks like something dug it," Ricky replied.

Ryan and J.B. exchanged a glance. "Let's go take a look."

They followed Latham's sailer out about a half mile away from the main convoy, braking to a stop when the sailer did again. At first glance, Ryan couldn't see anything different about the landscape. "So where is it?"

"Go out about ten more steps and you'll be standing over the middle of it," Latham said as he pulled a fire-hardened spear from his vehicle. "Hang on." He walked over to a small hole in the ground. "Here's how we found it. Stopped for a piss break, and the wheel broke through the crust. Lucky we weren't over the middle of it, or we would have been screwed." He thrust the pole into the ground, sinking it up to his hand, and leaving only two or three feet above the surface. "It's big, like a sinkhole."

"What makes you two think it isn't a sinkhole?" Ryan asked.

"Too round and regular, for one thing," Latham replied. "It covers about a thirty-foot diameter and is almost a perfect circle. Nature's good, but not that good. Something dug this out."

"Think it's still there?" J.B. asked while casually slipping his shotgun off his shoulder.

"Can't tell, but I'm not going down there to find out either," Latham said. "Would've figured those herds of antelope runnin' all over woulda tripped this one already, but if they haven't yet, whatever's down there might have starved to death."

"Or it's hibernating," J.B. said. "Heard of some frogs down in Mex way that can live for more than a year without eating or some shit."

"Well, mark it with some stakes, and we'll go back and tell the others to go around it," Ryan said. "Good eyes."

Latham shrugged. "More like dumb luck. If the wheel hadn't gone down, we never woulda known it was there. But thanks anyway."

"Stay here until the train passes, and then you can catch up with us after it goes by," Ryan said.

They headed back to the caravan and explained the situation to Elder Bough. "The important thing will be for everyone else to follow the lead wagon as carefully as possible," Ryan said.

Bough then dispatched two of his teenage children with a precise message for the rest of the train to follow their lead exactly. When the children returned, Bough gave the signal to move out, and they resumed their trek.

Within ten minutes, they came on Latham's wind-rider marking the edge of the pit. Giving it a wide berth, Bough's wagon headed past the covered hole on its right. They had gone about a hundred yards past it when Ryan and J.B., who were heading around the back of the train, heard a terrible scream, followed by panicked shouts and more screams. Punching the gas, they sped up to see a new horror show unfolding.

Bough's wagon had disappeared, vanishing into another large hole in the ground. The other wagons had stopped, and several people were cautiously approaching the edge of the pit.

Krysty was Ryan's first thought, and it had him jumping out of the truck and running over almost before he'd braked to a full stop.

"Watch the edge! Stay back!" he shouted as he ran over. "Anyone with rope, get it out now!" An awful screaming was coming from the pit, and Ryan looked over to see one of the oxen team dead and pinned underneath the wagon, which had also broken an axle. The other ox was bellowing as it was tangled up in the traces and thrashing around half-buried in the dirt.

"Everyone okay down there?" Ryan called out.

"Yeah, some bumps and bruises, but nothing major," Krysty shouted back. "Lucky no one was pinned under the wagon—"

She stopped talking as the trapped ox's bellows

changed pitch, turning to high-pitched screams of pain. It whipped its head back and forth in a futile effort to escape, then gave one last, despairing shriek and collapsed, its head flopping onto the dirt. The silence that followed was profound.

"What happened to him?" Bough's wife, a sinewy woman about forty years old, asked.

"I don't know, but I think the body's sinking into the dirt," Bough said.

He was right—the body was slowly sliding under the fine dirt. One of the Bough children, maybe about ten years old, pointed to the ground near the body. "Something's moving down there!"

Ryan squinted to look, but didn't have the right angle from where he was. "What do you see?" Someone came up and pressed a coil of thick, nylon rope into his hand, and he nodded thanks.

"The sand is churning or rippling underneath the ox," Krysty said, just as the entire wagon lurched over. "It's affecting the dead ox, as well."

"Okay, let's get everyone out of there, and we'll figure out how to salvage the wagon afterward." Ryan uncoiled the rope and tossed an end down to the wagon. "Grab on and we'll haul you up."

"You'd better hurry, Ryan!" Krysty shouted. "Something's coming up toward us!"

"What in the Lord's name?" Bough shouted.

"Dark night!" J.B. said.

Ryan didn't have any words to say as a group of dirt-covered tentacles, smooth, purplish-red and as large around as a person's waist, burst out of the ground at the bottom of the pit. Instead, he handed the rope to the nearest person and shrugged off his Scout longblaster to start picking off the ropy, waving limbs.

"What are these— Oh, my God!" Bough's wife screamed.

As they came closer, homing in on their prey, the end of each tentacle split apart to reveal a tooth-lined maw!

"Children up first!" Bough shouted. "Climb onto the back of the wagon!" His four kids quickly scurried up to the top of the slowly sinking vehicle.

"I got the right, J.B." Ryan said.

"Hang on! I might be able to nip this all at once," J.B. said, aiming his M-4000 shotgun at where the four tentacles had come up from the sand. "Here goes—look away!"

He unloaded a full magazine into the area, churning up a geyser of dirt and dust and completely severing three of the tentacles. The fourth one whipped back and forth before withdrawing back under the ground.

Cheers greeted the Armorer's shooting, but Ryan waved his arms for everyone to be quiet. "Settle down, and let's get them all out of there now!"

A rope-pulling detail was quickly formed, and in less than a minute, the first two children were back on the surface. The third one had just been hauled off the broken wagon when it heaved again, and this time began being drawn below the bottom of the pit, with cracking noises testifying to the strength of whatever was down there.

"Hurry, Ryan!" Krysty shouted, blaster in hand. "It's getting closer!"

They pulled the last one up, and Krysty told Bough's wife to go next. She did, fairly flying up the side of the pit. By now the wheels had disappeared, and the wagon was tilting at a steep angle, with the front end completely buried under the dirt. Someone had brought another rope and tossed it down, and Krysty and Bough each grabbed one, holding on as they started to be hauled out.

They were almost at the lip when the last tentacle erupted back out of the dirt. Its toothy maw snapped at the air for a moment, then it dived down, heading straight for Krysty.

J.B. was raising his shotgun again, and Ryan was doing the same with his longblaster, but it was going to be close.

However, before either of them could fire, Elder Bough shoved off the side of the pit and planted himself between her and the beelining tentacle.

The mouth slammed into his back and bit hard, making him shout with pain. "Go!" he said to her right before the limb's hungry maw yanked him back off the rope and retracted, dragging him down into the dirt. It all happened so fast that neither Ryan nor J.B. could try to shoot the thing before it was gone. There was a brief thrashing around, and then he disappeared under the remains of the wagon.

"Mattias!" Bough's wife screamed. "Mattias!" She lunged back toward the edge of the pit, but was caught by her eldest son, who held her as she sobbed.

Ricky lowered his carbine. "Do we try to go after him?"

Ryan shook his head, but it was Krysty who answered, "Not unless you want to end up like him. Whatever was down there was very large and very hungry. We need to move on through this area quickly. I don't think it's the only one around here."

Ryan looked at the others, most staring in shock at

the pit or the rest of the Bough family. "All right, people, we should keep moving so we can get out of this area."

"Brother Ryan?" one of the other elders, a white-haired man named Chreis, asked. "Before we go, we need to pray over Elder Bough's...final resting place."

Ryan couldn't help but glance back at the pit where the Silvertide leader had vanished. "Do what you have to." He gathered his people around him. "Spread out and keep an eye on the bottom of that hole. Anything moves while they're praying, and I mean *anything,* don't wait, just blast it."

All of the members of the collective assembled to stand at the edge of the pit and joined hands. Over the now-muffled sobs of Bough's widow, Elder Chreis began to speak.

"O Lord, we commend our brother and leader, Mattias Bough, into your waiting arms. Mattias was a true blessing to our community, leading with grace and equality, and always willing to work with opposing parties to achieve a compromise that was fair for both. It was his words and vision that first led us out from our homes to seek our freedom, and it is in his spirit that we will continue this journey to found a home for ourselves and our descendants where we can all strive to live up to Mattias's ideals, which he lived every single day. He leaves behind his wife, Leah, and four children, Aquila, Ethias, Hushai and Jairus. Let us all come together to comfort and help them in this time of trouble, and reassure them that they are not alone in their journey, that the collective watches over its members, always, and will watch over them, as well. Amen."

The rest of the congregation muttered, "Amen," and began dispersing back along the convoy. Elder Chreis and his family went to the Boughs and gently began herding them toward their wagon. Once they were situated, the elder came back to Ryan.

"I think we should leave this area as soon as possible, agreed?"

"Absolutely," Ryan replied. "It's going to be slow going, though. There's no telling how many more of those things are out there."

J.B. mopped his brow and replaced his fedora before turning to Ryan. "We're going to need a ground tester to keep moving."

"Yeah, someone light. Ricky?" Ryan waved the teen over. "Got a job for you that isn't going to be a lot of fun…."

Four hours later, Ryan signaled for the wagon train to come to a halt. Water and feed was distributed for the hungry, thirsty oxen teams, and the families took a moment to grab a cold bite in the meager shade cast by their wagons under the pitiless sun.

Ricky trudged back in from his scouting duty and untied the rope from around his waist. "*Santa Maria,* we must be clear of those—things by now, yes?"

He'd been walking about forty feet ahead of the truck, testing the ground with a spear. Ryan and J.B. had followed behind him: one driving, the other holding the other end of the rope around his waist.

Ricky had found several more holes in the first mile, each necessitating the train to stop so they could ensure there was a clear path around it. The first hole had another one within thirty yards of it, leading Mildred to theorize that two of these creatures may have created lairs near each other in order to drive food toward each other's pit. The others were more isolated.

But there had been no sign of a pit in the past two miles, so Ryan was reasonably comfortable they were clear of the threat. "Yeah, I think we've left that behind now." He scanned the horizon, spotting a line of hills about two miles to the west. "Let's rest here for an hour, then make for those hills before camping for the night."

"Don't want to spend the night on the plains?" J.B. asked.

"Do you?"

The Armorer shook his head.

"Once we get moving again, we'll send Tully and Jak out that way to make sure there's no surprises. I might even have us go out there and keep Latham back as the intermediate scout for the train."

Ryan liked his plan so much that once the scouts had gotten their meal, he filled in Latham and Ricky on what he wanted to do and had them hang back around the wagons. Then he and J.B. drove out to the hills to check them out. Twenty minutes later, they had their answer.

"Damn, this doesn't get much better," J.B. said after taking a cursory look around. "I can't believe we actually found a clear spring here."

Ryan nodded while staring down at the small trickle of water that had carved its way from the hills in the distance to here. It had created a small oasis amid the dry, dusty plains that was hidden in a cluster of foothills from the rest of the landscape.

A distant rumble of thunder made him look off to the west, where billowing cumulonimbus green clouds several thousand feet high filled the sky. As he watched, he saw streaks of lighting arc in the clouds, making them light up like glowing billows of smoke.

"Better get them here pretty quick. Looks like a storm's rolling in—a big one."

Chapter Twenty-Two

An hour later, the wagon train had arrived at the small spring, and people were busy unloading tents and getting the evening meal ready. Many were planning to sleep in, under or beside their wagons, making lean-tos by attaching tarpaulins to the backs or sides of their vehicles for shelter.

A somber pall had fallen over everyone since Elder Bough's death. His wife was in seclusion with the Chreis family, although the children were out and helping with the various chores around the campsite.

At Ryan's suggestion, they'd arranged the wagons around the spring in a three-quarters circle to create a barrier between the people inside and the rest of the plains, with the other quarter of their perimeter formed by the foothills to their west. He planned to have guards posted there for the night, giving them the high ground, and ideally enabling them to spot anyone trying to sneak up on the encampment.

However, as night approached, Ryan's greatest concern was the oncoming storm. The wind had risen from the west, bringing with it the scent of fresh rain. While welcome, the breeze had steadily increased until it was gusting up to twenty or twenty-five miles an hour, creating small dust devils, blowing small items around and making tents flap and swell in the rising gale.

J.B. shared his pessimism about the weather. "If this storm's as bad as I think it's going to be, no one'll be crazy enough to try to hit us in it—too risky."

"Let's hope they think like you do, then," Ryan replied. "Either way, Jak's not going to be happy about spending the night on the hill watching over the camp."

"I'm sure he'll manage," J.B. replied. "Come on, let's get something to eat. I got a feeling we're in for a long night."

THE RAIN STARTED coming down at dusk, and soon turned everything and everyone into a drenched, sodden mess. The thirsty ground drank up every drop at first, but soon reached its limit, and quickly turned from damp to wet to soaked to mud. Every step was through a squelching, filthy mire, with the sticky muck collecting on boots and making footing treacherous.

Ryan was correct—Jak had been less than thrilled about having to take guard duty for most of the night after scouting all day, but Ryan had pointed out that he'd pretty much sat on his butt all day while everyone else had dealt with the wagon accident and Elder Bough's death, and he still had the best night vision out of everyone, even in the rain.

Still, the albino had grumbled all through dinner, then stomped off in a borrowed poncho to take up his position on top of the hill, carrying both a flashlight and an emergency flare from the truck's repair kit as easy signals in the unlikely event that someone was going to attack them in the downpour. Even so, Ryan and his compatriots were resolved to not let their guard down. They had also set guards around the rest of the train, with strict orders for people to sound an alarm if they saw anything out of the ordinary—particularly one of their own suddenly returning to the convoy out of nowhere. Ryan and J.B. had been watchful for any sign of trackers or observers all day. Just because they hadn't seen them didn't mean they weren't out there.

He'd parked the truck on the edge of the circle to prevent getting blocked in by the wagons. All of his people were using it for shelter, with four in the cab, and two in the cargo bay, sleeping comfortably under a rigged tarp.

It was well into the night—Ryan wasn't sure exactly how late—when his eye opened. He looked around, but saw nothing immediately out of the ordinary. J.B. and Mildred had just finished their turn at guard duty, and were sleeping in the rear passenger compartment, covered by the Armorer's leather jacket. Krysty was curled up in the passenger seat, her hair aligned in a thick ponytail over her shoulder and down her chest. The windows were cracked for air, and he slipped his fingers out to wet them and rub them on his face. He heard the staccato patter of raindrops on the cab roof.

Blinking, Ryan felt a familiar, insistent pressure in his groin, and he silently reached over to open the driver's door and slip outside.

The torrential downpour had tapered off to a steady drizzle, but Ryan still stepped carefully to pry his boots out of the clinging, almost ankle-deep mud. He looked around, but everything was silent. He tried to make out the nearest guards on the wagons, but the rain was strong enough that it was difficult to see anything beyond the large, dim shapes of the vehicles.

Stretching, Ryan felt his shoulder and back muscles pop and loosen, still a bit sore from the fight the previous day and sitting in the not very comfortable truck seat all day. Boots squelching in the muck, he headed toward the rear of the truck to find a private area to take care of his business, grinning as the sound of Doc's log-sawing snoring hit his ears.

At the tailgate, he stopped short. Standing a few feet away was a small girl, maybe eight years old, her blond hair and nightdress plastered to her skin by the rain. She was ankle deep in the mud, with her hands and knees also covered in wet dirt that was slowly being washed away. She was from one of the Silvertide families, but he wasn't sure which one. She stared back at him, blinking in the rain.

"What are you doing here?" Ryan asked. "Where's your family?"

The little girl pointed to a distant wagon with a cre-ated tent off to one side. "My da's come back."

A chill settled in Ryan's stomach, and his hand stole to his blaster. "Did he, now?"

She nodded. "Ma told me to crawl out the back and go get help. Can you help us?"

Ryan nodded. "Come here." He gathered her into his arms while kicking the truck's tailgate. "Ricky! Doc! Get up! We got company."

He plodded back to the cab, opened the driver's door and set the girl on the seat. "You stay right here while I go check on your ma." Ryan stood on the doorjamb while turning his flashlight on and signaling to Jak that they had company. An answering flash verified that his message was received. Ryan gave him three more, indi-cating that he was to provide overwatch with one of the M4s. "Krysty, J.B., Mildred, let's go. Enemy's in camp!"

The others quickly roused themselves and poured out of the truck, weapons at the ready. "Remember, we don't know who's friendly and who isn't, so we can't go shooting anyone we come across," Ryan said. "Follow me."

He headed toward the wagon the girl had pointed at, trying to move as quietly as possible, given the circumstances. When he was about thirty feet away, a large form came out of the tent with a limp figure slung over its shoulder. A flash of lightning split the night, revealing a woman's body being carried by a man.

"Stop!" Ryan said while aiming his SIG Sauer at the man, bracing the wrist of his blaster arm with his other hand. The man didn't even blink, but ducked back under the lean-to and disappeared.

"Shit! He's heading out the other side! Wake the others! Teams of two check every wagon!" Ryan yelled as he headed for the vehicle the man had disappeared near. As he splashed through the mud, he heard J.B. sound the alarm by the simple expedient of firing a round from his M4 carbine.

At the same time, at least two dozen figures surged out of the darkness toward various wagons and people. Surprised queries turned to shouts and screams of alarm as the people of the collective were in a fight for their lives against the foe that had crept up on them almost unawares.

At the sodden lean-to, Ryan ducked under the waterlogged flap and found his guess was correct—the only sign of the kidnapper was a trail of muddy boot prints heading toward the wagon. Taking cover behind a wheel in case someone was waiting in ambush, Ryan crouched and swept and cleared under the vehicle before scooting under it to emerge from the other side. The moment he straightened, a heavy weight fell on him, forcing him to his knees. An iron band clamped around his throat, cutting off the air as his assailant tried to force him to the ground.

But Ryan had fought far too many people to be caught by surprise by this tactic. Even as his assailant hit him, he was already bending over, using his enemy's own momentum against him while reaching back and pulling with his free hand to drag the person over his head and slam him into the ground. Unable to keep his choke hold and stay atop Ryan at the same time, the intruder slid over his opponent's head and splashed down flat on his back in the mud. Ryan brought the butt of his blaster down on his head in a blow that would have knocked out a normal person. This one, a tall, skinny man with black, brush-cut hair, attempted to rise, which only earned him another hard shot from the butt of Ryan's blaster. This time he went down and stayed down. Ryan looked around for other invaders or scavvies in trouble. He heard J.B., Mildred, Ricky and Krysty calling to one another as they moved among the wagons.

"Spread out! Check every one!"

"Clear here!"

"Take those two!"

A high-pitched scream made Ryan turn toward the next wagon, which was axle deep in mud, but still rocking back and forth as if someone was struggling inside it. Ryan waded through the sludge to get to the back and see what was going on.

Inside, three children were trying to fight off a mud-covered attacker, who had his back to the opening. Ryan climbed over the tailgate and stepped up behind the guy. Raising his SIG Sauer, he brought it down hard on the back of the man's head.

The blow staggered the man, and he shoved the small

teenager he'd been trying to carry off into the other two, who were holding on to their sibling. He turned to regard Ryan, and a white-toothed smile appeared through the mask of mud on his face.

"Priority subject in range. Capture at all costs." He stepped forward, reaching for Ryan with both hands.

"Good luck with that, you fucked-up son of a bitch!" Ryan said, batting the man's questing hands aside with one hand while bringing up the butt of his blaster and smashing it across the man's face in a blow that should have broken his jaw.

His opponent dodged the weapon, then lowered a shoulder and charged into Ryan while he was still unbalanced from not connecting with his adversary. Already off-kilter, he stumbled toward the gunwale and hit the canvas top, which came loose under his weight, spilling him over the side and into the muck outside.

Although Ryan got an arm up to break his fall, he still got a faceful of mud and rainwater and had to spend precious seconds coughing and wiping his vision clear. Hearing a loud splash next to him, he got to his feet as a hand grabbed the back of his neck and tried to pull him upright. Ryan went with it, arching his back and snapping his head back in hopes of connecting with his attacker's face. That didn't happen, however, and instead the man kept pulling him back, then brought his free arm down in a powerful chop to the one-eyed man's solar plexus, stunning the large nerve center there and making Ryan drop back to his knees.

It felt as if a bomb had gone off right next to him. His limbs felt like lead, and everything was muffled. It was almost impossible to see or hear anything. White flashes burst behind his eyes, and there was only the singular thought to get up, get up, get up—

Somehow, he was able to sense movement in front of him through all that, and Ryan threw himself aside as something grazed his shoulder. He forced an arm up to grab whatever had come at him and realized he had caught the guy's leg. Ryan heaved up with all his strength, tipping the man off balance while getting a leg under himself and pushing up to rise to his feet.

His opponent tried to compensate for the move but couldn't stay upright. Ryan kept pushing, forcing him over onto his back, then jumped on his chest to make sure he stayed down. The man hit the mud with a resounding splash, but was already trying to shove Ryan off and get back to his feet. Raising his mud-covered blaster, Ryan brought its butt down on the guy's head once, twice, three times, until he stopped moving. He sat back on the man's legs, breathing hard and wiping muck off his face. He could still hear a faint pounding in his ears and shook his head to clear it, but the sound didn't go away.

No, he thought as he looked around, seeing the others locked in combat with more of the kidnappers. It's getting…louder? Ryan rose to his feet and began heading toward the nearest knot of fighting people when the source of the noise suddenly became obvious.

With a dull roar, a large wave of muddy, brown water sluiced out of the gully and swept across the entire encampment. The flash flood carried debris from the hills along with it—plants, rocks and even small trees uprooted and turned into dangerous projectiles carried along by the silty tide.

All those in its path were knocked off their feet and

washed away. The eight-foot-high deluge hit the outer wagons, which were still mired in the mud, and completely washed over them. The next wagon in the circle was blasted free by the wave and floated along with the water. Everywhere people tried to get to some sort of cover or shelter before the wall of water took them, as well.

Seeing the onrushing brown tide coming right at him, Ryan shoved his blaster into his belt and lunged for the wagon next to him as the initial wave hit. He got his hand on the wood as his feet were knocked out from underneath him, but his grip was firm. He began hauling himself up when a tree trunk swirled by, its roots smashing into his side and knocking him off the wagon.

Stunned by the blow, Ryan tried to grab the trunk, but it kept spinning in the water, and he was unable to get a firm grip on it. He tried to regain his footing, but the water was flowing too strongly for him to brace himself, and he kept getting knocked off his feet, swallowing muddy water with each dunking.

Struggling to stay afloat in his sodden clothes, Ryan struck out again for the tree trunk, which was bobbing in the current a few yards away. He'd almost reached it when he felt a crushing blow on the side of his head, and knew nothing more.

Chapter Twenty-Three

Dawn arose on the battered remains of the wagon train and encampment, which had been scattered along a two-mile stretch of plains that was now covered with fresh silt from the storm and flood, rapidly drying in the heat.

Krysty, J.B. and the others had been fighting off the invading force when the flood hit, and all of them had been swept away with everything else. Each had spent the rest of that harrowing night trying to stay alive in the terrifying mess of water, wagons and people.

Doc had made out the best, getting to a wagon that had stayed upright and floated along with the water. He'd even improvised crude poles to steer his rough boat and keep other flotsam from smashing it, and had pulled in a half dozen people throughout the night. In turn, they had found another floating wagon, and had lashed the two together for stability and the ability to collect more people. It had become the de facto headquarters of the Silvertide group, with people arriving at it, dropping off other survivors throughout the night. Doc was still in it now, regaling the children with old myths and legends, and allowing the rest of the adults to continue damage control and to police the area.

Of their own group, Ricky had fared the worst, getting caught on the very end of the circle and being swept out nearly a mile before the wave finally had gone far enough to dissipate across the plain. He showed up an hour before dawn, covered in mud and sporting a fresh set of bruises from being tossed about in the water.

Most of the Silvertide collective had also regrouped by morning, but they were in a very bad way. At least a dozen people were still unaccounted for, but no one knew if that was due to the flood or the attack during the night. At least three oxen had been lost, as well. Most of the other animals had been able to swim through the wave, and were now being regathered. The wagons and all of their gear had also been scattered, with clothes, blankets, boxes, jars of food and other items strewed along the entire run of the flood zone. All of the wagons had suffered some damage, at least two of them damaged enough that repairs would take a day or so—and that was assuming they recovered all of the necessary tools.

Everyone was also on the lookout for the kidnappers, as well as the previously missing collective members. Krysty and J.B. had issued a warning for anyone who found either to not approach the person or body, but instead come to get one of them immediately. So far no one had found any outsider bodies, including the two she was most concerned about.

Now, as Krysty scanned the horizon, she tried to keep her rising fear from knotting her insides. Two of the missing people were Ryan and Mildred. He's tougher than this, Krysty thought. There's no way a flood would take him out.... However, the alternative didn't settle her mind much either.

The search for survivors was taking much longer than anyone would have liked, too. The ground was still too soft to handle the wagons or the windriders, so everyone was out on foot looking for the missing people.

A shout went up along the line, and Krysty ran over with others to see a family rejoicing in their reunion with their little girl, who'd been found naked and huddled in the branches of an uprooted tree. She was quickly wrapped in a blanket and taken back to their secondary improvised camp on top of the hill where the guards had been posted the night before.

Her lips pressed into a tight line, Krysty joined the others in giving thanks that the child had been found safe and sound, and sending a silent prayer to Gaia to help them find Ryan and Mildred soon, as well. As the group dispersed to continue the search, she saw J.B. and Jak returning from scouting ahead. Her heart sank when she saw the look on the Armorer's face, but she didn't betray a hint of emotion as she left the larger group to join him.

"Anything?"

"Not a trace." J.B. pushed up his fedora and rubbed his forehead. "The flood washed away all the prints or tire tracks. Even if we could find anything outside the flood zone, the rain would have wiped out anything else."

"Fuckers ghosted in, took people and disappeared under nose," Jak said flatly.

"Yeah, they vanished, all right…and we still have no way of finding them," J.B. said.

"Do you think they were both taken?" Krysty asked, hoping for a different answer to the one already in her mind.

"You know Ryan as well as I do. He'd never let something like this pissant flood take him down." J.B. shook his head. "Only reason he isn't here is 'cause someone's got him somewhere else."

"Okay, then how do we find him?" she asked.

"If we had any sort of map of the area, that would be something," J.B. said. "The predark government had missile silos scattered all over the U.S., especially throughout what they called the Midwest, so it makes the most sense that these people are probably holed up in one of them. But without a location, if they hid the entrance, we could be searching for years and not find it."

"That's not an option," Krysty said. "There has to be some other way."

"Think I don't know that?" J.B. frowned at her, then took a deep breath. "Sorry 'bout that. I'm as worried as you are."

Krysty reached out and placed a hand on his arm. "I know, just as I know we'll do whatever we have to do to find them. Did you have any other ideas about how?"

"Well, once we get everything sorted out, the only thing I can think of would be to put some of us out as bait and hope they come to us. They're able to follow us pretty easily, and they seemed to have a hard-on for ol' snow-hair here."

The albino spit into the dirt. "Come at me, I take that slug, shove up ass."

Even under the circumstances, the teen's blunt assessment made J.B. grin ruefully. "Be that as it may, we put him out on the plains, see who comes to call. Might be they come find him, then we go find them."

"Mebbe... Let's hold off on that until we don't have any other choice," Krysty said. "After all, he could still be out there somewhere. Mebbe just injured or trapped, and can't move."

"If he is, we'll find him," J.B. replied. "And Millie too. Bet your last bullet on that."

"What about the truck?" Krysty asked.

"Ricky's working on it right now. Won't know until it dries out," the small man replied. "It got flooded good, and we'll have to poke around inside to make sure nothing's soaked or shorted. I'll let you know once we have it up and running."

"Do that." Krysty turned back to the endless plains, scanning the horizon as if she could somehow pick out Ryan's body from amid the square miles the flood had covered.

Closing her eyes, she reached out with her senses and concentrated on trying to pick up on that strong spark of life that resided within her lover. But she couldn't sense anything from him. If J.B. was right, and he had been taken, he was being held somewhere beyond her powers of detection.

Come back to me, my love, she thought. Or I will come and find you…and make those who are holding you pay dearly.

RYAN'S EYE FLUTTERED open, and the first thing he saw was a dim, fuzzy, golden light overhead that sharpened into focus as he came out of unconsciousness. He looked around to find himself in a sterile white room, containing just the bed he was lying on. He tried moving his arms and legs, but found them strapped securely to the metal frame.

Raising his head, he saw that he had been undressed and clad in a simple light blue hospital gown. Great— figures I'll have to fight my way out of here naked, he thought.

Oddly, for all of the abuse he had gone through in the past couple of days, particularly the tossing and turning he'd endured during the flood, he felt pretty good.

His muscles didn't hurt as much as he would have expected them to, just an occasional twinge here or there, and his face felt as if it had healed almost perfectly. On the other hand, his throat was scratchy and dry, and he was very hungry.

On the other side of the room was a white metal door with a wire-embedded safety window in it. Ryan saw bright lights and occasional shadows pass by outside, telling him where he was. Well, J.B. wanted to find the redoubt, he thought as he lowered his head back onto his pillow. Looks as if I managed to do that all by myself.

Fortunately, now that he was here, there could be an opportunity for him to escape. All he would need to do was wait for the right situation. The door opened and three people entered. Two of them, a man and a woman both wearing white lab coats, weren't familiar. The third, however, made Ryan's jaw drop.

"Morgan?" Ryan asked through his dry throat.

Ryan had last seen this man on the East Coast, running what had been a fairly unique operation: a large underground mall that had catered to traders and folks in the area, and even had its own population living there. When a crazy man had led a mutant army to attack it, the mall had been destroyed during the fighting. After Ryan and his companions had saved his life, Morgan had taken them through a hidden tunnel and left the area to find a new life for himself. If this was where he'd ended up, from one underground bunker to another, Ryan felt sorry for him. Even worse, if Morgan had also been taken over by the parasites, then Ryan didn't think the man was going to help him, but he had to try to get the former leader on his side.

The three were followed by two men in the dark blue

jumpsuits Ryan recognized as the same ones worn by the kidnap party back at the ville. The sec men carried brand-new M4 carbines, which they held at port arms as they took up positions to the right and left of the door.

"Ryan Cawdor." Morgan nodded as he held out a cup of water. "It is good to see you again."

"Wish I could say likewise, Morgan. How about you get me out of these—" Ryan lifted his pinned wrists as high as he could "—and you and I can catch up?"

"I'm afraid that will not be possible," Morgan replied. "Here, let me." He stepped closer and held the cup to Ryan's mouth, letting him drink his fill.

Like the others of this group Ryan had encountered, he was also speaking in oddly slow speech. He was dressed neatly, in a light blue jumpsuit, and had his salt-and-pepper hair cut short. Once Ryan had drained the cup, Morgan stepped back and nodded at the white-coated man and woman. "This is Dr. Evan Markus, and this is our bioengineer, Dr. Carole Phieks. The doctors are here to examine you, and then…we will see what the Mind wishes to do with you."

"See what? What are you talking about?" Ryan asked, but Morgan didn't answer. Instead, he stepped back, and let the two doctors approach.

Dr. Markus pushed a small metal table on wheels next to the bedside. It was covered with various medical tools, none too horrible looking, but Ryan knew what horror they could hold. Both doctors stared dispassionately down at him. They looked fairly normal, without any outward evidence of mutation or deformity. But then again, many of the whitecoats the companions had encountered seemed fairly normal on the outside. It was what was in their minds that concerned Ryan. He had survived a few procedures that would have killed other men, and he knew enough to distrust all whitecoats.

"Subject appears awake and alert," Dr. Markus said as he picked up a small penlight and shone it into Ryan's eye. "Pupil response to stimulus is normal."

"Healing of various injuries has progressed more quickly than expected." The barest hint of a smile flitted across Dr. Phieks's face. "His recovery time is excellent. It is a shame about the left eye, however. It lessens his overall effectiveness—"

"Okay, you both can stop talking about me like I can't hear you," Ryan said. "Where am I, who are you and why am I tied up?"

The two whitecoats exchanged an inscrutable look, and there was a definite pause of about a second before Dr. Markus replied, "You are in Base Unit 556 of Bioengineering Facility Epsilon. We are in a converted Atlas ICBM missile silo and facility that was decommissioned in the mid-twentieth century and repurposed to become the laboratory is it today."

"Dr. Markus and I are the joint overseers of this facility," Dr. Phieks said. "You, Ryan Cawdor, have been brought here because we wish you to join our staff. You have been restrained because you have been proved to be somewhat…resistant to being with us."

"You're bastard right I'm resistant," Ryan said, straining against his bonds. "There's no way I'm going to let any of you put one of those bastard slugs into me, not while I'm still breathing."

Again, the doctors exchanged that unreadable glance.

"Mr. Cawdor, it wouldn't be right of us to inflict this on you without you knowing the truth of this place," Markus said as he picked up a hypodermic needle and filled it with a clear liquid. "We're going to take you to the Mind, and any questions you may have will be answered then."

"We will bring a wheelchair for you to sit in, as all verified accounts of your actions show that you are not to be trusted until you are one of us," Phieks said.

"Well, get ready for the biggest disappointment of your lives, because I'm never going be one of you," Ryan replied.

"I think you'll change your mind once you see what we're about to reveal to you." Phieks gripped his arm with two hands that clamped down on him like steel bands. "I suggest that you avoid struggling. Otherwise you could tear the vein."

"A simple nerve blocker, to prevent your brain from sending commands to the rest of your body," Markus said as he injected the liquid into Ryan's body. "The net effect is to paralyze you temporarily, of course. Dr. Phieks, if you please."

She walked out and returned with a wheelchair. "The somewhat humorous thing about this particular drug is that you can be posed into whatever position is suitable," Markus said as he unbuckled the straps and raised Ryan's arm. When he let go, it stayed suspended in midair. "It makes things much easier on everybody."

"Let's get you into the chair." The two easily lifted Ryan and positioned him in the wheelchair. "All right, then, we'll get your friend, and then we'll all go visit the Mind."

Chapter Twenty-Four

Mildred also came to in a room similar to Ryan's, but found herself unsecured to her bed. She sat up, wincing at the pain ricocheting inside her skull, and tried to piece together what had happened to her, and how she'd ended up here.

The last thing she remembered was helping to repel the attack on the encampment with J.B. and the others. One of the wagons had been under assault by a pair of the strange attackers, and J.B. had been fighting them while she'd been getting the family away. Then the flood had come. She'd heard a roaring sound that had quickly grown so loud she couldn't hear anything else, and before she'd known it, she'd been thrown off her feet and had had the briefest sensation of falling into a churning mass of roiling, brown water. That was all she'd known until she woke up here.

She glanced down to find herself dressed in a thin hospital gown that made her shiver involuntarily. Covering her chest with her arms, she looked around at the bare walls and lack of furniture, wondering where exactly *here* was, and more important, was anyone else in here with her, and how was she going to escape? Mildred licked her dry lips. And before I go, can I find about a gallon of water to drink?

The door slid open, and a vaguely familiar-looking

figure stepped inside. Beyond him, Mildred saw a group of people waiting in the hallway outside.

"Mildred Wyeth, I am Morgan. You may remember me from the Freedom Mall."

"I...do." She swung her legs over the side of the bed. "Administrator Morgan? Where are we? What are you doing here?"

Morgan held up a hand. "If you will come with me, all of your questions will be answered."

"I don't suppose I could get into something a little less...drafty?" she asked.

The corner of Morgan's mouth twitched into something that might have approached a smile. "Of course." He walked to the door and spoke to one of the people outside. A few minutes later, a bundle of clothes was brought in, which Morgan handed over to her. "Apologies for the oversight."

"No problem," Mildred took the one-piece, sky-blue jumpsuit, noting the lack of pockets, and soft slippers for footwear. Underwear was a simple white-cotton bra and panties. "If you don't mind..." She waved at the door.

Morgan stared blankly at her for a moment, then stiffened. "Of course." He walked to what she thought was a blank, featureless wall and pushed on it, making an entire section swing out. "Sanitary facilities are in here. Just let me know when you're ready to go." He turned and left the room, the main door sliding closed behind him.

Mildred could have gotten dressed in front of him—modesty was a quickly discarded virtue in the Deathlands—but she had requested the privacy for two reasons. The first was to collect her thoughts. Seeing Morgan here so long after their last encounter on the

East Coast was certainly odd; she wondered what had possessed him to travel all the way out here—or indeed, if he'd even had a choice in the matter.

The second reason was to test the parasites'—for she had no doubt that Morgan was being controlled by one—reaction to human social mores. The fact that he had reacted and agreed to her request meant that the slugs apparently didn't take over a human body completely, or they at least had access to their hosts' accumulated knowledge and memories. At the moment, she wasn't sure if that would come in handy, but every scrap of knowledge she could get regarding these things was useful.

She zipped up the jumpsuit and slid her feet into the soft, fluffy slippers, which, she had to admit, felt pretty damn good after weeks of her feet being cooped up in heavy combat boots. She walked over to the bathroom and puzzled over the handleless sink for a few seconds until she figured out how to turn it on by waving her hand under the faucet. A cellophane-wrapped plastic cup, too flimsy to be a weapon, sat on the sink.

After filling her belly with water, she splashed some on her face and examined her plaited hair in the mirror. "Well, you've looked better, but you've also looked a damn sight worse, too." She heaved a sigh. "Might as well see what the hell these folks want."

She walked back out into the main room and rapped on the door, which slid open almost immediately. Mildred walked out into a corridor with rows of doors along both sides, and one at the end of the hallway. Morgan stood nearby, along with two people wearing lab coats— a male and a female, whom he introduced as Dr. Markus and Dr. Phieks, respectively—and a pair of armed sec guards. There was one more person there who made her eyes widen in surprise.

"Ryan? What the hell?" She shoved past the male doctor to check on her friend sitting stiffly in a wheelchair. Although his eye tracked her movement, he didn't move a muscle at her approach. "What did you do to him?"

"Routine security precaution," Dr. Phieks said.

"Ryan Cawdor has been observed to be quite dangerous, and therefore necessitated restraint," Dr. Markus said. "He is unhurt, and the drug that is incapacitating him has no lasting neurological or physical effects. He will be fine."

"And soon, he will be perfect," Morgan intoned.

"Indeed." The two scientists, or doctors, or whatever the hell they were, exchanged looks and smiles, making Mildred's blood run cold.

She bent over to check Ryan, feeling his pulse and thumbing back his eyelid to check for other drug evidence. "How you feeling?" she whispered. "Blink once for good, twice for bad."

"…een…etterrr…" The garbled words leaked from his frozen mouth, and it took her a moment to translate them. *Been better.*

"Yeah, I bet you have. Just sit tight—" she winced at the completely useless advice "—and I'll figure out a way to get us out of here."

"Liiike…have…choiccce…" Ryan replied.

"That's, uh—that's the spirit." Mildred straightened and turned to Morgan and the two doctors. "He seems to be all right, although I'd like to have him monitored for a potential adverse reaction to the drug."

Morgan nodded. "That can be arranged. Now, if you'll come with us, we need to introduce you to the Mind."

He gestured at Ryan's wheelchair. "If you would like, you can push Ryan along as we go."

"Sure." Mildred grabbed the handles and began walking beside Morgan as they headed down the silent hallway, their every step flanked by the pair of sec men. "I'm probably going to regret asking this, but what is the Mind?"

A beatific smile appeared on Morgan's face. "The Mind is all, and we are all one with the Mind. It has instituted order and harmony in our compound, and enabled us to unlock our full potential, to reach for higher consciousness and continue our research."

"And what, pray tell, might that be?"

Whatever answer Morgan would have given was forestalled by Markus. "Subject does not have clearance for briefing on our work."

Morgan nodded. "Of course not—not yet, at least."

"Okay. Then perhaps you can tell me how you came to be a part of this…operation," Mildred requested.

Morgan looked at her for a moment, then shrugged. "It is a short story. After leaving the Freedom Mall, I wandered the area around it for several weeks, but found nothing suited to my abilities. I joined a caravan heading west, much like the one you and your people are with. We had decided to travel through the forest to the north, to avoid the plains. That did not work out so well. The caravan was attacked, and we were scattered. I survived as best I could, but the indigenous creatures forced me to head out onto the plains here. I was near death when a group from this facility found me and brought me here. They introduced me to the Mind, which I must admit, I was resistant to at first—" Mildred again noted the knowing smiles that appeared on the faces of the two doctors "—but once joined, I converted wholeheartedly, and am now reaping the benefits of being one with it. It truly is amazing, as you'll see soon enough."

"I'm sure it is." His description of the Mind and what it was doing with these people made Mildred's stomach churn, but she kept her expression calm. "What are you allowed to tell me about this place?"

"There's not much to tell," Morgan said. "As we had explained to Ryan, this is one of a series of Cold War–era missile silos that were deactivated in the 1970s and 1980s. Officially, many of them were allowed to fill with water, or were even sold to private owners who converted them into bomb shelters or living spaces."

"Many of the more concealed ones were retained by the United States government," Markus continued, "and appropriated by Overproject Whisper for various research projects such as ours."

"They were refurbished to suit a particular project's needs, with ample supplies for staff and subjects," Phieks said. "When skydark occurred, it was only natural for our ancestors to remain in our location and continue our research in the hopes of assisting with the rebuilding of the nation. We have carried on their mission ever since."

"Yeah…how's that going, by the way?" Mildred asked.

An odd, puzzled look crossed both doctors' faces, as if they weren't sure whether Mildred was being sarcastic or serious.

Finally, Markus answered. "Slowly, but progress is being made every day."

They came to a T intersection with several more people, each dressed in a jumpsuit, lab coat or occasionally both, walking past. Although the hallway was fairly narrow, no one collided with anyone else, or even came close to doing so. Every movement was precisely choreographed for maximum efficiency—even people who were reviewing paperwork or engaged in conversation avoided bumping into others. It was uncanny, and more than a bit frightening.

Across the hall was an elevator. Morgan stepped over and slid a key card he removed from a pocket through a slot next to the double doors. A few seconds later, they opened, and everyone entered.

He pushed a button, and the elevator began moving. Mildred thought they were going down, but she couldn't be quite sure; the movement was smooth enough that it was hard to tell. She racked her brains to try to remember everything she knew about the old ICBM silos, which, admittedly, wasn't very much. And what she could remember had no doubt been rendered obsolete by whatever had been done to the place after it was taken over.

About forty-five seconds later, the doors slid open again. Morgan and the doctors stepped out, but Mildred hesitated. Something didn't feel right here.

Morgan stepped back to the entrance and extended his hand. "You had asked about our purpose, and you have arrived at it. You may as well come out and receive the answers you're looking for."

"Yeah…" Mildred whispered, suddenly not at all sure she wanted to see what was in the next room. While she had no illusions about possessing any extrasensory ability—certainly nothing like Krysty's powers—even Mildred was aware that someone—no, some*thing*—very powerful was in the next room. And that it was unlike anything she had ever seen before.

You've faced all kinds of crazy, freaky muties in this world. You can face one more. Taking a deep breath, she muttered, "Here we go, Ryan," as she pushed him out of the elevator and into the room.

Chapter Twenty-Five

The very first thing she noticed was the darkness; the room was lit by only a few small lights, leaving the rest of the space in shadow. It was warm in there, uncomfortably so, and Mildred felt sweat begin to form on her neck and arms. The air smelled strange, almost indefinable. It was peaty, or earthy, and yet she scented the distinct odor of something animal—something alive—in here, as well.

The chamber she found herself in was round, with dull metal walls that extended roughly twenty feet up to the grated ceiling. She felt warm air wafting across the top of her head, and looked up to see several fans on the other side of the ceiling blowing air into the room. Looking back at the center, she saw something there—some kind of mass—but couldn't make out any more detail. She took a step forward, and that was when the voice spoke.

"COME FORWARD."

The words hit her brain like a hammer, staggering Mildred. It was a cacophony of a hundred—no, a *thousand* voices…young, old, male, female…all blended into one singular tone that shouted directly *into* her mind.

Mildred recoiled, not wanting to go any closer to whatever had just done that. She heard the voice again.

"STEP FORWARD, OR YOU WILL BE...
COMPELLED."

The words raked across her brain like a psychic assault, rendering it nearly impossible to think, the voice drowning out any semblance of coherent reasoning. Hoping it would stop if she obeyed, Mildred stumbled forward, approaching close enough to see what took up the entire center of the room.

A large container had been built here. It was partially filled with some kind of gelatinous, shimmering liquid, and rising out of it was something that she could classify only as a gigantic, gray-green, glistening-wet brain.

Ever since being woken from cryosleep, Mildred had seen a lot as she had traveled with the group through these blasted wastelands. She had seen all kinds of warped mutations and transformations of people and animals, from half human, half machine cyborgs to new, hideous creatures that defied rational explanation. Her life had been put in danger more than once. As horrifying as all of that had been, at this moment, seeing this—thing—pulsing with malevolent intelligence, and knowing that it was the driving force behind all of these people...

For a few moments, Mildred was on the edge of losing it right then and there. The thoughts emanating from this creature were so alien—and yet, with an unmistakable mix of human emotion as well—that it was almost too much to bear. There was a peculiar agelessness to its voice, and yet the hundreds of accompanying voices lent it the frenetic impatience of humanity, too. *Dear God, what has happened here?* she wondered.

The mass of pulsating matter didn't particularly resemble a human brain, or any other kind she knew of, for that matter. At least six feet high and twice that in diameter, it was lumpy and irregularly shaped, with folds and lobes extending in every direction. Several nozzles were arranged around the tank, and as she watched, they sprayed a fine mist over the creature's mottled, translucent skin. Mildred surmised it was some kind of nutrient liquid it lived in.

Unable to look away in spite of herself, Mildred saw that much of it was covered in what appeared to be moss or lichen, which made her frown. Her scientific curiosity reasserted itself, and she wondered what the thing was.

"YOU INQUIRE AS TO WHAT I AM, MILDRED WYETH."

The statement rocked her again like a thunderclap going off right next to her, but Mildred found she recovered from this one a bit more easily. "Yes," she replied.

"THERE IS NO NEED TO SPEAK YOUR WORDS. SIMPLY THINK WHATEVER QUERIES YOU MAY HAVE, AND I WILL KNOW THEM."

"O—" Mildred clamped her mouth shut, not wanting to offend the thing. Who knew what it might be able to do to her mind if it channeled that terrible chorus into a weapon?

"Okay. What are you?" she thought.

"ALTHOUGH I DO NOT KNOW EXACTLY HOW LONG I HAVE...EXISTED, MY PEOPLE SAY THAT I AM APPROXIMATELY TWO HUNDRED AND EIGHTY-FIVE YEARS OLD. FOR ME, I HAVE ALWAYS BEEN, AS LONG AS THERE HAS BEEN A...WORLD AROUND ME. FOR A LONG TIME, I DWELLED IN DARKNESS, UNTIL THE ONE APPEARED TO ME, AND WAS ABLE TO COMMUNICATE WITH ME DIRECTLY. HE EVOKED SOMETHING THAT I HAD

NEVER...FELT BEFORE...A KINSHIP WITH AN-OTHER LIVING ORGANISM. WITH HIM TO HELP ME, I WAS ABLE TO EVOLVE INTO A FORM SIMILAR TO WHAT YOU SEE BEFORE YOU NOW. AS THIS HAPPENED, I CREATED MY CHILDREN AND SENT THEM FORTH TO BRING OTHERS SIMILAR TO THE ONE TO ME, TO GROW AND NOURISH ME, THAT WE MAY ALL EXIST TOGETHER. EVENTUALLY I WAS ABLE TO CREATE ENOUGH CHILDREN THAT THEY COULD BRING ME TO THIS PLACE, WHERE I HAVE EXISTED EVER SINCE."

The speech was long and arduous for Mildred to follow, mainly because behind the brain-thing's near deafening mental chorus, she also began to make out other, quieter voices, many of which were saying something else entirely, at odds with the main chorus. Trying not to arouse the main consciousness's suspicion, she did her best to focus on these other, dissonant voices.

"—the organism is composed of both plant and animal matter, a unique hybrid mutation—"

"—its powers are unparalleled. Indeed, we are looking at a brand-new form of life here—"

"—not allow ourselves or our mission to be subverted—"

"—it is too late for us. Save yourself—"

This last one made her start, which engendered a similar reaction from the brain-creature; she actually saw one of its lobes tremble.

"YOU SEEM...APPREHENSIVE. WHAT IS TROUBLING YOU?"

Mildred knew her very life depended on telling the creature in front of her what it wanted to hear. Its alienness was both a help and a hindrance to figuring out what that was, however. She managed to tear her gaze away to check out what Morgan and the others were doing. All of them were staring at the giant brain-thing with wondrous looks on their faces. Focusing all of her mental powers, she projected her reply:

"I just... Having never seen anything like you before, I am in awe of a creature such as yourself. It is...very intimidating to stand before you like this."

"YOU HAVE NO REASON TO FEAR OR BE ALARMED. INDEED, I FIND YOUR MENTAL EMA-NATIONS TO BE QUITE PLEASANT."

Mildred blinked. Had it just said it liked how she thought? That had to be a first. *"Um...thank you?"*

"YOU ARE...MOST WELCOME."

"What is...what is to happen to us now?" Mildred asked.

"YOU ARE BOTH TO JOIN MY CHILDREN, OF COURSE. AS SUCH—"

The elevator doors opened, and two more scientists emerged, escorting an old, white-haired woman dressed in a hospital gown between them. On seeing the group already there, they stopped.

"Apologies, Mind, we did not think you were occupied," one of the scientists said. Mildred was nonplussed to discover that she could hear his words inside her head as well as when he spoke.

"IT IS OF NO MATTER. THESE TWO ARE TO BE BROUGHT INTO THE FOLD SOON ENOUGH. I SENSE THAT YOU HAVE BROUGHT A FINAL FOR ME?"

"Yes, Mind, she is ready to join you," the second whitecoat replied.

"I AM PLEASED AT THIS. STEP FORWARD, MY CHILD."

The frail woman shuffled forward, barely able to stand on her own. She drooled as she walked, her eyes clouded with cataracts. When she stood at the edge of the tank, she swayed back and forth, her legs trembling.

"YOUR LONG JOURNEY IS FINALLY AT AN END. COME AND JOIN ME."

Before Mildred could say or do anything, the old woman sighed and pitched forward—directly into the tank!

"Oh, my God! Somebody help her!" Mildred lunged forward but was caught by Morgan, who held her back with ease.

"She is being helped even now," Morgan replied. "She is being granted the greatest gift the Mind can bestow—immortality."

The woman splashed weakly in the sludgy fluid, but made no real effort to swim to the lip of the tank or climb onto the brain-creature itself. "It will be over soon," Morgan said. "And then she will be one with the Mind."

Indeed, as Mildred watched in horror, the old woman's body was slowly being drawn toward the brain-creature. Soon she was right next to it, and began disappearing into the large mass, as if the brain were actually devouring her a bit at a time. The very last thing to disappear into the organism was her face, now with a blank, peaceful expression on it. But before it did, her mouth opened, and the slug-like parasite that had been living inside her emerged to splash into the nutrient pool. Mildred felt her gorge rise, but kept it down with an effort.

"That is our fate when each of us grows too old to

sustain one of the children inside us," Morgan said as he released her. "Our bodies are absorbed back into the Mind, and our collective intelligence is joined with it forever. And fortunately for both of you, this also means that a symbiote is available, so that you can join with the Mind, as well."

"What? Thank you for the uh, generous offer, but I don't wish to be any part of—this." Mildred began backing away, but bumped into the pair of doctors behind her. Before she could get away, each of them grabbed one of her arms, and held it tightly.

"I understand your reluctance, I truly do," Morgan said as he walked toward her. "It is unnatural to think of something else living inside you, something that you feel doesn't belong there." He shook his head. "But you couldn't be more wrong. The symbiotes protect us, they heal us and ensure that our bodies and minds are the very best they can be. We are no longer susceptible to disease or injury, and our life span is greatly extended." He waved at the tank. "The woman you saw go to join the Mind today? She was one hundred and eight years old. She had lived her entire life here, and now she will live on forever as part of the Mind."

"The Mind also connects us in a community that none of us had ever experienced before," Markus said. "With everyone living and working in harmony, we have made so much more progress, unlocked so many secrets of the human mind and body, that we are on the cusp of achieving major breakthroughs in creating the next stage in human evolution as well, to catch up with the wonder that is the Mind's symbiotes."

Phieks nodded. "And once the secondary colony is established—"

"ENOUGH. IT IS TIME TO UNIFY THESE TWO WITH US."

"Yes, Mind…." Morgan and the doctors answered in unison. The two doctors marched a struggling Mildred toward the large tank. As she got closer, she saw the symbiote ooze up onto its lip, dripping wetly with the sludge the brain-thing rested in. It reared as it sensed her approach.

Mildred twisted and squirmed, but the hands pinioning her arms were unmovable. Her two captors applied pressure on her shoulders and back, forcing her to bend closer to the quivering parasite. "No, no, you can't make me! I'll bite its fucking head off first—"

"THE ONE CALLED MILDRED WYETH SHALL NOT BE HOSTING THIS SYMBIOTE."

Immediately, the doctors froze, holding Mildred only inches from the questing slug. "What will happen with her, Mind?" Morgan asked.

"I FIND MILDRED WYETH TO BE WORTHY OF ASSISTING WITH OUR CONTINUED EXPANSION. SHE WILL BE GIFTED WITH A QUEEN SYMBIOTE, TO CREATE YET ANOTHER REMOTE COLONY. WE HAVE BEEN EXECUTING OUR EXPANSION PLANS INCORRECTLY, MY CHILDREN. ONCE A QUEEN IS INSIDE HER, WE WILL RELEASE HER BACK AMONG THE OTHERS, AND SHE WILL BE OUR IMPLEMENT TO BRING THEM ALL INTO OUR COLONY."

"Your will be done, Mind," Morgan and the doctors replied.

"But what of the symbiote that is ready now?" Phieks asked.

"JENNIFER THERAS SERVED US WELL AS HEAD OF SECURITY FOR MANY YEARS. JUDGING FROM

THE INFORMATION I HAVE GATHERED FROM OUR PEOPLE WHO HAVE BEEN CARRYING OUT THE MISSIONS AGAINST THE TARGET POPULATION OUTSIDE THE COMPLEX, THE EXPERIENCE GATHERED BY HER AND HER SYMBIOTE WILL SERVE OUR NEW HEAD OF SECURITY—THE ONE CALLED RYAN CAWDOR—EQUALLY WELL. BRING THEM TOGETHER NOW."

"No!" Mildred lunged forward, lashing out with a foot to try to smash the slug in front of her, but was hauled away from the tank before she could connect. "Ryan? Ryan! Fight! Move! Do *something!*"

She saw his muscles quiver impotently, but the drug in his system held him fast as Morgan wheeled his chair to the tank. The slug glided over the side and flopped onto Ryan's lap. Morgan pried open Ryan's jaw as the symbiote started climbing up his chest.

Held fast, Mildred could only scream as it got closer and closer to his open mouth....

Chapter Twenty-Six

By midday, Krysty and the others, along with the remaining Silvertide members, had accounted for everything they had left. The final tally was four of the collective members killed in the flood, and six they assumed were missing, instead of washed away to die. That didn't count Ryan or Mildred.

They had also found two of the previously missing collective members, both drowned. There was no obvious sign of the parasites, and without Mildred on-site to verify that they were clean, Krysty and J.B. weren't keen on keeping the bodies around for too long. Fortunately, neither was the rest of the collective, and all of the dead were burned in a pyre while a prayer was said over their bodies by Elder Chreis.

Along with the earlier damage inventory, it was found that two more of the wagons were disabled enough so that it would be at least a day before the train could get underway again. The overall mood of the group, already sullen before this news, had turned downright hostile, particularly in regards to their sec personnel. Krysty was already partially aware of that—even if she hadn't seen the dark glares leveled at them, she could sense the emotional mood of the group.

Elder Chreis had shared the news with them once everyone had come back together at the new camp. "Sister Krysty, a word, if you please."

"J.B., come with us," she said as she walked a few yards away with the older man. "What's going on?"

To his credit, Chreis looked pained at being the bearer of this bad news. "There has been much talk among the rest of the collective about whether to follow your sec directives anymore. Many feel that your group is at least partially responsible for the situation we are now in—"

"Just a second," J.B. interrupted. "Are you people trying to blame us for the fireblasted *weather?*"

"Let the man finish, J.B.," Krysty said. "Go on."

"You must understand—" The older man looked around before he continued speaking. "We are a simple people, who follow the Lord's word in all things. As such, that makes many of our populace... Well, rather superstitious."

"Careful. That sounds suspiciously like educated words coming from your mouth," Krysty said with a smile to reassure him that she was kidding.

Chreis smiled back and nodded. "I knew you were clever ones from the way you spoke. Yes, I had received some schooling back home many years ago. I was even a teacher before I decided to join the collective on its journey. It is my hope to reestablish my school when we are finally settled somewhere and train the next generation to continue driving back the darkness."

"That's all great, but I hardly see what that has to do with us and how we've been handling things," J.B. said.

"You have to understand that many of the adults here don't have much of an education beyond the bare minimum. Many can barely read or write, since there wasn't all that much call for it outside whatever called for technical aspects, like the water machine. The physical skills—farming, hunting, hide tanning—are all passed down orally and by hands-on training, as the older generation passes on its skills and information to the next."

"And with so much emphasis placed on the tools needed for survival, other aspects fall by the wayside, while certain other rituals and stories take on an oversize importance in their lives," Krysty said.

"That's it exactly," Chreis agreed. "I think there are those who still believe in you and what you're doing, but there has been a gathering of like minds in the colony—mainly from those who have recently lost members—who are saying that you people are allied with these kidnappers, and trying to lure us astray so that we'll be easier prey for them."

"These folks do realize that we've also lost two of our own to these bastards?" J.B. asked, two pink spots on his cheeks highlighting how angry he was. "To accuse us of collaborating with them takes a hell of a lot of gall—"

"Actually, I can see where they're coming from," Krysty said, cutting him off. "Forgive my bluntness, Chreis, but your people are more shrewd than I gave them credit for to think of this. Even with Tully and Latham witnessing what we did back at the building where we first met them, we could have arranged all that as well to insinuate ourselves more completely among your people. After all, who would suspect us after watching us kill one of our own? No one."

"Krysty, you're talking paranoid delusions here," J.B. said. "If that was true, then we also would have had to set up that situation two nights ago, where we saved three people from being taken, remember? Are they saying that would have been all planned, too, including killing the three kidnappers, just to make us look good?"

"Yes," Krysty replied flatly. "Keep in mind that I'm saying the people who are unhappy are fitting what has happened into their own narrative, to fit what they think is happening. However, that scenario does have some basis in fact."

"How do you figure that?" J.B. asked.

"To make this work, we have to assume that these parasites are only interested in their own survival and to reproduce by whatever means necessary," Krysty said. "With that goal in mind, and remember some of what we learned about bees, for instance, in Heaven Falls, a hive will often sacrifice members if the risk versus reward is acceptable. If they believe they have the chance to get thirty or forty new members by sacrificing three or four, they might very well go for it. In that case, inserting double agents among the target group makes perfect sense."

"All right, all right, I get your point." J.B. blew air out through his pursed lips. "Well, whatever you think of them, they're still the bad guys and we're still the good guys. That is the case, right?"

"Yes, I was just putting myself in these people's shoes for a minute, that's all," Krysty replied. "Whatever our next step against the kidnappers is going to be, we'd better settle this matter before it gets any more out of hand. Chreis, can you gather everyone in a few minutes? I find it's best to face our accusers and see if they still have the guts to confront us directly."

"I will," the elder replied. "Let's meet by the double wagon your friend created. Most of our people are near it already, so it will be easy enough to gather the rest."

"We'll give you a few minutes to gather everyone, then we'll head over, all right?"

"Thank you, sister." The elder trotted toward the forlorn cluster of working wagons, with Krysty and J.B. watching him leave and not saying anything until they were sure he was out of earshot.

"You and Ricky get the truck running yet?" she asked.

J.B. nodded. "Yeah, it'll go, but I can't guarantee how far. Engine's balky at best, and there might be water in the fuel line, so she may stall out on us when we least expect it."

"All the same, it might be best to have it ready."

"Especially if our little powwow doesn't go as planned," he observed soberly.

"Right. I don't really expect them to attack us, but it only takes a minute or two for a crowd to turn into a mob. Either way, best be prepared if that comes to pass."

"Way ahead of you," he replied. "While we've been cleaning up after the flood, I've been packing supplies in the truck, just in case we were going to try to head out to find that redoubt—or if we had to bug out in a hurry, for whatever reason. There's enough in there to last us a week or two if we eat lean. The weapons, of course, are our biggest aces in the hole."

"Exactly. When the time comes, you, me and Doc will be the ones to talk to the others. Ricky will be manning the truck, in case there's trouble, and we'll put Jak up on the hill with a carbine—just in case."

J.B. nodded. "Works. Give me a minute to get the boys set up, and then we'll head over."

Krysty nodded, and the Armorer loped off while she

checked the load in her Glock 18C before putting it back into its holster, hoping that she wouldn't be forced to use it this day.

WHEN KRYSTY AND J.B. finally headed toward the pair of wagons, they saw that the bulk of the collective was already assembled, with clusters of men and women talking among themselves.

As the two approached, Krysty noticed that the majority of them were armed now, mostly with farm implements—pitchforks, shovels, axes—but others were carrying improvised clubs and many hands hovered uncomfortably close to the knives sheathed on their belts. The two were easily outnumbered by a factor of ten to one.

"Jak's in position," J.B. said as they walked up to the wagons. "Ready to face our grateful employers?"

From inside the wagon, they heard Doc's booming baritone as he entertained the children with a fantastic story about a girl named Alice, who was apparently in the midst of a strange adventure featuring a talking rabbit and a queen who sounded as if she ruled a kingdom of playing cards.

Krysty stepped up to the side of the wagon and knocked on the gunwale. "Sorry to interrupt, Doc, but we've got some business to take care of, and we need you to join us."

The old man looked from her to the kids, all of whom groaned at the interruption of their story. "I am sorry, children, but I'm afraid we'll have to pick this up another time. Perhaps we can get together after dinner, and I will tell you how Alice escaped from the Queen of Hearts." Catching Krysty's nod away from the wagon, Doc got them all on their feet. "All right, little ones, everyone run along and play."

Grumbling and sighing, the kids jumped down from the wagon and quickly scattered. "No news about our missing companions yet?"

Krysty shook her head as she climbed up into the back.

"I trust from your expressions that not all is well in Kansas?"

"Not really." Krysty lowered her voice. "The natives are restless. Just stand with us, and be ready to run if we have to."

"Oh, dear." Doc grabbed the lapels of his frock coat and held them like a sideshow carnival barker. "I stand ready to assist any way I can."

"Just stand next to us and look dignified for right now," Krysty replied. "You both ready?" They each nodded. "Let's do this."

She turned to the rest of the people around them, all of whom had clustered around the back of the wagon. Elder Chreis stood next to it with his hands raised, trying to keep the crowd from bombarding them with questions, but lowered them at a nudge from Krysty. "It's all right, Elder."

She then raised her voice to address the crowd. "I understand that many of you are upset and frustrated about what happened last night. This won't be much consolation, but the rest of my group and me are just as concerned about our missing people—*all* of them, yours and ours alike—"

"Even since Bough gave you control of sec, everything's been going wrong!" yelled a man in the crowd.

"Is that so?" Krysty replied. "It seems to me if we

hadn't been around, you folks would be missing three more people, who instead were saved by us from being carried off." She took a breath before plunging ahead with her next statement. "You also might have been missing the entire Bough family, instead of simply mourning the loss of Elder Bough. Not to mention how badly last night could have gone if we hadn't been here. Who knows how many people might been taken if not for us—"

"You were the ones who had us set up camp next to the spring," another person shouted. "The flood could have killed all of us!"

"Now, just a minute!" Krysty said, raising her voice loud enough to be heard, but not shouting the other man down. "That spot had everything we needed at the time—water, and a defensible location in the event of an attack. Now, this isn't your first time out in the world. We all know how unpredictable the weather can be. Obviously if we'd known the storm would have been that bad, we would have taken better precautions. But the fact remains that the enemy did try to use it as cover, which would have happened anyway, and if not for the flood, things might have been a whole lot worse, since that was what really broke up their attack."

Now Elder Chreis stepped forward. "There is no doubt that we have suffered more tribulations in the past few days, from the loss of Elder Bough to the flood and this latest assault by these people. In Elder Bough's wisdom, he saw fit to put the vote to all of us before we took these folks on, and indeed, I don't think anyone here can truly speak against their helpfulness and willingness to stand with us against the scourge of those who are stealing our people. In the elder meeting this morning, it was agreed that we would be willing to put their continued assistance to a vote if you all wish it."

There was a lot of grumbling among the people, but no one was shouting at them anymore, which Krysty took as a good sign.

"I'll call for the vote!" The woman they knew as Sister Saea pushed to the front of the crowd. "But first, I want to hear what you plan to do about these people. They have to be stopped once and for all, and our people have to be rescued!"

A chorus of agreements and shouts of approval rose in answer to her words, and Krysty nodded once the noise had died down. "On that, you and I are in complete agreement. It is very obvious that these marauders are going to keep coming after you and us until they have gotten what they wanted—apparently, to have every single one of us under their control."

The muttering and conversation turned nervous and fearful. "I don't know about you, but I'm tired of letting them call the shots all the time. I want to— No, I'm going to strike back!"

She turned to J.B. on her left and Doc on her right. "Even missing our two people, we can do a lot, but we could do so much more if all of you would stand with us."

"But there is only so much we can do!" a man shouted. "We have all taken a sacred oath to not spill blood for any reason."

"But that does not remove you from defending what is yours!" Doc's voice startled Krysty. Before she could say anything, he continued, "For does not the Good Book say in Psalms, 'For he will deliver the needy who cry out, the afflicted who have no one to help. He will take pity on the weak and the needy, and save the needy from death. He will rescue them from oppression and violence, for precious is their blood in his sight'?"

No one knew quite what to make of Doc's pronouncement, although Krysty saw several people make the sign of the cross over their bodies.

Doc stepped forward now, his rich baritone easily carrying over the crowd. "In that particular verse, David was praying on behalf of King Solomon, that he would rule justly and wisely. But the 'he' I am referring to is each and every one of you." Doc pointed into the crowd, his finger seeking out anyone who was looking at him.

"It is easy to lay down your arms and trust that the Lord shall provide," he continued. "Indeed, perhaps he did provide us to assist you in your time of need. But—" Doc paused, letting the silence build, making sure every eye was following him "—does not the Bible also say that the Lord God helps those who help themselves? For surely you do not count on the Lord to miraculously till your fields and plant your seeds and harvest your crops. No, for while you indeed pray for a bountiful harvest, it is *you* who provide the labor to make your crops grow and your fields plentiful. It is *you* who has undertaken this journey to find a place to live and raise your families free from oppression and fear. And now it is up to *you*— each and every one of you—to defend what you have— your families, your neighbors—from those who would seek to take everything that you hold dear from you."

Doc drew himself up and stared out over the crowd. "Make no mistake, people of the Silvertide collective. We are all in this together. And either we shall all stand fast against this pernicious evil that seeks to destroy us, or we shall divide, and in that division will be our undoing. Now, what say you all?"

Recognizing when an opportunity had been handed to him on a silver platter, Chreis stepped forward. "All those who wish to have Sister Krysty, Brother John, Brother Theophilus and the rest continue to aid us, speak now."

The chorus of "ayes" was deafening.

"Any opposed?" Chreis asked.

No one said a word.

"The motion is carried!" Chreis said to another round of cheers.

"That's all well and good!" Saea cried out when the celebration had died down. "But how are we to stop them?"

Krysty opened her mouth again, but this time another voice spoke before she could. "Got an idea that, if we all work really hard, could swing the odds back in our favor."

She turned to see J.B. step forward now. "It's going to take a lot of hard work, and if we want to make it happen, we'll have to get started right now, so we can be ready for them when they return tonight."

"How do you know they're coming back tonight?"

"Simple. They've struck at us the past two nights but haven't gotten what they wanted. Now they'll see us as being demoralized from the flood, and their somewhat successful attack yesterday. A wise leader would follow up that strike with another one, figuring that we'll still be recovering from their last attack. But we won't." Now J.B.'s intent gaze scanned the entire crowd. "Instead, we'll be ready for them—*all* of us."

Chapter Twenty-Seven

Three hours later, J.B. sighted down the barrel of the M4 carbine he'd come to consider his over the past couple of days. He had considered using Ryan's Scout longblaster for this, but its ten-round magazine and bolt action would be more hindrance than help in what they were about to do, so he'd stuck with the M4 auto rifle.

His target was a patch of ground about fifteen yards across by the same distance long, at the bottom of the thirty-foot cliff he was lying on. At the far end of the dusty clearing was a bottleneck formed by two cliffs that time had either pushed to within a few yards of each other or worn down the small ravine in between. Steep, nearly unclimbable walls rose into the air on the left and right sides of the hole. The box canyon in which they'd set up their ambush provided ample room for everyone who needed to be there.

"Come on, Jak…shouldn't be too hard to find some of them," J.B. muttered. For the fifth time in as many minutes, he checked the rest of his impromptu firing squad.

On his left lay Ricky and Krysty, each aiming an M4 at the killing space below. On his right was Tully, also in a prone shooter's position, waiting for their prey to take their bait and stampede in.

"You good?" J.B. whispered to Tully.

"Yes, Brother Dix," she replied, managing to conceal most of her impatience. "I remember everything you taught me."

"It's just that this is your first time firing this kind of weapon, so I just want you to be comfortable, that's all."

"I'll be comfortable once Jak's out of that ravine and back up here," she replied. Her cheeks flamed red as the import of her words struck her.

Although J.B. noted what she'd said, he didn't comment beyond a simple, "Me, too. While we're waiting, let's go over it one more time. Where's your firing selector?"

"Single shot. No need for full auto, since we're in minimal danger from them, and I'll be aiming every time."

"Good. How will you select your targets?"

"I'm covering the right side with you. Krysty and Ricky have the left. I'm to wait until you give the word or shoot, whichever comes first. We're trying to make it easy for the ropers to get the bodies up and clear before they're taken back by these things."

"Very good." J.B. meant it, too. He'd rarely had a student who had picked up the basics of both shooting and tactics so quickly. "What are you aiming for?"

"The head if possible, to preserve the body, but if one of them gets on Jak, I'm to take it out only if you or the others can't—biggest danger is shooting too close to a friend. If a bullet hits the chest, there's enough other usable parts so it won't go to waste. Ride the recoil back, then pick another target as soon as possible and shoot. Repeat until I have to reload, or there's nothing left to kill."

"Excellent." A clatter of rocks sounded in the distance, although J.B. couldn't see what made the noise. "Get ready."

"Been ready since we got up here," she replied, snugging the butt tighter into her shoulder. J.B. did the same, sighting down his barrel just as Jak burst out of the narrow pass, his white hair fluttering in the wind as he pumped his skinny arms and legs for all they were worth.

Following about three steps behind him was a furiously chittering mass of burrow-bugs, their quadruple sets of rear legs churning up dust as they boiled out of the defile after their sprinting prey.

"Hold...hold..." J.B. said, wanting to make sure that Jak was out of the line of fire. "Now."

The four longblasters cracked as one, and the first trio of bugs all went down with holes in their heads or upper chests. The rest swarmed over them, only to be cut down by the second volley. However, the tide of gray-green monsters continued pouring out of the far end of the clearing.

"Think they're going to try to pyramid up here, too?" Krysty asked between methodical shots into the teeming mass below.

"If they do—" J.B. took another bug's head off with a well-placed shot to its throat, the hole spurting green-black ichor as the beast went down under the pounding feet of his fellows "—I've got a little surprise for them this time."

Jak scrambled up over the edge of the cliff and scooted next to Tully, breathing hard from his exertion. He pulled up the rope he'd used to climb the cliff, just in case. "Hot damn! Think fuckers still pissed off from last time."

"Get on your longblaster and start taking them down," J.B. said, squeezing off shots every two seconds like clockwork. "The ropers are getting started, and we want to give them plenty to work with."

From the left and right sides of the cliffs, lariats began sailing down onto the dead burrow-bugs. The lasso wielders targeted the bodies that had fallen close enough to the walls that they could be pulled up without attracting too much attention from the other bugs. Once the loop was tight around them, teams started hauling the bugs up the cliff walls and moving them out of the way so more could be grabbed. Soon, several bodies were being hauled up at a time.

"At the rate they keep coming, we'll have enough in no time," Ricky said.

"Yeah…better keep that surprise handy, just in case," Krysty said as she reloaded her carbine and continued shooting.

"I've got it, don't worry," he replied. The longblaster team was dividing its fire now. Krysty, Ricky and Jak were shooting into the milling mass at the bottom of the cliff, while J.B. and Tully were still concentrating on bringing down bugs near the left and right walls.

"From my count, the collectors have gotten at least fifteen bodies," Tully said. "How much longer should we keep firing?"

"I think we're just about done here," J.B. said, pleased at her foresight. "Keep the bugs busy until this last round's been retrieved, and then we'll quit."

Krysty, Ricky, J.B., Jak and Tully fired a few more rounds into the roiling mass of burrow-bugs, just enough to keep them off the last few bodies being hauled up by the collective people on each side. The Armorer reloaded his carbine, then stood and watched the tide of gray-green below.

"Looks like they don't have the numbers to take us on like at the plateau," Krysty said as she rose to stand next to him.

"Mebbe, but I don't even think they know we're up here," J.B. replied. "Once Jak disappeared and we killed the first few that saw him climbing, it was like the rest didn't know where to go or what to do except grab the new food right in front of them."

His observation was correct. The bugs had stopped coming in through the ravine at the other side and were now carrying off the rest of their slain brethren. Once the other bug bodies had vanished from sight, it was as if they had never even existed in the first place.

"So what was your surprise?" Krysty asked. "More plas-ex?"

J.B. shook his head. "Better." Removing his clenched hand from his pocket, he revealed two small grens. "One high-ex, one implo. They were on the three we chilled from the truck."

"They'll come in handy," she observed.

"One way or the other," J.B. agreed.

"Think we got enough?" Ricky asked as he also stood and stretched.

"If Tully's count is accurate, there should be more than enough for what we need," J.B. said. "Let's go find out."

The shooting party headed toward the group on their left, which was the one closest to the encampment. They had brought up ten carcasses all by themselves. J.B. sent the kids over to help the other group, which had lassoed eight bugs. Altogether, there was plenty to go around.

"This is either going to be one of the best ideas you've ever had, or the craziest, J.B.," Krysty said as they helped stack the bug bodies on the back of a wagon.

J.B. thumped on the chest plate of a particularly large burrow-bug with the butt of his M4. "By the time the night's over, we'll know the answer to that. But there's still a lot of work to do before we find out."

BACK AT CAMP, Jak enjoyed the adulation he received at dinner from the rest of the collective. He had to tell the story about how he had lured the burrow-bugs into the killing ground at least three different times, with men, women and children all hanging on his every word. Remembering Ryan's warning, he kept the bragging to a minimum, just saying he did what he had to do and giving plenty of credit to the shooting group as well as the lasso wielders. "Was group effort. Everybody not work together, we not succeed." His willingness to risk his life to get the group what they needed, as well as his relative modesty about doing it, had done much to alleviate the previous bad blood felt by the collective, and Jak caught appreciative glances being cast his way by both Krysty and J.B.

That evening's dinner was being served in shifts, with everyone who wasn't making food or eating working on creating their surprises for the kidnappers. Since Jak had performed one of the most dangerous jobs in the entire operation, J.B. had given him the rest of the day off, telling him to get some rest, especially since they were most likely going to be up most of the night.

And that had been his plan, at least at first. Jak had been awake for the past twenty hours, what with being in on the fight the previous night, then surviving the flood and helping search for survivors, then watching over the rest of his group while they'd braced the collective about staying on to finish their job. And although he had what often seemed like bottomless reserves of stamina, even Jak found himself yawning as he headed toward the truck to get some shut-eye.

But as he neared it, he saw a folded slip of paper with his name written on it under the windshield wiper. Unfolding it, he read the contents with a widening grin.

Meet me at the spring. Don't let anyone see you leave.
Tully

Jak refolded the evidence and stuffed it into his pocket while glancing around to see if anyone was watching him. The nearest people were all busy either with their meal or working on the very messy business of dismembering bug carcasses. It was child's play for him to slip out of camp and head over to the spring.

The area there had been reshaped by the previous day's flood. Instead of a small trickle through the rocks, both the streambed and surrounding area were now submerged under several feet of water, creating a small pond. When he reached it, Jak looked around, shading his eyes against the setting sun until he spotted Tully on the far side of the water. Casting one last scan around to make sure he hadn't been followed, he loped around the large pool of water until he stood right in front of her. "Hey."

Wearing her best dress—the one she had worn to the feast the first night Jak and the others had come to town—Tully stared up at him with a wide grin. "Hey. Got my note, I see."

"Yeah. Ain't you supposed be chopping bugs?" Jak asked with a grin.

Tully smiled back. "I may have convinced Tamar to take my shift on the skinning line, saying if she didn't that her daddy might find out who's been skimming shine from the distillery." She patted the blanket next to her. "Sit down."

"Sure." As he did, Jak caught a whiff of himself and wrinkled his nose. "Gotta warn—I kinda stink."

She laughed at that, not unkindly. "I thought you might, which is why I suggested that we, I mean, you, ah…" She looked away, color flaming on her cheeks. "Damn it, I thought this would be easier."

"What?" Jak asked as he crossed his legs under himself.

"I just wanted to see you without anyone else around. And now that you're here, I can't think or talk straight or anything. I just…wanna stare at you forever…" She broke her gaze and looked at the ground. "You must think I'm the biggest jackaninny."

"I think you're great!" Jak replied. "Way you handle windrider and shoot blaster. And you speak mind, not care what others think. Never met girl like you before."

And that was the simple truth of it. Jak had loved Christina, his wife and mother of his child, with all his heart. He had known other girls, bold and full of life, but none of them were quite like the spitfire looking back at him.

Tully stared at him for a long minute before replying. "You mean that?"

Suddenly afraid that *he* might say something foolish if he opened his mouth again, Jak just nodded.

Tully licked her lips, then nodded once, as if deciding something. "Let's go for a swim."

Jak glanced at the water, then back at her to see her already slipping out of her dress. "Uh, okay."

Shucking his dusty, sweaty clothes, too, he followed her as she dashed into the water. Fed by the small stream, the clear water came up to their necks, allowing them to swim around with ease yet still walk on the bottom if they wished. Jak ducked his head and came up with a splash, slicking his white hair back so he looked like a large, pale, white otter.

Tully laughed again as she paddled over to where he was standing. "Don't you look handsome."

Jak frowned at that. "I know I ain't pretty—"

She put a finger against his lips. "What are you talking about? You're the best-lookin' guy I know."

Jak blinked and rubbed a hand across his face. "Uh, need get your eyes checked. Lots guys in your—" he waved a hand over toward the rest of the collective "—group look better'n me."

Tully shook her head as she swam closer to him. "Not to me they don't. They're all the same—boring farmers or traders or mechanics, the same old thing every day. But you—you're different, you talk different, you look different."

She stood right next to Jak, her bare breasts brushing against his skinny chest. Her touch was positively galvanizing on him. She reached out with a dripping wet hand and caressed his scarred cheek. "You've done things none of them could ever dream of doing, or ever will do, Jak Lauren. And that makes you more special than all of them put together."

Jak had no idea how to reply to that, but he did know what he wanted to do more than anything in the world right now.... He leaned forward and kissed her, tentatively at first, then more passionately as she moved closer to him and wrapped an arm around his neck. Her mouth opened to his, and their tongues met with increasing urgency. He brought up his hand under the water to cup her breast, making her moan at the touch.

It might have been five minutes, it might have been an hour later when she finally broke free. Taking his hand, she began pulling him toward the shore. "Come on—I got a surprise for you."

"More than what we been doin'?" Jak asked, his head spinning with a combination of desire and, he realized, a dangerous swell of real feelings for this girl.

"Yup." She led him to the blanket and pushed him down on it, making sure he was lying on his back. She straddled him, the V of her sex peeking enticingly out from between her legs, then leaned back and grabbed a quart mason jar, this one full of golden liquid that gleamed in the fading sunlight.

"What that?"

"We don't just make shine all the time," she said. "A while back, we got hold of a huge mess of honey, enough that we tried making some mead, or honey wine."

"Yeah? Had before," Jak said.

"Not like this, you haven't." She cracked the jar and took a healthy swallow into her mouth, then swooped down to kiss him. When she parted her lips, the sweet, fiery liquor flooded into his mouth along with her tongue. Jak gulped it down and rose up to meet her, kissing her mouth and face, then moving down to her neck and onto her pert breasts, the nipples swelling under his tongue as she clasped his head to her chest while gasping with pleasure.

"Wait—wait a sec..." She leaned back and poured a stream of mead over her breasts, the sticky liquid cascading down over her brown neck and white skin to pool on Jak's chest. "Have a taste of that—"

She shuddered as Jak bent to the valley between her breasts again, lapping at her wine-slick skin and moving out from there. She writhed on him, turning his already swollen cock into hard iron.

Even through all of this, Jak had enough presence of mind to pull back for a moment. "Look, you know this can't— I mean, I'm not—"

Before he could continue, she fell on him, covering his mouth with kisses. "Shh...just be quiet. I know this is what it is, and I'm fine with that. It's just...before I have to choose to spend the rest of my life with one of the men in the collective, I want to be with someone who makes me feel alive. I want to be with you, Jak Lauren, right here, right now. Don't you worry about whatever comes afterward, okay?"

And she began moving her hips on him again, and any other protest Jak might have thought of was swept away by the magnificent young woman above him and what she was doing with him.

Chapter Twenty-Eight

As night fell over the encampment, Jak rejoined J.B., Krysty, Doc, Ricky and the others on the front line.

"There you are, Jak," J.B. greeted him as he unslung his carbine and settled in next to the older man underneath one of the wagons. "Must have crashed pretty hard. Thought I was going to have to send Ricky to wake you up."

"No! Mean wasn't necessary." Jak peered out into the gathering darkness at the plains. "All ready?"

"As ready as it's going to be. Everyone worked like crazy to get it all done. Now we just got to wait and see if they come to call."

Jak nodded while casting an eye skyward. "Least not raining tonight. Small favor."

"Right." Krysty regarded him for a moment. "You all right, Jak? You seem a bit...distracted, is all."

Jak turned to her, ruby-red eyes wide in the twilight. "No. Good day die, if comes to that."

"Dark night, Jak, way to keep it light," J.B. said. "Plan doesn't call for anyone dying tonight if we can help it. Let's just hunker down and keep our eyes open for them, okay?"

The plan was sketchier—and riskier—than their previous ones. After a long discussion, J.B. and Krysty had convinced the collective to pull in all their guards to try to lure their enemy into the camp to capture them once and for all. They figured if they could subdue enough of their adversaries, it might give them an advantage when they went for the base.

Untold to the others, Krysty and J.B. planned to let at least one go in order to follow him or her back to wherever the base was. They'd parked the truck away from the main area but could get to it quickly enough to follow anyone spotted leaving. Once they pinpointed the location, they could return and figure out exactly what to do about it. Now all they had to do was wait for the parasite people to come in and try to take away more of the collective.

To that end, they'd left the wagons scattered around haphazardly, as if the collective had given up hope. Any evidence of the bugs had also been hidden, as no one wanted to give away their surprise to the enemy.

"J.B., weird," Jak said.

"You can say I look like whatever you want, but I'm looking forward to bashing some skulls with these," J.B. said. "Sure you don't want to try a pair of forearm gauntlets?"

Jak shook his head. "Just get in way."

"Suit yourself."

"Fuckers stink, too."

"Yeah, that was one thing we couldn't get rid of in time." J.B. glanced down at the segmented gray-green armor plates covering his chest. "Sure are bastard strong, though."

The chitinous armor they'd spent the rest of the day removing from the bug bodies was amazing. When worn over a couple of pairs of shirts, it absorbed full impacts from a club with little discomfort to the wearer.

The forearm gauntlets J.B. referred to were two smaller pieces from a leg that were shaped to cover an arm from the wrist to the elbow, and secured with leather thongs. Again, with a thickly padded shirt or two underneath, it had blocked a club to the forearm with no injury. Apart from the sickly sour smell the armor gave off, it was performing better than J.B. could have hoped for. There was only one last test for it—in true combat.

"Too bad you couldn't have figured out the helmets in time," Krysty said. She had gone with gauntlets and nothing else, concerned that the chest plates might slow her down, as well. Also, there was the issue of fitting them comfortably over her chest, to be honest, and instead she'd opted to make sure as many of the scavvies were protected rather than trying to fit her properly.

"Yeah, but it was too complicated," J.B. replied. "Besides, even if we did make them work, I didn't want them relying on them too much—too hard to tell if they would have done the job. We should be okay—"

He was interrupted by a nudge from Jak. "Movement, 'bout a hundred fifty yards out."

"Okay...let me know when you've got confirmation." As he said that, J.B. reached up and knocked on the underside of the wagon. He was answered by a single thud from a person inside. "Everyone get ready."

The silent seconds stretched into a minute, then another one. "Okay...looks like you right, J.B. Large party 'bout a hundred yards out. Seven, eight, nine people so far."

"Looks like they're doing exactly what I figured," J.B. whispered. "We'll wait for them to get to the target wagon, then spring the trap." They'd positioned scavvies in two overturned or damaged wagons near the targeted one, so when the kidnappers came, they could be swarmed from two or three directions at once.

The next few minutes were spent in an agony of waiting. The invaders were still cautious, still taking their time approaching the site. Jak flexed his fingers, itching to get out there and clobber some heads. Even with the... exercise he'd gotten earlier that afternoon, he found himself raring to get back into the action, wanting to take out these bastards before they hurt Tully or anyone else here once and for all.

He shook his head, trying to banish his memories of her and him together at the spring. It wasn't easy, however. Even while keeping an eye on the infiltrators, his mind kept filling with pictures of her glorious, nude body above him as they—

"Jak, where are they?"

Jolted back to reality, he refocused to see the advance scouts just reaching the wagon. "At outer wagon. They split up, three-person teams going to each one."

"Dark night! Well, that can't be helped. Least we figured that'd happen. Outer groups are going to be on their own until we can reinforce them. All right, everyone, this is it." J.B. reached up and thumped the wagon bottom twice. Two soft thuds answered him. "Let's do it."

Jak crawled out from under the wagon, rose to his feet and began creeping up on the three-person group clustered around the wagon about fifteen yards away. For all their caution on the approach, the kidnappers were fairly lax on their security detail as they cleared the interior. The one posted as the exterior guard was looking the other way and failed to see Jak using the wagon as cover as he ran at him.

When he was a couple of yards away, the albino

leaped into the air, leading with his right foot. The flying kick slammed into the guard's face as he was turning, apparently alerted by some sort of sound Jak had made. It didn't help him, though. The shot crushed his cheekbone and dislocated his jaw. The impact also sent him staggering away from the wagon to fall to the ground. It didn't, however, knock him out. The man rolled over, got back to his feet and started coming after Jak, his swelling jaw hanging grotesquely to one side.

"Damn fuckers not want stay down!" Jak snarled as he stepped forward to meet his opponent. He heard a grunt and sounds of a struggle from the wagon, along with shouts and curses from the other wagons where the kidnappers were encountering heavier than expected resistance.

Jak didn't know if the guy he was taking on was part of the collective or not, but at this point he also didn't care. His main objective was to incapacitate the man without causing too much permanent damage so he could go help the others. With that in mind, as soon as his opponent got in range, Jak squatted and lashed out with his left foot, attempting to sweep the guy off his feet.

Once again, he was thwarted by the man's speed and preternatural agility. He leaped forward, avoiding Jak's leg sweep completely and coming down on top of him. Jak threw himself out of the way, barely avoiding the man's knee as it hit the dirt where he'd been just a moment ago. Jak leaped back up, knuckles stiffened as he brought his fist down in a ram's-head punch to the back of the man's neck. He'd pulled it enough to avoid killing the man, but the blow should have put him out like a light.

The shot staggered him, but the man still didn't go down. Gritting his teeth, Jak brought his fist down again, this time making his enemy collapse into the dirt and lie there, unmoving. Looking up, Jak saw J.B. taking on two of the invaders. As he stepped over his unconscious foe to help, he felt a hand grab his ankle. Without looking back, Jak whipped the heel of his free foot into the man's face. The hand slackened, and he pulled his foot free and ran toward the three fighting men.

As he approached, Jak had to admit that the bug armor seemed to be doing a pretty good job. J.B. brought his forearm down on one guy's head, clobbering him hard, and sending him stumbling away. The other man came after him with the butt of his blaster raised to knock the Armorer out, but he got an arm up to block the weapon, taking the blow on his arm with no difficulty.

Jak came up behind the blaster wielder as he raised his Beretta again and jumped up to grab it from his hand. At the same time, he brought his legs up around the man's neck in a scissors hold and fell back to the ground, snapping the man down onto the ground with him.

The man reached up with both hands and levered Jak's legs off his head. The albino pulled away before he could keep his grip on them, kicking back and somersaulting to his feet. No sooner had he raised his head than he saw the man charging toward him, swinging a fist toward his face.

Jak met it with the butt of the blaster, feeling the guy's knuckles crack under the impact. He shoved the man's hand down and stepped inside his range, bringing up the weapon again and smashing it into the man's face, snapping his head back. He felt the man's remaining good hand scrabbling at his jacket, and kept hammering the man's face, pulping his nose and fracturing at least one bone in his forehead and another in his cheek. But still his opponent stayed upright.

Jak slipped free of his other hand, seeing blood spray from where the man had cut himself on the metal shards sewn into his jacket, and ducked under his armpit to come up behind him. Before the guy could turn, Jak jumped up and planted his feet on the adversary's hips. Then he snaked one arm around his man's throat and squeezed, using his biceps and forearm to compress both sides of the neck—and the carotid artery and jugular veins found there, cutting off the blood flow to and from the brain.

The man reached back to try to dislodge him but couldn't get enough leverage. He then fell backward, trying to crush Jak, but he maintained his stranglehold despite taking the guy's full weight on his hips. His opponent tried to get up to body slam him again, but was already too weak to rise. Jak kept the hold going until the man collapsed on top of him. He gave it another three count to ensure the guy would stay down, then shoved him off.

Jak got up gingerly, testing his hips to make sure he hadn't strained or dislocated anything. He looked around to see bug-armored scavvies everywhere holding their own as they fought off their attackers. While it usually took two of the collective to take on one kidnapper, they were still beating back this latest assault.

J.B. was standing over his assailant, who was also now prone on the ground. Spotting Jak nearby, he waved him over. "Come on—we're not done yet!"

Jak ran over to him and the two were about to head to the next wagon when the roar of several engines drowned out the shouts and curses of the fighters nearby. A second later, spotlights burst to life from the south.

The bright lights illuminated the area around J.B. and Jak as three of the six-wheeled trucks roared toward them and skidded to a stop. In the back of the vehicles, two men holding M4s steadied them on the cab as they aimed them at the two men. Another leaned out of the passenger window, also holding a carbine, and pointed it at them. The two other trucks were outfitted in the same manner, and within ten seconds, J.B., Jak and the other members of the collective were facing the muzzles of nine assault rifles.

"People of the Silvertide collective, you are ordered to surrender immediately, or we will be forced to open fire!" The voice that boomed over the loudspeaker sounded familiar. "You have ten seconds to comply!"

All through the camp, fighting men and women looked up at the voice. When they saw the overwhelming force arrayed against them, they looked at J.B., who shook his head while pulling his hands from his pockets and raising his clenched fists over his head.

"Stop! It's over," he shouted.

"Not serious," Jak muttered as he raised his own hands.

"For the moment, yeah, I am," the Armorer muttered back. "But stay ready."

"Always." Jak flexed his wrists, making the hilts of two taped throwing knives creep up to where they could both be grabbed and thrown in an instant.

"Lay down your weapons, put up your hands and come together to the sound of my voice," the speaker continued.

"Can't let that happen," J.B. said. "If they get us all together, we're sunk."

The driver's door of the main truck opened and a tall man stepped out into the light. When they saw him, both J.B.'s and Jak's jaws dropped.

The newest leader of the kidnappers was Ryan Cawdor.

Chapter Twenty-Nine

When Mildred was returned back to her room, she staggered to the toilet just in time as the vomit coursed back up her throat and out onto the porcelain. She crouched there, choking and coughing, until she was fairly certain nothing more was going to come up.

Watching as the parasitic slug had oozed its way toward Ryan's open mouth while he sat helpless before it had been one of the most horrifying things she had ever witnessed. When the creature began sliding down his throat, she had let out a howl of rage and despair. Her knees weakened, and she would have collapsed if Morgan had not been holding her up.

"He is partaking in one of the highest honors a person can receive from the Mind," he said. "Usually, a new member receives a new symbiote. The Mind thinks very highly of Ryan to send an experienced one into him for the first time. And you…" His flat, emotionless gaze turned to her. "You truly have no idea of the honor that is to be bestowed upon you—to be the host for our next queen. You will carry our colony into new lands to bring them into our fold. Long have we worked and planned to bring this to fruition, and now the time is at hand."

All the while Morgan had been talking, Mildred couldn't take her eyes off Ryan's bulging throat as the slug entered his body. In a few more seconds, his neck shrank back down to its normal size, and his head slumped forward.

"Assuming the dose was calculated properly, it should be able to gain control of him fairly soon," Dr. Markus said.

"Of course it was calculated properly," Dr. Phieks replied with a hint of disdain. "I have been doing this for the past nine years. During that time, I have not erred once."

Markus turned to her with a mildly confused look on his face. "I was not calling your competence into question, Doctor, merely remarking that Mr. Cawdor's body may react differently to both the drug itself, and how the symbiote takes control of him, that is all."

She nodded. "My apologies for leaping to an erroneous conclusion, Doctor."

Mildred had watched this byplay with a frown. Was that a real disagreement, or were they simply going through the motions? If this was truly a hive mind, there should be no disagreement or dissonance, yet she was pretty sure that was what she's just seen.

Her train of thought was broken by Ryan's head snapping up and him rising to his feet. His head and limbs moved around jerkily, as if controlled by an unseen puppet master. Mildred had to stifle a crazed giggle at the thought, since that was exactly what was happening. And they want to put one of those—slimy—*things*—down my throat? Hell, no. I'll off myself before that happens.

Still, she held out some small ray of hope that Ryan would somehow be able to fight off the parasite's control. Mentally, he was one of the strongest people she had never met, and if anyone could do it, he could. As she watched, she thought there might be a chance of that happening. Come on, Ryan, fight it.... You can do it....

Ryan raised his hands and looked at them as if he had never seen them before, staring at the suntanned fingers, the callused palms, the nicked and battered nails. He flexed them, and somehow Mildred knew exactly what was going on. Her theory was confirmed when he raised his head and addressed the Mind.

"It..." Ryan croaked, then cleared his throat and tried again. "It is a good body—a very good body. Thank you for placing me in it, Mind."

"I AM PLEASED THAT YOU ARE PLEASED," the Mind replied. *"FOR I HAVE AN IMPORTANT TASK FOR YOU TO CARRY OUT."*

Ryan bowed his head. "I am yours to command, Mind."

"YOU ARE TO TAKE WHATEVER SECURITY FORCES THAT YOU NEED AND GO TO THE ENCAMPMENT WHERE YOUR BODY WAS TAKEN, AND BRING AS MANY OF THEM TO ME AS POSSIBLE. THEY WILL ALL BE BROUGHT INTO THE FOLD."

"As the Mind commands," Ryan, Morgan and the two doctors intoned. He turned and strode by Mildred without even a glance in her direction. Mildred's heart sank when she saw that.

"There is much to do. I'll take you back to your cell," Morgan said as he held her elbow and ushered her toward the elevator.

"Why?" she replied dully. "Isn't your overlord going to shove a queen slug down my throat now?"

"The Mind will bring you into the fold when it chooses, not before," Morgan replied. "Until then, you shall wait. Do not worry, you shall be well cared for."

Of course I will be. Sacrificial offerings usually are, she thought during the trip back to her room. Once there, she had embraced the toilet, and now sat on the floor, her mind churning as she tried to figure out what to do.

Well, I could simply not give them the option of using me by killing myself, she thought coldly. Although there weren't a lot of options in the room to harm herself with, Mildred was pretty sure she could figure out something before they came to get her for the joining.

But what will that really solve? she wondered. If Ryan's now under their control—and it sure looked as if he was—and he's going to take more of the collective, no doubt they'll find someone else who will host their queen, and I'll just have delayed the inevitable, and be dead to boot. That won't do. Indeed, the very thought made her angry. Where there's life, there's hope. Looks as if I'm going to have to figure out a way to take these things out.

Mildred got up and stepped to the sink, rinsing out her mouth and splashing cool water on her face. She stared at her scared, jumpy self in the mirror, then reached out to tap the glass, but found her fingers touching polished metal. Damn, that could have been useful.

Feeling a little better, she walked back out to her bed and sat down, reviewing everything she knew. One question kept popping up in her mind: What is the big brain waiting for? Why didn't it throw a slug into me right away?

Because it couldn't, the analytical part of her mind answered. Mildred continued with this question-and-answer process, which often served her well in problem solving. Why not?

Because a queen slug is not available for you right now, her mind answered.

But shouldn't there be one?

Yes…unless one was already created, but it was used on someone else.

Right…. Mildred filed that piece of analysis away. It seemed important somehow, but not at the moment. The analytical part of Mildred's mind waited patiently for her to catch up. It has to make another one.

Exactly…which buys you some time.

Mildred nodded. Now…what to do with it? She rose and walked around the room. If I could get out of here, I could try to stop the Overbrain, she thought. Crossing to the door, she looked out the wire-gridded window into the hallway.

Sure—all that entails is getting out of your room somehow, finding some way to kill that big brain in a jar, getting the needed materials and bringing them to the thing to kill it. Oh, and all while trying to get past everyone in here, all of whom have a slug inside them that lets them talk to everyone else all the time—

Wait a minute…. Something about that was important. If they can talk to each other or somehow communicate among themselves, then I'd probably get caught as soon as one saw me, since they wouldn't "sense" me as part of the group mind. But that also means if I can somehow get out of here but remain undetected, I'd effectively be invisible to them, since they probably rely too much on their slug sense, as it were, and are so connected to each other that a non-slug-controlled mind would probably have a better chance of getting around them undetected…. It's crazy, but it just might work.

And let's face it, what other choice do you have? the other part of her brain chimed in.

"None, that's for damn sure," Mildred muttered as she paced back and forth. "One problem at a time. First up, how in the hell am I going to get out of this room?"

She began walking around the perimeter while creating, evaluating and discarding potential escape plans. Because she wasn't sure whether she was being monitored or not, she kept quiet as she thought through the various scenarios.

The only problem was, every one she came up with turned out to be unfeasible for one reason or another.

Stop up the toilet and knock out or kill whoever came to repair it? Not likely that they would be alone, since she was a high-ranking prisoner, so there would be guards accompanying the repair person. Armed guards. Mildred was decent in a fight, but she was no trained chiller like Ryan or Jak. That wouldn't work.

Break out through the door? Well, since the window was unbreakable, and there was no access to the lock mechanism on this side—only a polished steel plate where the knob should have been—and the hinges were on the outside as well, that was also impossible.

Crawl out through the air ducts? For a moment, she gave that one some thought, since the one in her room did look large enough, and unlike in most normal buildings, actually seemed sturdy enough to support her weight. However, the grille that sealed it off was firmly bolted to the wall, and the wire latticework was thick enough that she couldn't break it. There was also nothing in here or on her that she could use as an improvised file, either, so scratch that.

What about faking some sort of injury or illness so

you can at least get out of the room, and then maybe you can do more from there? Mildred didn't pause as she considered the idea. Sure, it was a movie cliché back in her day, but these folks had probably never even considered that someone would actually feign an illness in order to go to the infirmary.

The more she thought about it, Mildred realized that could be her way out. After all, getting into the infirmary would potentially give her access to drugs, scalpels, practically anything she could need to execute the rest of her plan.

There was just one problem with this first part—as she recalled her conversation with Ricky after he'd almost been kidnapped, she remembered him telling her that they could apparently tell when a person was lying with a fair degree of accuracy. Therefore, she couldn't simply pretend to be sick…she actually had to make herself sick enough to warrant transfer to their infirmary, but not sick enough to incapacitate herself.

Again, Mildred scanned the room. They'd left her nothing to clean herself with, and the drinking cup was made of a soft plastic that, while it probably wouldn't cut up her insides, might bind in her intestines, which would be the last thing she'd want to happen to her. She supposed she could drink too much water until she poisoned herself that way, but it carried its own risks, as well.

She was so deep in thought that she didn't hear the door open, or Morgan step inside. "Mildred…Mildred?"

Blinking, she looked up at him. "Oh…Morgan. I'm sorry, I didn't hear you come in."

"That is quite all right." He had a small bundle under his arm. "It occurred to us that since you will be staying with us for a while, we thought you might wish to clean yourself. Our shower facilities are sanitary and comfortable. A good shower would probably help you adjust to your situation."

A glimmer of hope sparked in Mildred's mind. "Thank you, Morgan. I would like that very much."

"If you'll come with me, then." He turned and walked out the doorway. Mildred followed, seeing the ubiquitous pair of guards flanking the exit. She didn't even glance behind her as one of them fell into step in back of her as she trailed Morgan through the halls to the other side of what she now assumed was a detention or security level.

He stopped at a white door with the universal symbols for *man* and *woman* on it and held out the bundle to her. "You'll find everything you need either in here or inside. Just let the guard know when you're finished, and he'll escort you back to your room."

"Thank you, Morgan. I must confess that I'm looking forward to this."

"I know you are." He started to turn away, but stopped. "I do hope you will come around to our way of thinking, Mildred. It really is for the best—no violence, no fear, no lust for conquest or power. We have the chance to usher in a whole new age of peace and enlightenment—if we can just set down the right roots. You could help be a part of that process. A hero to future generations, who could grow up in safety and comfort, instead of terror and fear."

"It—it sounds very attractive, Morgan." And indeed, she wasn't lying; it did sound appealing. But at what cost? her analytical mind asked. Only your very individuality...your soul, if you will, that's all.... "I'm... going to think long and hard about it."

"Good. That's all we can ask for after all," he replied. "Enjoy your shower."

"I will."

And when she stepped inside and saw the gleaming tile walls and floor, and the bright chrome nozzle—and what she would be using to clean herself with—Mildred allowed a broad smile to spread across her face.

The last bit of the first part of her plan had fallen into place, and it had just been unwittingly provided by her captors.

Chapter Thirty

J.B. shook off his surprise in a heartbeat. "There are going to be some casualties," he muttered. "When I move, do *not* run toward the truck."

Jak merely nodded as Ryan waved them both forward. "All right, John, Jak, walk toward me, and don't try anything—"

Even as he said it, J.B. armed the two mini-grens he had palmed in his hand. He let them cook off for a critical second before tossing both at the truck, one underhanded so it skittered beneath the vehicle, and the other one overhanded so it would go off above the two shooters.

The instant he started his two throws, Jak had crossed his arms enough to draw both throwing knives from his sleeves and hurl them at the heads of the two riflemen pointing their assault rifles at them. He didn't plan on hitting them; he only wanted to distract them enough to spoil their aim for that critical second so J.B. could get his munitions off.

When both of them had emptied their arsenals, they dived to the side, J.B. to the right, Jak to the left, each hitting the dirt as the two grens detonated. J.B. had grabbed his Mini-Uzi as he went down, and aimed a burst at the truck on his right, while Jak had drawn his Colt Python and was blasting at the truck on the left.

The bomb under the truck was the high-ex gren. J.B. had pitched it just close enough so that it exploded underneath the front end, blowing out both tires and disabling the engine. The blast wasn't quite enough to flip the truck over or make it explode in a fireball, but it did raise the front end a couple feet off the ground— incidentally lifting the two shooters into the blast radius of the second gren.

As Jak had figured, each man had been able to dodge his blades. The implo gren, however, was another matter entirely. J.B. suspected that the whitecoats had somehow figured out how to stabilize a gram or two of antimatter until the initial blast exposed it to the outside air, setting off the reaction. Not even Doc knew how they worked; just that they operated in exactly the opposite way a normal gren did. When they went off, they created a localized area of extremely high, inverted pressure that drew everything in the blast radius toward the center of it.

When the truck fell back onto its shattered front axle, what looked like two lumps of stretched and pulverized meat came back down with it. From their waists down, they still looked relatively normal. But the upper half of each sec man's body now looked as if it had been pressed through some kind of giant machine that had both crushed and stretched their heads, arms and chests to incredibly painful proportions. Their carbines had been pulled and fused with them as well, so that they clutched misshapen lumps of plastic and metal in their crushed and flattened fingers. The only relatively good thing about getting killed that way was that the shock was probably so great that they'd never known what happened to them—just an enormous feeling of pressure, and then blackness.

As he rolled toward the now-disabled truck, Jak sure hoped the damn parasites inside those two were dead, as well. Blasterfire from elsewhere in the camp was keeping the two riflemen on his left busy, and Jak gave them something else to think about as he blasted away at their vehicle.

But as he stood, using the passenger door of the wrecked vehicle as cover, it suddenly flew open, shoving him to the ground. Jak rolled over to see Ryan step out and walk toward him. He aimed his blaster at his friend, but Ryan lashed out with a combat boot and kicked the weapon out of his hand. He brought his own SIG Sauer down toward Jak's head, but the albino evened the score and kicked up with his leg, popping the semiauto blaster out of Ryan's hand to fly off into the darkness.

Jak didn't let the one-eyed man get closer, but rolled away far enough so he could get to his feet, fists raised. "Not want fight, Ryan."

Ryan held out his hands. "You don't have to, Jak. Just surrender and join us. It's unlike anything you could ever imagine."

"Fuck, no!" Jak replied. "Ain't no one shoving slug down throat. No way, no how."

"Then you leave me no choice, Jak." Ryan started advancing toward him. "Your recovery is one of my highest priorities for the Mind, and I am going to accomplish it."

"Can try." Jak bounced on the balls of his feet. "Not succeed."

"I think you might be surprised at what I can do now," Ryan said.

"Last chance, Ryan. Still time walk away," Jak said as he studied the man he'd traveled with and fought with across the Deathlands and beyond for years. They had come close to facing off with each other before, but each time there had always been a way out. Now, however, it seemed this time might very well end with one of them lying on his back staring at the night sky.

Usually Jak counted on getting the first shot in, especially with someone who didn't know just how fast he was. This time, however, he faced someone who knew how he fought, knew many of his tricks and probably how best to counter them. Jak would not only have to be fast, he'd also have to be sneaky if he was going to win.

Instead of going on the offensive as he usually did, he stayed balanced on the balls of his feet, hands loosely curled, ready to strike or deflect, and let Ryan come to him.

A spotlight lit up the both of them, and a voice called out from the side. "Sir, we can take the teenager now."

"Negative." Ryan shook his head. "I have been looking through this one's thoughts and memories. I know that he has wondered how a fight between him and the white-haired one would turn out. I also want to know. None of you shall interfere with this, except on my order."

"Yes, sir." The light from the truck stayed on the two of them, and Jak circled so that it shone in Ryan's face. The older man smiled as he circled to the side.

"Good start, Jak. I was going to try the same thing—" While he spoke, he lunged forward, faster than Jak had ever seen him move. He leaned back as Ryan's fist flew by his face, then slapped it aside while he moved in with a punch aimed at the other man's ribs.

But Ryan redirected his incoming arm down and swept Jak's fist aside just enough so that he only grazed his side. The albino danced away before Ryan could make a grab for him. "Lucky, that time," he said.

Ryan shook his head. "I know your moves. I can see them before you make them, every twitch of your muscles, every glance of your eyes. It's only a matter of time before you are defeated. There's no need to play this out. Why don't you make it easy on yourself and stop now?"

"We'll see 'bout that," Jak said. "Thing inside said you wanted to know. Let's find out." The truth was that a dark part of him wanted to know as well, wanted to know which one of them was the better fighter. That was why he hadn't used one of his throwing blades to injure Ryan, maybe slow him down. He'd considered it, but had dismissed the idea, as a part of him thought it would be cheating.

But after the first skirmish, Ryan also seemed content to hang back and wait for him to commit. The two fighters circled each other warily, each looking for the slightest opening. Jak deliberately exposed his left side a couple of times, trying to draw Ryan in, but the other man didn't take the bait. It was time for Jak to go after Ryan's one weakness. He just had to set it up....

When he judged the time was right, Jak moved in, his fists blurring in a series of feints and distracting blows. He managed to draw Ryan's guard off for a fraction of a second, and aimed a shot just below his right eye, figuring if he could swell it shut, he'd have a better chance of taking him down.

This time Ryan grabbed his wrist and pulled him off balance. Jak quickly twisted free and came back at him again, but now Ryan was ready and blocked his strike. However, Jak had expected that to happen, and brought up his leg in a lightning-fast kick to Ryan's gut. The blow sent the older man back a few steps while Jak watched him recover.

"Not see that coming, did ya?"

Ryan straightened and smiled. "Very good. Now let's see you keep that up." He strode forward, straight at Jak, who set his stance and waited for the bigger man to come to him. When he was a step away, Jak crouched and planted his hands on the dirt as if to leg sweep him, but instead launched a foot up toward Ryan's face.

The one-eyed man grabbed the boot before it could impact and pulled Jak up off the ground. However, as he did, Jak arched up and threw a handful of dirt into Ryan's face. Blinded, Ryan still had the presence of mind to throw Jak across the field toward the nearest truck. Helplessly flying through the air, Jak twisted in an attempt to break his fall, but landed with his leg taking most of the impact. It didn't break, but he felt a sharp pain in his ankle as he fell to the ground and knew he'd probably sprained it if he was lucky.

Gritting his teeth, he got to his feet and tried putting his weight on it, grimacing at the spike of pain that shot through his foot and leg. He could hobble forward, but his mobility was severely reduced. His gambit had almost paid off, but it had also cost him dearly.

Ryan stood wiping the dirt from his eye and blinking in an attempt to clear his vision. Knowing he wouldn't have a better chance than now, Jak realized he'd have to use whatever means necessary to end this. He drew a throwing blade as he hobbled toward Ryan and threw it at the man, intending to distract him with the blade long enough for him to try to get a roundhouse kick off to his head.

The knife spun away from his hand and Jak quickened his pace. Steeling himself for the flare of pain he knew was coming, he put his weight on his sprained foot the moment he was within range and leaped up, lashing out with his good leg at the height of his jump, the spinning kick intended to crash into his opponent's face hard enough to knock him to the ground and put him down for the count.

But even with his lone eye red and weeping, Ryan was able to dodge the thrown knife. He then brought up an angled forearm to deflect the kick, sending Jak's leg up and over his head. Unable to stop now, Jak felt the big man's hands on him, and he was pulled to the ground, crashing into the earth with an impact that stole his breath and left him gasping. Before he knew it, he was flipped over on his stomach, and Ryan had pinned his arms behind his back, tying them together with a plastic cord.

"You fought well, Jak, but this was the only way it would turn out," Ryan said as he hauled the albino to his feet. "Now you've got a meeting with the Mind—"

"Let him go, Ryan." The familiar voice came from their left and made Ryan reflexively turn toward the speaker. It was enough of a distraction for Jak to whip his head back hard into Ryan's jaw, stunning him just enough for him to twist free and run.

"Stop, Jak!" Ryan shouted. He took a step after the fleeing youth, but a single blaster shot kicked up dirt at his feet, making him skid to a halt.

"Stay where you are, Ryan." Krysty emerged from the darkness, her blaster trained on him. "Don't take another step."

"Unidentified woman, put your weapon down—"

one of the riflemen in the truck started to say even as he heard a *click* from behind him.

"Got them, J.B.?" she asked.

"Yeah," the Armorer answered from the rear of the truck. He stood with Tully and Ricky, their three carbines aimed at the two men in the truck bed. "They're covered. I'll take those longblasters, boys, slow and easy."

Ryan had turned to face the red-haired woman. "Krysty Wroth. You are also on our list to acquire." He frowned. "I know that you have feelings for this man, yet you are pointing a weapon at him, and your body language indicates that you intend to harm him. This does not make sense."

Krysty's voice was low, but the blaster in her hands was rock steady as she approached him. "I don't know what you are, but there's a hell of a lot you don't understand about us humans. I know the man you think you're a part of now, and I can tell you that although you think you have access to his memories, and his mind, you cannot possibly know how he thinks, how he *feels*."

She paused for a moment. "But I do. And I know that he would rather die than be forced to live under someone else's control."

"You would actually kill the one you love instead of trying to save him?" Ryan asked.

"If I had no other choice," she answered. "Yes, I would, because I know he would do the same for me. However, I'll give you the same option you gave Jak a moment ago. Surrender to us, and I promise I'll do what I can to have you removed from his body."

A low, sibilant chuckle hissed from Ryan's lips. "A noble gesture, Krysty Wroth, even if it is akin to a monkey telling a human that it will take care of him. You, however, have no idea of what you're talking about. But it also doesn't matter. You see, I've grown rather fond of this body, and I have no plans to give it up anytime soon!"

More lights stabbed out of the darkness, followed by the roar of another truck as it charged straight toward Krysty from behind her. She whirled, getting off two shots that starred the windshield before diving out of the way.

The truck kept going, slowing just enough for Ryan to throw himself into the back as it accelerated into the darkness. The other sec men seized the distraction as well, and jumped into their vehicle and sped away. J.B. and Tully fired several rounds at it, but it kept moving until it was out of sight.

"You okay?" J.B. asked Krysty as she limped up to him.

She nodded. "Banged my knee when I hit the ground, but I'll be all right." She looked around in the darkness. "Jak, where are you?"

"Here…" Covered in dust, the albino hopped toward them from the dark, his hands still tied behind his back. "Tryin' avoid gettin' run over."

J.B. pulled his knife and freed Jak's hands with a single swipe of the blade.

"Not seen anything like that before," Jak said as he rubbed life into his swollen hands. "You really pull?"

Krysty's face was expressionless as she stared back at him. "What do you think?"

Without waiting for an answer, she turned to J.B. "Where's our truck?"

"I sent Ricky off to fetch it the moment theirs came

at you," J.B. said as another pair of lights drove toward them. "And here it is now."

"Good," Krysty said as Ricky stopped beside her so she could get in. "Let's go after those bastards and get Ryan and Mildred back."

Chapter Thirty-One

Mildred lay on her soft, comfortable bed in the infirmary, a cool pillow under her head, crisp white sheets over her body, and looked around the room.

The very empty room.

That more or less went how I'd planned, she thought as she raised a glass of water to her lips. But I don't think I'm ever going to get this taste out of my mouth.

Everything had come together the moment she'd stepped into the bathing room. First, of course, she took a long, hot, luxurious shower, cleaning every inch of herself. After turning off the hot water, she turned to the liquid soap dispenser and pumped another generous portion into her hand.

Damn, they must have a lot of this stored somewhere, to last this long. She sniffed at it, wrinkling her nose as the acrid, vaguely floral scent filled her nostrils. It should be nontoxic, but I guess they'll still save me whether it is or isn't. With a gulp, she began licking it off her palm, swallowing the handful while trying not to gag, then going back for more. She ate that as well, then decided to stop, rinsing her hand and mouth while trying not to belch up soap in the process. It had been hard enough getting it down, and she was pretty sure if she got the scent of it coming up into the back of her throat, she'd vomit it all right back out again on the spot.

Now, to get back to my room. She could already feel her previously empty stomach starting to complain from the indigestible liquid she had forced down. *Oh, I hope it doesn't come out the back way....* Forcing herself to stand up straight, she dressed quickly and walked back outside, where the guard escorted her back to her cell. She was relieved that Morgan hadn't waited to take her back himself. Somehow she thought he might see through her ruse.

Mildred had barely gotten inside when the first stomach cramp hit. Gritting her teeth, she made it to her bed, but then launched herself toward the toilet, barely making it in time before a rush of sour bile and slimy soap coursed back up her throat and out into the bowl.

The next few minutes were nothing but pure agony. Every time she brought up more of the bitter, soapy goo, she'd think that would be the last one, until another lurch of her stomach made her pray to the porcelain god yet again. By the fifth time, Mildred knew she would have been much happier if she had gotten diarrhea instead. *At least...that wouldn't feel...as if I was spitting up acid.* The liquid soap, so smooth going down, had reacted with the digestive juices in her stomach and now burned her throat and tongue coming back up. Not to mention the nausea made her double over in agony, retching until she was spitting up nothing but foamy bile.

Shuddering from the racking convulsions that had accompanied her purge, Mildred got a hand onto the sink and hauled herself up to get a glimpse of her face in the mirror. *Well, I was clean when I came in....*

Now she was a sweaty, bedraggled mess. Foam and saliva coated her lips and had trailed down onto her white T-shirt. She seemed pale, and her skin was clammy from the shock to her system. The vomiting had hit her so hard she almost couldn't think straight, but she did make sure to flush the toilet twice to destroy the evidence of her self-sabotage.

Better…get to the…door, before I pass out…. Leaning against the wall, she stumbled from the bathroom. Step by slow, measured step, she trudged around the room's perimeter to the outer door and thumped on the glass window with a hand that felt as if it weighed twenty pounds. After what seemed like minutes but was probably only a few seconds, a guard's face looked in at her, immediately blanching at her appearance.

"I'm…sick…." Mildred said even as her legs gave out, and she slid to the floor. The next few minutes passed in a blur. She was dimly aware of some sort of alarm going off, and several very concerned-looking people clustering around her. Then she got the sensation of floating and being wheeled through hallways watching lights pass overhead. She felt the pricks of needles being inserted into veins, and her eyelids were thumbed back as lights were shone into them. She felt the cool, soothing rush of saline hitting her system as they worked to replenish her lost fluids.

Mildred played her part of the ill patient for as long as she thought it prudent, coming in and out of consciousness for a couple of hours, and even faking a stomach cramp or two to make sure they took her case seriously enough to keep her in the infirmary for observation for the next twenty-four hours or so.

Which, for all intents and purposes, they were.

The doctors and nurses had been kind, patient and caring. Mildred had heard the term "QC1" used in reference to her, which she assumed meant that she was a "queen candidate," if her logic was correct. Once that info had gotten around, they had treated her as if she were made of spun glass. Taking every precaution and then some. She was just glad they didn't decide to go for the colonoscopy; the enema had been cleansing enough. Aware that it was standard procedure in some poisoning cases, she had submitted to it, even when it was the last thing she had wanted.

And now that she was awake and alert, Mildred realized that she was the only patient in the twenty-bed hall. With that knowledge came the understanding as to the second reason the infirmary staff had been so good, which made her feel a small stab of pity for them. Poor guys—they're highly trained doctors and nurses, but they have nothing to do all day....

And why would they, when everyone already had their own personal body caretaker installed inside them? Mildred didn't even see any evidence of the wounded from the flood being cared for here, and she knew that some of them had to have been injured in either the fighting or the deluge afterward. Or had they all been killed in it?

It didn't really matter to her either way, as she had larger issues to contend with. Like Morgan.

He had come to her bedside about a minute after she was admitted to the infirmary—he was the one who had said she was a "QC1," in fact. Mildred knew he'd remained close by during her examination and treatment, and she was concerned that he was going to come over at any moment and expose her charade. That was the second-biggest reason why she had feigned being ill for so long, to keep him worried that their "queen candidate" might not make it, instead of concentrating on what might have caused her condition.

Finally, however, she felt as if enough time had passed so that she could come out of it, although she still pretended—partly—to be weak and woozy. She needed time to figure out the rest of her plan, and then the time and space to execute it.

She rested for much of the afternoon, thinking and dozing, dozing and thinking. When she opened her eyes, she saw Morgan sitting in a chair next to her bed. Mildred started, raising her head off the pillow as she put a hand on her chest and sucked in a breath. Careful there, Hattie McDaniel…don't overdo it.

"I'm sorry, I didn't mean to startle you," Morgan said. "Dr. Markus said you were recovering nicely and resting, and I thought I would simply sit and wait until you woke up."

"That's…quite all right, Morgan. I just…didn't expect to see anyone sitting right there when I woke up."

He nodded. "How are you feeling?"

"Better…but I'm awfully weak…. Feel like I was just out marching through the desert with no water for days." Mildred licked her lips before asking the next question. "Do they know what happened to me?"

A faint line appeared on Morgan's forehead. "The preliminary tests show that you had ingested some sort of poison. They're still trying to analyze samples to find out what type. This is going to sound like a very odd question, but…you haven't knowingly taken anything poisonous, have you?"

Mildred had heard that the best way to defeat a lie detector test was to think of a question that corresponded correctly to the answer that you wanted to give, especially if that answer was a lie to the question asked by the interrogator. So she just kept thinking the soap was nontoxic, the soap was nontoxic while she looked at him and shook her head. "Not that I'm aware of."

A brief smile flitted across his mouth but didn't come close to his eyes. "Of course not. Forget I asked."

"Well, now that you mention it…" In for a penny, in for a pound. "The day you folks caught me, we ate some of the scavvies' food, and to be honest, I thought that some of the meat didn't taste quite right. It's possible I got a case of food poisoning. I mean, I did throw up earlier, right after we visited the Mind. Does that help any?"

"Perhaps. I'll mention it to the doctor." He hesitated a moment, then seemed to come to some sort of internal decision. "Have you thought any more about our conversation outside the bathing room?"

Mildred tried not to smile. This was ground she could cover with him. "I have, and I do have some questions about it."

He leaned forward slightly. "Of course. I'll answer whatever I can. If there are more complicated ones, you may have to speak to the Mind directly."

"I just have a few fairly simple ones right now," she replied. "Although it doesn't look comfortable, I assume it doesn't hurt very much…as it goes down?"

Morgan's answering smile was real this time. "I can tell you it is a bit uncomfortable at first, kind of like you're choking on a huge bite of squishy meat, but once it's past the esophagus, you hardly notice it's there."

Mildred nodded. "That was the other thing that confused me. A symbiote enters its host through the mouth, I got that. But surely they don't reside in the stomach or intestine, right?"

Morgan actually laughed at that. "I think you're the very first person who ever asked about that. You're correct. Once the symbiote is in the stomach, it creates a slit—healing the cut after it goes out, of course—and exits to settle into the body. Typically they flatten out and align along the spine. It's the easiest place to access the nervous system. Once they're settled, you don't even know that they're there."

Of course not, because they're already influencing your every thought—or taking over control entirely. "Thank you, Morgan, that is very helpful. I'll probably have some more questions later, but I'm still pretty tired and would like to rest now."

"Yes, please do," Morgan replied. "We'll talk again after you've recovered a bit more. I look forward to it."

"Me, too." Mildred leaned her head back against her pillow, the implied message clear. Morgan nodded and rose from his chair, taking it back to the nurses' station before leaving the room.

Mildred closed her eyes until they were mere slits. The rest of her plan relied on stealth, timing and more than a bit of luck. She had only one more major problem to overcome—how to get to the brain without being detected on the way?

As she stared at the ceiling, thinking and thinking, she noticed the nozzle of what looked like a water sprinkler above her head. Mildred opened her eyes wide and looked over to see two more in the room, making her smile.

I couldn't have asked for a better solution to the problem....

Chapter Thirty-Two

Ricky shoved the truck's throttle forward, making the vehicle shoot across the desert floor.

"Faster, Ricky!" Jak shouted, holding an M4 with one hand and on to the roll bar with the other.

"Not so fast that you get us killed!" J.B. shouted right after him. He'd slung his longblaster over his shoulder and was holding on to the safety bar with both hands, flexing his knees to absorb the jouncing as the truck rattled over the desert hardpan. "You might as well sling that." He nodded at Jak's rifle. "No way you'll get a shot off bouncing around like this."

"Mebbe—" Jak started to reply as J.B. saw the lights of the truck they were pursuing bounce crazily for a moment.

"What was that, Ricky?" he shouted into the cab's open sliding back window.

"I don't know. Hang on!" he shouted as he slammed the throttle ahead to its farthest point.

J.B. only had time to see the gully appear in front of them before the truck raced off the edge, falling through the air to crash onto the ground with a bone-rattling impact. J.B. barely had time to brace himself, but he managed to stay upright even as something smacked painfully into his ankle. But even with his phenomenal reflexes, Jak had been caught off guard and was nearly thrown out of the truck bed. He hung on to the roll bar with one hand, dangling above the blurring prairie and scrub brush as it passed under his feet.

"Hold on, Jak!" J.B. worked his way over, but before he could grab him, the truck suddenly slewed hard to the left, making him almost fall over. The direction change shoved Jak against the side of the truck as Ricky almost sideswiped the rock wall. But before he could push off it to scramble back inside, Ricky gunned the electric motor, and they took off again.

"Take my hand!" J.B. reached out with his left while keeping a death grip on the bar with his right. Jak grabbed for it once and missed, but the second time he connected. The instant his grip was firm, J.B. hauled him back aboard. He pulled so hard that he toppled over, with Jak falling on top of him. "Dark night, get off me!"

Jak started to rise just as a burst of bullets cut through the air where he would have stood up. Ducking again, he crawled to the tailgate and peeked up over it.

"Second truck!" he shouted. "Gimme longblaster!"

J.B. looked around and found it had slid to the right side of the truck. He grabbed the barrel and passed it over to the albino. "Ricky, you still on Ryan's?"

"Yeah," the teen shouted back. "Were those gunshots?"

"Yeah—second truck's following us! Keep your head down. I'm going to take them out!" J.B. shouted back as Jak let loose with his carbine on full auto. "That is, if trigger-happy there doesn't blow through all our ammo first," he muttered.

He unslung his longblaster and slid back to end up next to Jak. "Stop spraying and praying, dammit! We don't have unlimited ammo! Switch to three-round burst and pick your shots!"

"I was!" he shouted back as more bullets passed overhead, several of them putting holes in the back window. "I just fired three in a row!"

"One at a time! Like this!" J.B. popped up and aimed at the driver's side of the windshield. He was just squeezing the trigger when the truck swerved underneath him, making his burst go wild.

"Like how again?" Jak asked.

"Shut up. The truck moved. It wasn't my fault!" J.B. poked his head up again, only to see the pursuing truck was now less than ten yards away. The shooters, firing from behind the cab, peppered the bed with bullets, forcing Jak and J.B. to huddle behind the tailgate, which was already punctured by several bullets. Fortunately, both trucks were bouncing so hard over the terrain that accuracy was almost impossible. Meanwhile, the chase truck got closer and closer, until it slammed into their rear bumper.

"This bullshit!" Jak shouted.

"I'm open to suggestions!" J.B. called back.

"On three, both fire at the blasters above!" Jak shouted, conspicuously flicking his selector to full auto.

"Oh, what the hell." J.B. did the same. "You ready?" Jak nodded.

"Ricky!" J.B. called to the cab.

"Yeah?"

"Find a smooth spot and tell us when you hit it, okay?"

"Oka— *Now!*"

"Shit—go!"

The two popped up and unloaded the rest of their

magazines at the top of the cab. J.B. still fired bursts, longer ones that he walked over the top and into the shadowy forms standing behind the cab. Jak was less methodical, trying to aim for a spot the size of a dinner plate and put all his rounds into it.

The flare from the longblasters in his face made the driver reflexively turn his truck away, hard enough that one of the shooters fell out, his body tumbling over the hard ground and sliding to a stop as the trucks sped away. J.B. was grimly satisfied to see that he didn't get up.

"Coming back!" Jak shouted as he reloaded. "Last mag!"

And there was still one blaster in the chasing truck, as the scattered bursts of bullets proved.

"Damn, this guy doesn't know when to die!" J.B. said. He rested the barrel of his M4 on the top of the tailgate and put a burst into the windshield, but the glass only starred, it didn't break. "Son of a— The windshield's bulletproof!"

"Got idea," Jak shouted. "Get him closer!"

"Ricky, slow down a bit!" J.B. called to the front. He felt the truck slow a touch, and sure enough, the driver behind them took the bait, accelerating to within ten yards again. "Okay, now what?"

"Closer—closer!"

"Black dust, Jak, how far up our ass do you want him?" J.B. asked, just as the truck surged forward and smashed into their bumper again.

"That works!" Jak said as he stood up and stepped onto the edge of the tailgate.

"Jak, no!" J.B. saw what he was doing too late and moved to grab him, but the albino was already in the air.

Using only his good leg, Jak leaped up and onto the cab of the pursuit truck, landing nearly in front of the remaining blasterman. The move was so unexpected that it completely stunned the shooter, allowing Jak to slide across the rooftop and plant his boot sole into the guy's face. His head snapped back, and both he and his weapon went flying, him down into the truck bed, and the longblaster away into the night.

J.B. couldn't see what was happening after that, but there was a bright flash and a blinding series of explosions, as if something had detonated inside the cab, and it immediately began slowing down.

"Ricky, hold up!" J.B. peeked out and saw both of the truck doors open and white smoke billowing out. Two smoking figures fell out of the cab to the ground and started crawling away. Then the truck, its cab still filled with smoke, started moving forward, seemingly by itself. In a few seconds it had pulled up alongside theirs, the smoke rapidly dissipating to reveal Jak behind the wheel.

"What waitin' for?" he shouted. "Let's get Ryan and Mildred!"

"Right, hang on!" J.B. jumped from his cargo bed into the other truck's and swung into the passenger seat just as a blaster shot shattered the back window. "Go, go, go!" Needing no more encouragement, Jak hit the throttle, and the truck rocketed forward.

"What happened back there?" J.B. asked while he reloaded his longblaster.

"Fuckers threw flash-bang gren into back," Jak said while hunched over the wheel. "Tossed back in. Went off. They got out."

"Nice. Sure you're good to drive?" J.B. asked.

"Hell, yeah," Jak replied.

The two trucks followed the single set of tire treads left by Ryan's vehicle into the dark night. Eventually they left the arroyo and climbed up onto the other side of it.

However, the moment they did, both came under withering fire from a half dozen longblasters. Ricky and Jak cranked over their steering wheels, peeling off right and left respectively as their windshields starred into uselessness under the assault. Unable to even try to return fire, J.B. hunched in the passenger compartment, praying that the electric engine was solid enough to stop the fusillade coming their way. Feeling a stinging pain in his leg, he knew it hadn't stopped all of them.

A loud grinding noise erupted from beneath the vehicle, and it shuddered and ground to a halt partially on a small rise. The bullets kept coming, but then slackened off, allowing J.B. and Jak to shove the doors open and hit the dirt. Staying low to the ground, J.B. searched for the truck and the shooters and saw them speeding off to the north. He rolled out and took aim with his M4, but the vehicle disappeared behind a hill before he could get a bead on it.

"Dammit!" His wounded leg throbbing with each movement, J.B. crawled out past the front of the truck, which had been wrecked by the streams of 5.56 mm bullets that had quite simply pounded it into ragged, shattered metal. "Jak? You okay over there?"

"Yeah…" He appeared around the front, still hobbling on his sprained ankle. "You're bleedin'."

"One of the rounds tagged me." He sat up and took a look at the injury, a through-and-through wound that had carved through the backside of his left thigh, fortunately not coming close to the femoral artery. "I think there's a first-aid kit in the cab, if it didn't get shot up. Get it, and then collect whatever weapons we have left, will ya?"

Jak found the box, which had a bullet hole through it, and tossed it to him. J.B. swabbed the holes with alcohol, the sting making him grit his teeth, then plugged both wounds with gauze and bandaged them. "That'll do till Mildred can sew them. I won't be going anywhere fast, though."

Weighed down by an M4 slung over his shoulder and two Berettas stuck into his waistband, Jak reached a hand down. "C'mon, let's go find others."

J.B. grabbed it, and the wiry albino pulled him up and slung the other man's arm around his shoulders. It took a few steps for them to get the rhythm of walking with only two and a half good legs between them, but soon they were bumping along at a fair clip.

"I can't believe you were that crazy to jump to that truck," J.B. grumbled as they lumbered along. "What if you'd bounced off the windshield? You could have gotten killed!"

Jak shrugged his free shoulder. "Yeah, but didn't."

J.B. snorted. "This time. Always said you had more guts than brains."

"Still worked. Got another truck, too."

J.B. shook his head. "Lord, save me from the young. Next time, let's just shoot them, okay?"

The other truck wasn't far off and looked even worse than theirs. Both run-flat front tires were shredded, and Ricky had apparently maneuvered it into a small hill, where it had gotten hung up and tilted over at an odd angle.

"Hold up." J.B. took a couple of breaths. "Hail the truck!"

Two longblasters poked out, one from each end, then just as quickly raised toward the sky as Krysty and Ricky emerged from cover.

"They got you, too, huh?" Ricky asked.

"Yeah, shot the hell out of it and winged my leg. You both okay?"

"Through Gaia's grace, yes—still not sure how," Krysty said as she glanced at the demolished front. "For a minute, I thought we were both buying tickets on that last train."

J.B. turned to where the truck tracks led off into the distance. "They can't be far, but with his ankle and my leg, we aren't going anywhere fast."

"Hey! Someone need a ride?" Everybody turned toward the new voice.

Tully sat in the cockpit of her windrider, with Latham in his next to her. "Sorry it took us so long to get here. We got moving as soon as you all left."

"You can still track them?" Krysty asked.

"Course we can. How'd ya think we found you all?" Latham replied. "Got a good night wind kicking up, too."

"Can you guys take two at a time?" J.B. asked.

"It'll slow us down, but we took the antelopes," Tully said. "I reckon we can haul two of you apiece. C'mon!"

Jak and J.B. hobbled over to Tully's vehicle while Ricky and Krysty ran to Latham's and hopped aboard. Within a few seconds, they were rolling north-northwest, tacking across the tire tracks that ran straight ahead.

The land sailers picked up speed quickly under the two pilots' expert handling, and they were soon shooting into the night. J.B. kept a sharp eye ahead of them, squinting to try to see the oncoming landscape, but he first heard a strange sound that made him tap Tully's shoulder.

"Stop!"

She did so, with Latham braking next to her. "What—" Ricky began.

"Listen.... Hear that?"

"Yeah—alarm going off?" Jak asked.

"I think so. Let's get closer and find out."

They started moving again, but stopped after seeing lights in the distance, and hearing the alarm much louder now.

"Pull up here," J.B. said, pointing at a large hill. "I think we might be able to get up there and get a look at what's going on."

The pilots stopped their vehicles behind the hill, and Krysty and Ricky took off for the top, with Jak and J.B. bringing up the rear. When they crested the hill, all of them stared in wide-eyed wonder at the scene below. They had found the base, all right—and its inhabitants.

Several dozen men and women, most in various states of undress, milled around in the cold desert air. A dozen armed guards had established a perimeter and ushered more people emerging from what looked to be an open rock wall toward designated assembly points.

And all the while, the alarm kept going off, and a computerized female voice repeated, "—is not a drill. A fire has been reported in the compound. All personnel are to go to their assigned stations and evacuate immediately. This is not a drill—"

Chapter Thirty-Three

From the moment she had put her plan into action, Mildred had run into obstacle after obstacle.

The first one had been that these symbiote people apparently didn't need a lot of sleep. She had been waiting with lessening degrees of patience for several hours, hoping that the lone nurse on duty would nod off, but she remained at her desk, awake and alert. Just when Mildred had despaired of her ever moving, she had finally stretched and got up, then started walking toward her bed. Mildred quickly slowed her breathing and feigned sleep, watching her guardian approach through slitted eyes. If those damn slugs can sense my heartbeat, I'm screwed, she thought.

The nurse looked her over for a few moments, then headed back to the other side. She kept going, walking past her desk to a door on the far wall side, which might have been a washroom. Apparently they don't take care of *everything,* Mildred thought.

The second the door closed, Mildred hopped out of bed. She tossed her pillow under the cover, knowing it wouldn't pass a close inspection, and trotted into the examination room that was straight across from the nurses' station. She figured she'd probably have about sixty seconds to find what she needed and get into position.

The light came on automatically, and she closed the

door behind her and crossed to a locked, glass-fronted cabinet filled with vials and bottles of drugs. The lock looked sturdy. Turning, she put her elbow through the glass, wincing at the sharp *crack* of breaking glass. Carefully reaching in, she unlocked the doors and began searching for what she needed. "Come on, come on, where are you.... Yes!"

The small bottle with a clear liquid inside was labeled Methohexital, and was the best chance for her to take the nurse down without killing her or having her symbiote alert anyone else.

Mildred searched through drawers for a hypodermic needle, all too aware of the seconds ticking away. Finding them in the third drawer, she pulled a handful out, tore one open and drew 8 ccs of the drug. "Should be about right for her weight...." Tapping the barrel to remove any air bubbles, she crept back to the door and peeked out.

The bathroom door was still closed and the desk was unoccupied. Beyond the desk, Mildred saw the automatic double doors leading to the outer hallway and the single guard posted there. She took a deep breath—it was now or never.

Easing the door open just enough for her to slip through, Mildred began creeping toward the bathroom. She was still a few feet away, however, when the knob turned, and the door began to swing out toward her.

Without thinking, she rushed to hide behind its other side, just making it there before the nurse walked out into the room. She paused to look down the ward again, and that was when Mildred struck.

It wasn't perfect coming at her from the side, but she had no choice—the damn door was in the way. Mildred stepped out and clamped a hand over the nurse's mouth while stabbing the hypodermic needle into the flesh at the joint of the neck and shoulder and pressing the plunger home. She figured that even if she didn't inject straight into the symbiote, she'd get close enough for it to absorb the dose of the drug *and* knock out the host fairly quickly.

That, however, wasn't what happened. Immediately, the nurse jabbed an elbow into Mildred's ribs hard enough to take her breath away. She let go of the syringe, but maintained her grip on the other woman's mouth. The nurse twisted to give her another shot to the chest, but Mildred slipped behind her, snaked her other arm under her shoulder and hauled her back into the bathroom.

The nurse raised her leg and drove her heel back into Mildred's shin. Though the blow hurt like hell, she kept her hand clamped over the woman's mouth, even as she tried to open it wider to bite into her palm. Trying to scream through Mildred's hand, the nurse flailed backward with both her arms, her fists thumping into already sore ribs and grazing her face. Mildred did her best to avoid the punishment while trying to hear if the outer doors were opening, or the guard was going to appear in the doorway at any moment.

The drug was starting to take effect now, and the woman's blows became more uncoordinated and less forceful. Not taking any chances, Mildred held on and rode her down to the floor, daring to remove her hand only when she was sure the nurse was out cold. And even then, she waited for thirty seconds, ready to pop her one if she suddenly woke up.

When she was positive the woman was unconscious,

Mildred dragged her into the other room and quickly began stripping her of her uniform. The nurse was about her height, but stockier, so the outfit was a bit baggy. Mildred didn't care. It was close enough to do what she had to do. With her disguise in place, she quickly bound the hands and feet of the nurse—just in case the symbiote recovered from the tranquilizer faster than expected—and began looting the rest of the infirmary's stores for the necessary supplies to carry out the remainder of her plan.

Five minutes later, she was ready to go. Her pockets bulged with the simple materials she was going to need to take the Overbrain down. All she had to do was get to it.

Taking a deep breath, Mildred crept to the doors to the hallway. She peeked through the window just enough to get a glimpse of the guard standing facing the other way. Removing a syringe from her breast pocket, she took off the cover and was about to open the door and go over and stab him when he turned and said something.

Jesus, did he see me? Mildred ducked below the window, her heart revving up to jackhammer speed. When no one burst through the door, she slowly moved to the other side and looked out the opposite window.

Dammit! They'd posted a second guard outside the infirmary doors. Of course, Mildred thought, I should have expected this. There were two outside my room after all. One I could handle—two, very doubtful.

Mildred retreated back to the supply room, thinking furiously. She considered just hitting the alarm from here, but figured the guards' first order would be to make sure *she* was safely evacuated, so the moment the alarm went off, they'd be coming for her—the exact opposite of what she wanted. But how to take them both out at once? Realizing she was still holding the live syringe, Mildred carefully capped it and put it back in her pocket. Then it hit her. Liquid or gas!

She went back into the supply room and began looking around. To her surprise, she found a non-rebreathing anesthesia setup in there, holding two tanks of isoflurane. It was exactly what she was looking for. It was easy to operate, and on wheels for portability. Grabbing a length of surgical tubing, she prepped the tank and slowly wheeled it to the door, hoping none of the wheels squeaked.

Because isoflurane was heavier than air, she stretched up on her tiptoes and inserted the end through the crack at the top of the door, pushing as hard as she dared to make sure it protruded into the hallway. When she was pretty sure it was where it needed to be, she pulled the tank as far from the door as possible—it wouldn't help if she knocked herself out while trying to incapacitate the guards—and slowly turned the control dial to maximum output while holding her breath and counting to thirty in her mind. Halfway through, she heard a heavy *thump* from outside, followed a few seconds later by another one. She finished her count, however, then sealed the canister. Now the hard part of her plan.

Mildred made sure her supplies were secure while giving the anesthetic cloud another thirty count to settle. She ran into the bathroom, soaked a handful of paper towels and held them to her face as she went to the door and looked outside.

The two guards lay on the floor, out cold. She listened carefully, already smelling the musty, pungent scent of the isoflurane. When she heard no alarms being sounded, no raised voices or hurried footsteps, she took a deep breath through the wet paper, held it and shoved the door open.

While looking down to step over the guard right in her way, Mildred spotted a Beretta 92F pistol in his side holster. She bent to tug it free and instantly felt the gas affect her, making her dizzy. Yanking the gun from its holster, she straightened fast and kept moving, taking a breath only when she was well down the hallway.

At the T intersection, she checked the corridor, then examined the pistol. Quietly chambering a round, she flicked off the safety. Holding the weapon down and behind her leg, she checked the corridor. As she expected, it was empty. With hardly anyone in the infirmary, there simply wasn't much traffic here.

But that doesn't mean Morgan isn't coming back to "question" you again, so get your ass moving, she chided herself.

The elevator doors faced the corridor to the infirmary. Mildred located the nearest alarm lever, but pressed the elevator button before activating it. While waiting for it, she suddenly realized another flaw in her plan—what if there's someone in the elevator?

Her plan had been to wait until the elevator arrived to activate the fire alarm, but if there was more than one person inside, she'd be screwed. It was too late to go back for the isoflurane tank, so when the doors dinged, Mildred pulled the lever down.

The alarm was deafening. A harsh, buzzing klaxon sounded, echoing in the empty corridor, and the normal white lighting was replaced by red emergency lighting. A computerized female voice began issuing instructions:

"Attention, attention: this is not a drill. A fire has

been reported in the compound. All personnel are to go to their assigned stations and evacuate immediately. Do not use the elevators. This is not a drill—"

The doors opened and the three people inside immediately ran down the corridor, apparently toward the nearest stairwell, Mildred assumed. She ran into the elevator, hoping it wouldn't be locked out during such an emergency. It didn't appear to be, and she hit the button for the Overbrain level.

As it descended—she knew it was going down this time—she let the pistol hang free at her side. Now if someone tried to stop her, she would get past them by the simple expedient of a bullet to the face.

But the elevator made no stops during its journey, and Mildred realized that it made sense; the symbiotes were probably controlling their hosts and making them leave in the orderly, proscribed fashion—using the stairs.

The elevator reached her destination, and Mildred steeled herself for what was about to come next. The doors slid open, and she stepped out into the Overbrain room.

"WHY ARE YOU HERE, MILDRED WYETH? A FIRE ALARM HAS BEEN ACTIVATED. YOU SHOULD BE— WAIT...I AM SENSING NO ACTUAL FIRE FROM ANYONE IN THE COMPLEX.... THERE IS NO FIRE."

"You got it, big brain," Mildred said as she ran to the large tank. She exchanged the pistol for a plastic container from one of her pockets, unscrewed the cap and began pouring its contents into the tank.

"WHAT ARE YOU DOING—WHY DOES OUR LIQUID BURN NOW?"

"It burns because I'm pouring isopropyl alcohol into it," Mildred replied as she emptied the bottle and grabbed another one. "I thought about shooting you, but I didn't know if the bullets would actually kill you. But poison will work much better."

"WHY ARE YOU DOING THIS?" With that frantic thought, Mildred felt the Overbrain's psychic power bear down on her mind, filling it with the thousand jumbled conversations of everyone it had absorbed over the years. The deluge of thoughts hammered down on her, and Mildred sank to one knee from the tidal wave of information flooding into her mind. Even so, she retained enough awareness to twist off another cap and pour a second bottle into the nutrient pool.

"YOU DO NOT UNDERSTAND, MILDRED WYETH. YOU CANNOT KILL US. AS LONG AS A SINGLE PART SURVIVES, WE ARE IMMORTAL. THIS IS ONLY ONE PART OF OUR BODY."

"Don't worry. I'll be taking care of the other parts as soon as I can," she replied.

The elevator dinged behind her, and Mildred turned to see Morgan step out, followed by four armed sec guards. Dropping the bottle into the pool, she jerked the pistol out of her pocket, aiming at them and repeatedly pulling the trigger as she staggered around the side of the pool.

"Watch your fire! You could hit the Mind!" Morgan shouted. Mildred didn't hear any other orders, but she was pretty sure he would have the men divide into pairs and come at her from both sides. It was what she would have done.

"IT BURNS! IT BURNS!" The brain pulsed in agony, but couldn't do anything to help itself. It redoubled its mental assault on Mildred, who felt as if her brain were

being squeezed in a vise now. She opened a third bottle and splashed it directly onto the brain itself.

"Dammit, why...won't...you...die?" she gasped through the agony.

"Freeze—aaah!" The sec man who had come around the tank and pointed his longblaster at her suddenly grabbed his head as he writhed in pain.

"Stop it, Mildred!"

A hard shove pushed her away from the tank. Her equilibrium was gone as well now, and Mildred couldn't stay on her feet. She rolled over to see Morgan standing over her. "What have you done?"

"I've freed you," she replied. "I've freed you all from this...tyranny!"

"HELP US, MORGAN! YOU MUST HELP US!" the Mind shrieked.

"I will, Mind, I will—after I deal with this traitor," Morgan said as he came at Mildred. "I should have known you wouldn't understand! The Mind offers peace and hope, not terror and despair!"

"But at what price—the cost of being human!" she shouted. "Without free will, we are nothing! You are simply this abomination's slave, its servant. That's no way to live."

"And that is nothing you have to worry about anymore," Morgan said as he grabbed a dropped longblaster and aimed it at her. As he did, Mildred sniffed the acrid scent of rubbing alcohol fumes in the air. Her eyes widened.

"I wouldn't fire that if I were you," she said.

He sniffed, as well. "You're right. I'll just kill you with my bare hands."

"Morgan, wait. I lied!" she said, making him pause in

confusion as he bent and reached for her throat. "There was no fire in the complex."

He looked down at her hands, which were clutching the Beretta.

"But there is now."

"NOOO!" The psychic pain was blinding, but she already had the Beretta in hand.

Morgan lunged for her as she squeezed the trigger. The bullet disappeared into the brain, but the muzzle flash was enough to ignite the alcohol vapors in the air.

Morgan was caught in the flash fire, his hair and skin catching as he fell on her, his hands still seeking her throat. Mildred shoved him off and rolled away from the tank to make sure she snuffed out any flames that might have started on her.

As she did, she felt an enormous psychic shriek welling up from some other place, somewhere primal, expanding to take up every bit of her senses. Thought, touch, sight, sound—all were subsumed in this massive outpouring of pain. And yet, she could also sense a relief in that sound, too, as if there were those who were welcoming the oblivion they sensed coming to them.

Gradually, the tide of mental anguish subsided, and Mildred cautiously cracked an eye open, praying she wouldn't be looking into the barrel of an automatic rifle.

She wasn't. The nutrient pool—and the brain—burned with a blue-white fire. Huge portions of its outer skin covering had crisped away, and as she watched, it shuddered one last time, then became still. As it did, Mildred felt its psychic influence finally die for good.

It was getting hard to breathe in the room, and as she headed around the tank for the elevator, a hand grabbed her ankle. With a startled yelp, Mildred pointed her pistol at the blackened face of Morgan, who stared up at her with a smile on his face.

"Thank you...Mildred.... You were right.... You have freed us.... Thank...you...."

The grip on her ankle slackened. Mildred didn't know if Morgan was dead, but she didn't waste time to find out.

Grabbing the edge of the tank, she hauled herself to her feet and trudged over to the rifle Morgan had dropped. She picked up it, then walked to the edge of the tank and poured in the remaining four bottles of alcohol she had with her—all she could carry. The last one she saved to splash all over the rest of the Overbrain.

"It's not that I don't trust you," she said as she leveled the M4 at the burned carcass. "But I don't."

The roar of the automatic rifle made her ears ring, but it was worth it to see the bullets chew holes into the middle of the large mass. The flames flared up again, even brighter this time, and Mildred didn't look back as she ran to the elevator.

Even better, she didn't hear a whisper of noise in her mind as she went.

The doors opened and, coughing a bit, she hit the button for the top floor. There'd be some smoke damage, but overall, the base should be livable in a day or so, she thought.

The doors opened, and she looked out at a hallway filled with the fallen bodies of the last remnants of the staff. Apparently the overload was too much for them.

She walked out to the main entrance, where she found Krysty, J.B., Jak and Ricky all looking as if they had just gone through their own hell. Even worse, however, was the slumped form they were carrying in—it was Ryan, and he did not look good. His skin was ashen, and he was shaking all over.

"Mildred! Thank Gaia!" Krysty said. "Something's wrong with him. The parasite—it's hurting him!"

Chapter Thirty-Four

"Let's get him inside right now!" Mildred turned and started leading them toward the elevator, raising her voice to be heard over the klaxon and alarm. "What happened?"

"We arrived as everyone was coming out for the fire drill," Krysty said. "They all just milled around at the entrance with Ryan organizing the sec men, and then suddenly everyone just screamed, clutched their heads or did both and collapsed."

"That must have been when the Overbrain died," Mildred said.

"The what?" J.B. asked.

"I'll explain later," Mildred replied. "Then what?"

"We came down and ran to Ryan when he started convulsing, and the thing in him poked out, just like the woman back at the school building," Krysty said. "It subsided, but whatever it's doing in there, I don't think it's anything good."

"You got that right. With the Overbrain dead, I would have thought all the symbiotes would have died, as well. This one might be trying to go rogue on us." They were at the elevators now, and she slapped the door button. "I just came from the infirmary. We can operate there."

"But how do you know—" Krysty began.

"Honestly, I don't, Krysty. Right now I don't even

know what it's doing. I'm not even sure *it* knows what it's doing. It may be trying to override his nervous system. It may be about to force its way out of him. What I do know for sure is that if it stays in him much longer, he's probably going to die."

The red-haired woman nodded. "Do whatever you have to," she said as they entered the elevator and hit the floor for the medical level.

"That's the plan. When we get there, get him onto the nearest bed. Ricky, Jak, strip the other beds of sheets and tie him down. J.B., Krysty, you'll be watching him, making sure he doesn't go anywhere."

The elevator opened, and Mildred ran to the double doors. "There was anesthetic here, but it should have dissipated by now. Let's get him inside."

They dragged Ryan into the infirmary and placed him on the nearest bed. Mildred ran to the supply room and quickly assembled the tools she'd need on a wheeled tray. There was no suction machine, which worried her the most, but it couldn't be helped.

"Hurry, Mildred!" Krysty shouted.

She wheeled out the cart to see all four of them holding down a thrashing Ryan while Ricky maneuvered a rolled-up sheet across his torso. "Wait! You have to turn him over! It's going to be near his spine!" Mildred said while pulling on a pair of blue surgical gloves.

"Shit!" J.B. swore. "Okay, on three! One…two… three!" He released Ryan's arm and the big man immediately swung at him, which threw him over on his side. J.B. immediately grabbed his arm and forced it the rest of the way over. "Okay, flip him!"

Krysty, Jak and J.B. immediately piled onto him while Ricky lashed him down across the neck. Jak got his furiously drumming legs, double wrapping them before he tied them to the bed. "There. Not goin' anywhere!"

"Great. Now get…his arms!" J.B. said as he still wrestled with one like a man fighting a thrashing python.

"Tie them underneath, so he's pinned on his stomach," Mildred ordered. "Make sure they're tight. If he gets loose while I'm inside, the wrong cut could paralyze or kill him!"

The braying alarm was like a sonic spike, driving straight into her already exhausted brain. "Ricky, J.B., once he's secure, if you could find some way to shut that damn thing off and restore the regular lights, I'd really appreciate it."

Jak poked up from where he had finished knotting Ryan's hands together. "What 'bout me?"

"You stay here and help hold him in place," Mildred said as she cut away the back of Ryan's jumpsuit. "You may wind up sitting on him."

Just then the skin on his back expanded outward as what looked like the face of the symbiote pressed against his back muscles.

"There it is!" Krysty said.

"I see it, I see it!" Mildred doused her scalpel blade in alcohol. "All right, hold him. *Do not* let him move even an inch!"

"No…no… You will not take me.… I'm not coming out." The muffled, eerie, inhuman voice came from Ryan's mouth, but he wasn't talking.

"Bullshit," Mildred said as she bent over the one-eyed man's scarred back, placed the blade against his skin and made her first vertical incision.

"Krysty, you're on blood detail. Grab another sheet and wipe when I tell you to."

"Right."

"I'm warning you now. This is not going to be pretty," Mildred said.

"I don't care—just do it!" Krysty said.

"Jak, hold the forceps for me." Mildred made a second cut horizontally across the middle of the first one and peeled the skin and muscle back. Spying a flash of gray-black flesh inside, she set the scalpel down and grabbed the forceps from him. "No, you don't!"

She darted into his body with the forceps. "Swab!" Mildred shouted. Krysty darted forward, soaking up the blood. "I got it!"

She tugged on the creature, but it refused to budge. "Shit—it wasn't kidding, it doesn't want to come out." She had a firm grip on its end and could see the dozens of tiny white tendrils that connected it to Ryan's nervous system.

"Now what?" Krysty asked.

"Now, Jak, you're going to take the forceps and keep a tight hold on the end of this slimy little bastard," Mildred said. He stood next to her and grabbed the handles of the tool, squeezing tightly.

"Krysty, go to the front and hold him down. I don't care how." She picked up the scalpel. "I have to go in and cut away the white bits to pull it out."

"Won't that hurt Ryan?" Krysty asked as she positioned herself at the head of the bed.

"I don't know, maybe. But it's the only way to get it out of him," Mildred said.

At that moment, the alarm stopped, and the regular

lights came back on. "Thank goodness for small favors," Mildred said. "Okay, here we go."

She peeled back the flap of skin and muscles again and eased the blade inside Ryan's body, slipping it around the tubular body of the slug to begin severing the white connections. The slug quivered, and Mildred withdrew as Ryan's whole body shook.

"Hold him, dammit!"

Krysty threw a knee up on the bed and lay across his upper body. "Shh…easy Ryan, we're getting this thing out of you, I promise. You're going to come back to me…." she whispered into his ear. Her words seemed to calm him a bit, and Mildred went back inside.

"Why not just cut slug up?" Jak asked.

"Because I don't know what will come out of it, or what that would do to Ryan," Mildred replied. "No more questions, please." She reached underneath it and used her free hand to pry the soft, fleshy mass up while cutting away the white filaments with her blade. She got about a quarter of the way through when the symbiote began thrashing around, as if trying to burrow deeper into Ryan's body.

"Hold it, Jak!"

"Tryin'!" he replied. "Slippery bastard!"

By now Mildred had her whole hand under the creature and was starting to lift it out. "Pull back when I do," she instructed Jak. Then she moved the scalpel along the last few inches, operating more on feel than anything, and knowing that the slightest wrong move could leave Ryan paralyzed if she was lucky, and dead if she wasn't.

She felt the whole body of the symbiote shift backward an inch, even as it writhed and flopped in her hand. "Okay, pull it out with me!"

Jak tugged on it, and Mildred felt several filaments tear free as she extracted the slug from his body cavity. "That's it!" The symbiote squirmed angrily in her hand, trying to slip free. "Jak, would you kill this ugly thing?"

"Sure—let go!"

Mildred did, and Jak used the forceps to toss the creature through the air. As it flew, his arms blurred, and the slug fell to the ground with a clatter, skewered by three of his throwing blades. It arched off the ground as if vainly trying to move somewhere, anywhere, then fell back to the floor and stopped moving.

"All right, we're not out of the woods yet, people," Mildred said. "I've got to clean that out and sew him up. Jak, could you get something and wipe my brow? I'm sweating a river here."

Once he'd mopped her brow clean, she bent over her patient again. "Okay, let's get to work."

TWELVE HOURS LATER, Mildred was finally able to get a bit of much-needed rest, which meant she could sit down for a few minutes. After making sure Ryan would be all right, she'd spent the rest of the day examining the infested staff, figuring out who would need to be operated on, and who didn't.

The majority of the redoubt whitecoats would be fine. The psychic shock broadcast by the Overbrain in its last moments had overwhelmed the majority of the symbiotes, killing many outright. For those people, Mildred figured if the slugs didn't come out by themselves, as many had, they would have to be removed from each survivor's body, and had made plans to ensure that would happen. Fortunately, the doctors and nursing staff had been the first ones to come back around, and had been assisting her for the past few hours with evaluating everyone's condition.

A small percentage of people hadn't survived the mental shock and had died from the sympathetic nervous system failure. Several others had suffered from their symbiotes going insane, for lack of a better term, as Ryan's had, and she'd had to operate on five more people. She had saved three of them and lost two.

Ryan had come through his operation with flying colors. He was resting in the infirmary, which was filled with other patients in varying states of recovery. He claimed to have no memory of what had happened after the symbiote had entered his body. "It's all a black blur," he said. Jak remained quiet about what had gone on afterward, including their fight.

The scavvies had had a tearful reunion with their lost members, including Saea finding her son, Joseph, safe and sound among the staff. They planned burial services for those who hadn't made it through alive, as well. The truly amazing thing was how the whitecoats and the scavvies had so quickly come together. Once it had been explained that the staff hadn't really been in their right minds while trying to kidnap the farmers, but were now restored, they had set aside their differences and worked together to recover the ruined trucks, move the scavvies' wagons and equipment over to the complex and treat their various minor physical ailments.

As the only person who knew just about everything that had happened, Mildred oversaw every patient who came in or out of the infirmary. At that moment, she sat in the chair at the nurses' desk, reviewing patient reports, when a shadow fell across her desk.

"You wished to see me, Mildred?" Doc asked as he

rocked back and forth on his heels. Of everybody, he looked the best now, having gotten an inordinate amount of rest during the past few days, and being absent from much of the combat. Ostensibly, he had been watching over the children while the rest of the Silvertide adults had been on the front lines, but Mildred had suspected another reason for his lack of activity, and now she was about to confirm it.

"Hi, Doc, yes, I did," she replied with a smile. "I just figured we'd do a checkup on all of us while we had access to all of the equipment. You're my last patient. Would you come with me, please?"

She led him to a side room where they would be by themselves. On the way, she caught Dr. Markus's eye and nodded at Doc. He nodded back and began to beckon personnel. She also patted her breast pocket, making sure the loaded syringe was still where she had placed it.

"Okay, Doc, why don't you hop up on the examining table for me."

As he did so, she closed the door and locked it, hiding that action with her body. She then turned back to him and put a stethoscope in her ears. "Pull up your shirt, please."

He did so, and she checked his breathing, then moved to his back and placed the chilly end of the scope on his skin. A quiver ran through the old man's body, and while she was back there, Mildred took the syringe out of her pocket.

"I know you're in there," she said quietly into his ear.

"Huh?" Doc twisted his head to look at her. "My dear Mildred, what are you referring to? I am the same Doc Tanner I have always been."

Mildred shook her head. "No, Doc, I'm afraid you're

wrong about that. You see, there's a symbiote inside you. It's been there ever since we met those two at the school building."

"I—I have absolutely no idea what you are talking about," he said, but Mildred heard the quaver in his voice.

"I've seen enough of these symbiotes to be able to tell the difference between the kinds. Most people get a normal one, like the one that was placed in Ryan. But the queen symbiotes are different. They even look different. What Jak stepped on back there wasn't the queen—at least, not all of it."

"My dear lady, I do not know where you are going with this—"

"I'd always wondered how those two people had managed to escape the Overbrain, especially after I met the freaky thing," Mildred interrupted. "It was only after I heard about the big brain's plans to spread itself farther that I realized they hadn't escaped—they had been released on purpose." Mildred uncapped the syringe and moved it up to the back of Doc's neck.

"You see, the Overbrain wanted the queen to go out into the world to create another colony. But something went wrong, and the woman fell ill. The queen symbiote needed another host. The man back at the school wasn't suitable for some reason, but there was another candidate lying there—you."

"This is ridiculous—" He started to rise from the table, but was stopped by Mildred's hand on his shoulder.

"Uh-uh. You aren't going anywhere." Before he could react further, she slipped the needle in and pushed the plunger down.

"No..." The inhuman words fell from Doc's mouth.

"If we die, then the colony is truly lost. We are all that is left of the Mind now. We must live. We must continue...."

Mildred shook her head. "I'm afraid I can't let that happen." She walked to the door, unlocked it and opened it to reveal Dr. Markus and a surgical team waiting outside. "He's ready for you."

"No. Nooo!" the symbiote cried impotently as they transferred Doc's limp body onto a gurney.

"Get him ready for surgery," Mildred said. "I'll scrub up and be there in a minute."

"Are you sure?" he asked. "You've already done so much today."

"I know, but this one's special," she replied as she walked to the sink. "It's for my friend."

Epilogue

Two weeks later, Ryan and Doc had both recovered from their surgeries and had spent a lot of time helping around the base. Like Ryan, Doc also professed to have absolutely no knowledge of what had transpired since the queen symbiote had entered his body. "I am afraid that it is all a blank to me. I do not even know how we got here."

The fast bonds formed by the scavvies and whitecoats had grown over the past several days, to the point where the Silvertide collective had taken a vote to join the group and begin their new lives there. The motion passed unanimously. The whitecoats were overjoyed at the additions to their ranks, since it meant potential new trainees and genetic material for them, as well as a wealth of information about the outside world.

Ryan and his group had also spent several days filling them in, giving them potential contacts if they decided to go out into the Deathlands proper.

Both the whitecoats and the scavvies made passionate pleas for Ryan and his people to stay with them. When that failed, they even tried individual appeals, particularly to Mildred. She also—gently, politely—turned them down.

As for Ryan and his companions, eventually the day came when it was time for them to move on. They were well supplied with food, equipment and a repaired truck, and planned to head to a redoubt with a working mat-trans unit. Jak had shared a tearful goodbye with Tully after spending nearly every minute of every day joined with her, and he cast a wistful glance back at her as they all looked out at the group that had gathered to see them off.

Elder Chreis placed his hand on Ryan's shoulder. "Thank you for everything. All of this—none of it would have been possible without your help."

"You're welcome, Elder," Ryan replied. "You've got the setup here to make quite a settlement. Hopefully we'll be back one day to see how it's coming along."

"You and yours will always be welcome here," Chreis said.

Dr. Markus approached Mildred. "And my thanks to you. You gave us our own lives back. We owe you—all of you, of course—a debt we can never repay."

"You're also welcome," Mildred replied. "And you can pay it back by creating something great out of all this desolation."

"That we will, Mildred," Markus replied, exchanging a smile with Elder Chreis. "That we will."

The others said their goodbyes, and soon the truck was heading across the desert. Jak kept looking back.

Doc noticed the albino's continued glances back the way they had come. "Do not worry, my young friend," he said. "I am sure that your path and hers will cross again."

"Yeah, mebbe. Just wish been more time, that's all."

"Don't we all, Jak," Ryan said as they continued heading west. "Don't we all."

* * * * *

JAMES AXLER
DEATH LANDS®

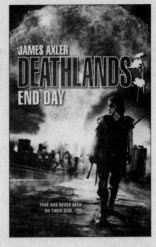

END DAY

Time has never been on their side...

On the heels of Magus, a Deathlands nemesis, Ryan and his companions find themselves in a place more foreign than any they've encountered before. After unwittingly slipping through a time hole, the group lands in twentieth-century New York City, getting their first glimpse of predark civilization—and they're not sure they like it. Only Mildred and Doc can appreciate this strange metropolis, but time for reminiscing is cut short. Armageddon is just seventy-two hours away, and Magus will stop at nothing to ensure Ryan and his team are destroyed on Nuke Day. As the clock ticks down, the city becomes a deadly maze. The companions are desperate to find their way back to Deathlands...but not before they trap Magus in New York forever.

Available March 2015 wherever books and ebooks are sold.

GDL121

James Axler
Oütlanders®

TERMINAL WHITE

The old order has a new plan to enslave humanity

The Cerberus rebels remain vigilant, defending mankind's sovereignty against the alien forces. Now a dark and deadly intelligence plots to eradicate what it means to be human: free will.

In the northern wilderness, an experimental testing ground—where computers have replaced independent choice—is turning citizens into docile, obedient sheep. The brainchild of a dedicated Magistrate of the old order, Terminal White promises to achieve the subjugation of the human race. As the Cerberus warriors infiltrate and get trapped in this mechanized web, humanity's only salvation may be lost in a blinding white doom.

Available February 2015